Snow Furries

Susan C. Daffron

An Alpine Grove Romantic Comedy

Book 4

 Published by Magic Fur Press
An imprint of Logical Expressions, Inc.
P.O. Box 383
Ponderay, ID 83852

Snow Furries

ISBN: 978-1-61038-029-4 (paperback)
        978-1-61038-030-0 (EPUB)

Like all of my books, *Snow Furries* is dedicated to
my husband James Byrd,
my best friend and biggest supporter.
Thanks for everything!

<u>Books by Susan C. Daffron</u>
The Alpine Grove Romantic Comedies
Chez Stinky
Fuzzy Logic
The Art of Wag
Snow Furries
Bark to the Future
Howl at the Loon
The Good, the Bad, and the Pugly
The Treasure of the Hairy Cadre
The Luck of the Paw
Daydream Retriever
The Hound of Music

The Jennings & O'Shea Mysteries
Sensing Trouble
Sensing Secrets
Sensing Truth

Chapter 1

Big Flurries

"Alpine Grove?" Rebecca Mackenzie put her hands on her hips and glared at her uncle. "Why do you want *me* to go? I thought Joanne was doing that appraisal. I'm going to be at Thanksgiving dinner with you. Mom wants me to make my world-famous mashed potatoes."

Patrick Radcliffe ran his hand over his smooth bald head. "I'm sorry, Becca. I already talked to your mom about it. I know your mother is my sister, but I was unaware she knew such colorful words to describe her feelings about this situation. The problem is Joanne has to go back East to see her family. Her mother hasn't been well lately."

"You told *Mom* about this before you told me?" Becca turned toward the copy machine, opened the lid, and slapped a piece of paper on the glass. "You know what happened the last time I went to Alpine Grove."

"I know."

"I don't understand why that place has no road signs. All the directions are things like 'turn at the ugly green house next to where that feed store used to be.' I'm not psychic. How hard would it be to put up road signs?" She jabbed the green button on the machine. "And how am I supposed to get a reservation *now* for Thanksgiving weekend? Alpine

1

Grove is a touristy place. I'm sure everything is full. Can't we just put this trip off until later?"

Patrick leaned against the file cabinet, crossed his arms across his chest, and faced her. "No. The bank needs the appraisal by December first, and they tend to take deadlines pretty seriously. You're the only one, other than me, who has enough experience with the area. Joanne already had a reservation at the H12 motel. You can stay there."

"Do they take dogs? I can't just leave Mona here. And Mom and everyone else are going to be way too busy with the whole family Thanksgiving party to take care of her."

"Can't you board her somewhere?"

"I guess I can call around." Becca sighed melodramatically. "But Pat, I can't believe you're making me miss Thanksgiving!"

"Hey, you're the one who wanted to get into the wild and wacky world of property appraisal, you know."

"I know." Becca collected the papers from the copier's output tray and placed them on top of the machine. She reached out and gave her uncle a hug. "And you know I appreciate you letting me be an appraisal trainee here all this time. I really do. I'm so close to getting certified now and I'm grateful. So I'll be a big girl and stop whining. I guess I need to go make some calls."

Pat patted her shoulder and turned to walk back toward his office. "I'll miss your mashed potatoes. Thanksgiving 1995 won't be the same without them."

"Mine are the *best!*"

"There's always next year."

Becca picked up her copies and held them to her chest. A career change had definitely been in order, but starting over at the bottom rung of the corporate ladder had some real down sides. Her glory days as a property manager were over, and after what had happened, she certainly could never go back to her old job. She'd tried, but she just couldn't do it. In the end, she'd had to quit. Then when Uncle Pat had suggested that she become an appraiser, it seemed like a perfect fit. She already had experience working in a somewhat related field and she had enjoyed all the courses she had to take to get her trainee license. Pat had even let her bring Mona into the office with her.

Becca opened the door to her small, crowded office and found Mona curled up in the monogrammed dog bed located in a dark corner under the desk. The small shepherd mix lifted her head, waved just the tip of her tail slightly, and put her muzzle back down on the pillow to return to her nap. It was way too early for her walk, and the dog clearly knew there was no point in getting up.

Although Mona had decided Becca was okay as a human being, the dog was extremely shy and seemed to be mortally afraid of everyone and everything else. With the exception of her lunchtime outing, sleeping under the desk was Mona's preferred way to spend the work day.

The irony was not lost on Becca that the dog she had adopted from the humane society "for protection" turned out to be a total scaredy-cat. At least Mona had mostly stopped randomly piddling on the floor. Uncle Pat had really not appreciated that aspect of Mona's behavior. The fact that Becca had paid to have all of the office carpets cleaned had helped, and now Pat and Mona had reached an uneasy truce.

Because almost no one in the office ever saw Mona, having her around wasn't a problem. She loved hanging out under the desk while Becca worked on her computer.

Before Becca became the most junior associate at her uncle's company—Radcliffe and Associates—her office had been a storage area for files. The office was so small, it was almost impossible to move around. It was a good thing Mona didn't take up much space.

The dog loved going for car rides, and she seemed to welcome the excursions to visit properties with Becca. It was too bad the dog couldn't read maps, because Becca desperately needed a navigator. She spent a lot of time at the side of the road trying to decipher directions and flipping through her tired old *Thomas Guide* book of street maps.

The prospect of going to Alpine Grove was daunting, since *Thomas Guides* for the middle of nowhere didn't exist. And as she had told her uncle, the Alpine Grove town leaders apparently were not big believers in road identification. It was way too easy to end up on some meandering dirt road that went off into the deepest, darkest depths of the wilderness. Becca sighed. Maybe she'd buy some bear spray before she left the city. Becoming snack food for a grizzly was not how she had envisioned spending her holiday weekend.

～

Becca navigated her car down the long driveway, clutching the piece of paper with directions in her hand. This *had* to be the correct house. Maybe. After Becca arrived in Alpine Grove, she'd checked into the H12 motel and verified the directions she'd received from the boarding kennel owner with the guy at the front desk. He had patiently answered all her navigational questions, and yet here she was, still wondering if she was in the right place. Turning up in some stranger's front yard would be more than a little embarrassing.

As Becca had predicted, every boarding kennel in the greater Los Angeles area had been full for the holiday weekend. And the H12 motel in Alpine Grove didn't take pets. However, they said there was a new boarding kennel that might be able to take Mona. It had taken a complicated, frustrating series of phone calls to actually find out where the rumored kennel was located. Becca shook her head. Everyone seemed to know someone who knew someone else.

First Becca had to call some web site company and the guy who answered the phone had her talk to a woman named Tracy, who gave her a phone number for Kat Stevens, who owned the dog boarding kennel. At last, she'd tracked down the person. But what a production!

Becca was already sick of Alpine Grove and she hadn't even dropped off Mona yet. It was going to be a long trip. At least Kat had seemed nice enough on the phone, if a little concerned about Mona's shyness issues. But at this point, Becca had no choice. She looked over the seat at Mona. The dog seemed to be enjoying looking out the window at all the huge trees.

"It's okay, Mona. I'll do the inspection and the photos just as fast as I can. I know it's going to be a little scary at first, but I promise I won't leave you here any longer than I have to. We might still be able to make it back to Mom's for Thanksgiving. I've got everything all laid out on my list. We'll be back home before you know it."

Mona wagged her tail in response. At least the dog didn't seem too worried. Mona was probably less concerned than Becca was about the stay at the kennel. Maybe the knot that was lodged in her stomach would finally go away once she had Mona settled in.

Becca tapped her fingers on the steering wheel. It was taking forever to get out to this place. A real estate listing would probably euphemistically refer to it as *private*, as opposed to *remote* or *in the middle of nowhere*. Maybe Kat was some type of recluse or granola-eating back-to-the-land type.

The weather was starting to look ominous, with heavy dark gray clouds that hung so low it seemed like they were curling around the treetops. Snow flurries had followed Becca all the way up the mountain to Alpine Grove, and now that she was outside of town here in the sticks, it was snowing with significantly more enthusiasm.

The car didn't have snow tires, but the roads still seemed okay. After dropping off Mona, next on Becca's extensive to-do list was to get back to various offices in town and look up legal information before everything closed for the holiday. With any luck, she wouldn't get lost again trying to get back to Alpine Grove. This whole trip was a nightmare. Best to get it over with as fast as possible.

The car slammed into a giant pothole and slid sideways a little as it came up out of the crater. Becca's heart lurched in her chest as she jerked the steering wheel and caused the car to fishtail back and forth. She let off the gas and pressed her foot on the brake, and the car slid to a stop. Taking a deep breath, she berated herself for hitting the brake so hard. That was stupid. There was hardly any snow on the ground and she was going two miles an hour. After another long breath, she carefully put her foot back on the accelerator and eased the car forward. At last, the forest opened up and a log house came into view. It was nestled in a clearing surrounded by huge evergreen trees. With the dusting of snow on the pines, the scene looked like a Christmas card. Becca's heart finally slowed down, returning to a more normal rate as she carefully nosed the car under a tree and parked.

She grabbed her coat from the passenger seat and turned to look at Mona. "Be good for a minute. I need to check and make sure this is really the right place." She got out and walked up the steps to the house. The sound of barking came from inside and as Becca raised her hand to knock, the door opened. A petite woman with long wavy dark hair smiled and said, "Hi. You must be Becca. I'm Kat." She peered out the doorway. "Where's Mona?"

Becca put out her hand. "Yes, I'm Rebecca Mackenzie. Mona is in the car. I got a little lost and I wasn't sure I was in the right place."

Kat glanced at her quickly, and shook her hand. "Well, you found it." She moved inside and grabbed a coat off a hook. "Let's go get Mona."

Becca followed Kat down the steps back to the car. As her left foot slid, Becca shrieked and circled her arms like a windmill as she tried to regain her balance.

Kat looked back at her, "Those might not be the best shoes to wear here."

"I'm fine." Mortified, but fine. She loved these pumps and they made her look professional. The shoes had been a gift to herself after she got her first check from Uncle Pat. They went perfectly with her outfit, which was a grayish-blue suit that matched her eyes and looked great with her light brown hair. Unfortunately, the cute bouncy curls created by the hot rollers she'd used this morning were starting to look a little tired. It had already been a long day and it was far from over. She still had a lot of items on her list to deal with.

Becca motioned toward the house. "This is a very pretty log house. How big is it?" At Kat's surprised expression, she added, "Sorry…appraiser curiosity. I love finding out about houses and their stories."

"I inherited the place from my aunt. Or grandmother." Kat waved her hands dismissively. "It's a little complicated. Anyway, it's three bedrooms. The master bedroom, bathroom, and kitchen are upstairs and there's an open great room with the living and dining area. Downstairs, in the daylight basement, are two more bedrooms we use as offices, plus a hallway and some storage areas."

"Sounds nice. How much property do you have?"

"I guess you could say the house is nice in a kind of vintage rustic way. It's on eighty acres. The house sits right in the middle. That's why the driveway is so long. I think my aunt wanted privacy."

"There aren't many big parcels like this available anymore, even out here."

"My aunt bought the land a long time ago."

"Interesting." Becca moved around Kat and unlocked the car door.

"You locked your dog in the car? Here?"

Becca opened the door and clipped a leash on Mona. "Force of habit." Mona peeked her nose out and then daintily leaped out of the car. "Good girl!"

Kat crouched next to the dog. "Hi Mona. How are you?" Mona wagged her tail happily, seeming to enjoy all the fun snowflakes falling around her.

Becca squinted at the dog. "Like I said, she's really shy. Don't be surprised if it takes her some time to warm up to you." Mona was remarkably relaxed, just sitting there. What was that about? Mona was *never* relaxed.

Kat reached out and scratched Mona's shoulder. "She seems fine to me. What do you think, Mona?" Mona's tail flapped back and forth cheerfully. "Do you want to walk around a little and sniff? You'll love it. There are all kinds of great sniffies here."

Becca handed Kat a manila envelope. "Here are Mona's veterinary records. I also wrote up some details about her history and behavior, so you know what to expect. It should only be one night. I'm still hoping to make it back home for Thanksgiving, if I can get everything done quickly today." Becca looked back toward the driveway. "I really do need to get going. I still have to get back to town and look up some information at the assessor's office before they close." If she could find it again.

Kat took the envelope and leash from Becca. "That's fine. You have my number. If you have any questions or just want to check in, feel free to give me a call."

"That would be great." Becca reached out and grabbed Kat, hugging her fiercely. "Thank you so much for taking Mona right before the holiday. I know it's an imposition. You're really saving me." In the city, a last-minute holiday drop-off like this would never happen.

Looking bewildered, Kat said, "It's no problem. A couple of people are stopping by later, but other than that, it should be a quiet holiday here."

Mona sat next to Kat, not even having the decency to look sad that Becca was leaving. Traitor.

Kat looked up at the sky and said, "I'm glad we're not going anywhere. Please drive carefully. It looks like there might be a storm."

Becca shook her head and fat snowflakes flew off her hair every which way. "No. They said it would just be flurries. I'm sure it will be fine."

"These are some big flurries." Kat bent to sweep some snow off Mona's back. "I haven't lived here very long, but I've noticed that the weather guys don't seem to be particularly accurate. Usually I find it's better to just look out the window."

Brushing a clump of snow off her head, Becca said, "I think I see what you mean."

~

After giving Mona a short walk around the yard, Kat led the dog inside the house and put the envelope on the entryway bench. She removed her coat and Mona sat quietly, looking on with interest as the human shook snow off her outerwear. Kat grabbed a towel from a hook on the wall and rubbed the melting snow off Mona, which the dog enjoyed immensely. She writhed and wagged madly, delighting in the free massage.

Kat grabbed the envelope and brought the dog through the kitchen into the living area, where Joel was sitting on the sofa. Even after months of living together, she never failed to appreciate his quiet, loving presence in her life. He had his feet on the coffee table and was flipping through a magazine with one hand and rubbing the side of his leg with the other. Looking up at Kat, he said, "I guess Mona made it here after all."

Kat sat down next to him and Mona settled onto the rug in front of her. "This doesn't seem like the scared, freaky dog Becca described. She talks really fast though, so maybe I missed something. I did look up how to deal with shy dogs in my books again and Mona isn't acting skittish or nervous like they said. In fact, she loved being toweled off. It was so cute." Kat leaned over and picked up the manila envelope. "So far, Mona seems really sweet. Not to mention relaxed."

Joel looked down at the dog, who had already settled in for a nap. "She certainly seems a lot easier to deal with than Swoosie the spaz dog or the dachshund with the warped sense of humor. Is she going to be okay with the other dogs?"

Kat scanned the vet records and the neatly typed information sheet Becca had provided. "I think so. When we talked about it, Becca said Mona has never met a dog she didn't like. It looks like she's got a million notes about Mona's behavior on this piece of paper. But there's nothing about problems with dogs or cats. It sounds like they aren't a big deal for her. I'm thinking we can introduce Mona to the gang in here instead of going outside into the freezing cold again."

"You just don't want to go outside."

"True. Did I mention it's cold out there? Would you go open the gate and let Linus upstairs? I thought we could start by just letting him up. Some dogs seem to find him a little intimidating at first, until they discover he's just a big marshmallow." She gazed intently into Joel's dark green eyes. "By the way, is there something wrong with your leg?" Sometimes he wasn't exactly forthcoming with information, so it was best to inquire.

"It's sore. I probably shouldn't have gone running with Swoosie."

Kat gestured toward the windows. "Well, unless you have ice cleats, I think your fitness program is over for the year.

It's really snowing hard out there. Big fat clumps of snow. It looks like a holiday movie where they use those plastic-looking soap flakes for the fake snow."

Joel frowned. "I hope Cindy will be okay. She was already whining about coming 'all the way out here.'"

"Apparently to your sister, your world-class stuffing is worth the trip over the river and through the woods to our house. A few hours with her won't kill you." She looked down at Mona. "Okay little dog, are you ready to meet everyone?"

Joel got up, stumbled on the rug, and grabbed the bookshelf to keep from falling. "I'll be right back."

"Are you sure nothing is wrong?" Kat scowled. What was going on with him?

He darted a glance at her. "It's cold and I was outside for hours moving that firewood under cover. I'm just sore. You're not going to worry about the fact I tripped, are you?"

Kat crossed her arms in front of her chest. "I am a worrier. It's what I do. But I'll shut up about it." For now.

"Okay. Watch out for thundering canines."

Kat narrowed her eyes as Joel left the room. Was he limping? He had been out working out in the forest for ages dealing with firewood. Maybe he hurt himself. It would be like him to not say anything about it. The gate opened downstairs and the sharp clattering sound of claws hitting the stairs broke the silence. Mona shot straight up from her nap and was back on all four paws, looking alarmed. Kat held the leash and said softly, "It's okay Mona. Sorry about the noise. Linus is a big guy and he can't help himself."

A huge brown hairy dog ran into the living room and skidded onto the rug, which slid in front of Kat toward

Mona. Kat reached out her hand to pet his head. "Hi Linus. Meet Mona."

Mona's eyes were wide and she looked startled, but she wagged her tail tentatively at the larger dog. After engaging in some reciprocal sniffing, the two dogs seemed to determine that all was right in the canine universe. Kat relaxed her hold on the leash. That was a relief. One down. Four to go.

The gate creaked open again and the rest of the dogs thundered up the stairs. At the noise, Mona jerked the leash and Kat got up off the couch as the remaining four dogs came into the living room. She pointed at them. "Okay, you guys, be nice to Mona." A golden retriever, border collie, collie mix, and an Australian shepherd mix joined Linus in a friendly group wag.

Kat led Mona over to the dogs, who continued to wag merrily at the visitor. Mona's tail waved back and forth in response. "So are we all cool?" More wagging and sociable sniffing ensued and Kat walked back over to the sofa and sat down again. Mona settled back in on the rug in front of her. Kat reached down to pet her back. "You're being so good, Mona. I think Becca was too hard on you. Maybe you just don't like loud noises. I can relate to that."

Joel returned to the living room, picked up his magazine, and sat down. "That seemed to go okay."

"You're limping." She had paid more attention as he walked toward her, and she definitely wasn't imagining it.

"Sorry."

Kat reached out and touched his arm. "Did you hurt yourself and neglect to mention it to me?"

"Not lately."

She tapped his arm more playfully. "Yeah, I know. You're probably still annoyed about hurting your arm. But the dachshund won't be back for a while. At least Mona is bigger, so it's less likely I'll lose her."

"We can only hope."

Suddenly, all of the dogs leaped up and ran for the door, barking hysterically. Mona stood at the end of her leash, looking confused. Kat stood up and smiled at Joel's expression. "I think your sister has arrived."

Joel sighed heavily and pushed himself up off the sofa again. "Great."

~

The repetitive pounding on the door was incredibly annoying and Mona was obviously not happy about it. Kat stroked the dog's head. Cindy's visit wasn't likely to be easy on anyone. "I'm sorry, Mona."

At last, Joel shoved aside the pack of dogs and opened the door. A small boy ran by Joel, screaming his way through the kitchen and into the living room. The dogs looked on in interest. Kat was holding Mona's leash, trying to prevent her from ducking under the sofa. The blonde child crashed into Kat's knees. She bent and grabbed his shoulders. "Ow, that hurt!" At least, the impact caused him to stop screaming for the moment.

"I'm a fire engine!" he shrieked.

Kat sat down on the sofa and faced the boy. "Johnny, remember how Joel talked to you about using your 'inside voice' when you're here? It's really important now because we have a dog here that doesn't like loud noises."

"No! I have a voice. I can be loud whenever I want to. I don't have to listen to you. Mommy says you're strange. And my name is not Johnny. I changed it."

"Okay, whatever your name is, I might be strange, but it's my house. When you're inside my house, you need to talk quietly." She pointed down at Mona, who was lying at her feet with her eyes wide. "See how you scared the dog? You need to be careful not to scare dogs. They don't like it and it's mean."

"It wasn't mean!"

"Say that more quietly and maybe I'll believe you. Try whispering." The kid had been here twenty seconds and he was already trying her patience. It was going to be a long evening.

Johnny whispered melodramatically. "It was *not* mean!"

Kat pointed at Mona again. "See how she looks more relaxed now? That's because you were nicer and respected her feelings."

Johnny ran back into the kitchen and wrapped his arms around Cindy's legs. "Mommy, it wasn't mean. *I* wasn't mean!"

Cindy looked over at Kat. "What did he do?"

"Nothing," Kat said. "We just have a dog here that doesn't like loud noises. I tried to explain that to him." Whether he understood was another story.

"Good luck." Cindy turned to Joel, who was placing a grocery bag on the counter. "I don't see why you couldn't come to my place and make the stuffing there."

Joel pulled a bunch of celery out of the bag and put it on the counter. "I refuse to make anything in your kitchen. You have no decent pots, pans, or knives. I don't know how you cook anything."

"You are such a cooking snob." Cindy squinted at Joel appraisingly. "What's wrong with you?"

Joel looked up. "Nothing." He held a bunch of carrots and flopped the green tops toward Johnny, who was systematically opening and closing the lower kitchen cabinet doors. "You might want to keep an eye on him. Did you bring any games or anything?"

Cindy grabbed Johnny's hand. "Why don't we sit down at the table over here?"

The small child pulled away. "I want to go outside in the snow. I want to build a snowman!"

"No honey, we need to stay inside for a while. There's not enough snow for a snowman. It's just supposed to be flurries today. You'll get to build a snowman soon though—I promise." Cindy pulled out a chair and lifted him onto it. "I brought your coloring books."

"I don't want to color."

Cindy pulled books and crayons from her bag and put them on the table. "You love to color, Johnny."

"I'm not Johnny, I'm Sparky the Fireman."

Cindy pulled out a big picture book and laid it on the table. "I brought that book too. We can read it later."

"I want to play with Smokey and Snozzle and Squirty!"

"I know. Why don't you color first?" Opening the coloring book to a page with a fire hydrant on it, Cindy said, "I have to help Uncle Joel with the food for the party tomorrow. Remember we talked about that?"

"I know." Johnny picked up a red crayon and waved it. "Fire hydrants are red!"

Kat led the resident dogs downstairs, closed the gate, and returned to the kitchen. She said to Cindy, "All of our dogs are secured, so I can help Joel chop up the veggies. I can keep an eye on Mona if you want to keep an eye on Sparky over there. Do you want something to drink?"

Cindy shrugged. "What I really want is about six glasses of wine, but I still have to drive home. So I'll settle for water."

"Okay. Have a seat."

Cindy walked over to the table and bent over Johnny, who was looking industrious, coloring hard. "That's really nice. I thought you said fire hydrants were red."

"I changed my mind. This one is in outer space." He put his finger on a squiggle. "That's a space man."

Kat gave Cindy her water, then went to the counter and grabbed a knife. She turned to Joel, "So what are we chopping?"

He handed her the carrots. "Start with these."

She went to the sink and said over her shoulder, "I think Mona likes Chelsey. Maybe it's a shy-dog thing, but I think they are bonding."

Joel whacked a pile of celery. "They're probably comparing notes."

Cindy leaned back in her chair. "There is something wrong with you."

Kat turned to look at her. "Sparky tells me you think I'm strange."

Cindy blushed slightly. "I'm sure I didn't say that. He has an active imagination. I wasn't talking to you anyway. Joel, what's going on with your leg? You're standing funny."

He turned around and aimed the knife blade toward the great outdoors. "Nothing. I went running with a dog. It's just sore."

Cindy thumped her glass down on the table. "You idiot. Why would you do that?"

Kat turned to face the living room. What was going on here? Although Cindy could pick a fight with Joel in thirty seconds flat, this was a new tactic. "We had a dog stay here that needed a little extra exercise. I'm not a big fan of running or exercise in general, so Joel ran with her a few times."

"You *know* you're not supposed to do that!" Cindy said. "Your days on the track team are long over."

Joel put down the knife. "It's not a big deal."

"Yes it is! You know what they said."

Kat turned to Joel. "What *who* said?"

Cindy threw up her hands in exasperation. "You didn't tell her? Do you guys ever actually talk to each other?"

"Tell me what? What are you talking about?" Kat said. It was like they were speaking some bizarre foreign sibling language.

"I broke my leg a long time ago," Joel said. "I told you I broke a bone. But it's not a big deal."

Cindy got up and walked into the kitchen. "Yes, it was a big deal, you idiot. You had what, eight surgeries? Nine? It's a miracle you can even walk!"

Joel leaned toward his sister. "I'm fine. Could you just drop this? I don't want to talk about it."

"You are such a pain. I hate it when you do this, Mr. Clam-Up-And-Never-Say-Anything." Cindy looked out the kitchen window. "Oh crap! Look at the snow. It's a white-out! I can't even see my car out there." Her shoulders slumped. "Poor little Myrtle is buried. It was *supposed* to be flurries."

Kat peered out the window at the small Mazda hatchback that Cindy referred to as Myrtle. It looked like an igloo rising up from an expanse of frozen tundra. She turned to Cindy. "I think the snow had other ideas."

Cindy crossed her arms across her chest. "I'll take that glass of wine now. Clearly, I'm not going anywhere."

"I can plow everything out in the morning," Joel said. "By then the snow will have stopped and you can just go home and get ready for your party."

Kat walked toward the pantry to get the wine. It was going to be very a long night. Maybe she'd pour a glass for herself too.

~

Kat returned to chopping carrots as Johnny yammered on about outer space and Cindy sipped wine. Periodically, Cindy offered advice or commentary on the cooking process, which Joel studiously ignored. The phone rang and Johnny leaped up out of his chair. "It's the space men calling. I knew it! They're making contact!"

Fortunately, Johnny was too short to reach the wall phone and Kat answered it. She smiled at the sound of her friend Maria's voice.

"What is going on there, girlfriend?" Maria said. "What's with all the screaming? Are you and the engineer doing something kinky?"

"No. Joel's nephew has decided to be a fire engine again. Hold on for a second. I need to switch to another phone." She waved at Joel and indicated that he should hang up the extension after she got downstairs.

Kat ran down to her office and picked up the receiver. "You can hang up now, Joel."

The line clicked and Maria said, "You know, I never thought about it before, but the engineer has a sexy phone voice. He sounds different than in person. Maybe it's just that he has to say something, so you don't think the line went dead and hang up on him."

"Oh give me a break. He speaks all the time and you know it." Kat picked up one of the books on her desk and put it in a pile. If Johnny and Cindy were going to stay here in her office, it might be a good idea to tidy up a little. "So hey, what's up? Happy Thanksgiving! Did you find a job yet? I thought you were going to go see your family this weekend."

"No. Gas is expensive and my personal financial situation is what you might call precarious at the moment. It's hard to believe that with as many people as there are in this city, that it would be so hard to find a job. My landlord also has no sense of humor when it comes to tardiness on my rent payments."

Kat paused in her book-relocation program. "I didn't know it was that bad. Do you need a loan?"

"No. I have decided to return to my former profession, since it seems that my secretarial and organizational skills are not in high demand at this particular point in my career."

"You mean bartending? I thought you said you never wanted to do that again. I believe you made some disparaging comments about the men who tend to frequent those establishments." Disparaging was a polite way to put it.

"These are desperate times, girlfriend. I went back to the fern bar."

"The creepy Fern Oasis? With the disgusting Lemon Drop drinks and aggressive plant life?" The place even smelled weird.

"You know it. The bartender there still thinks I'm cute and we had a discussion about part-time work after I showed him my mad mixing skills. I made him a killer Queen's Part Swizzle and dazzled him with my technique. If you're really good, you can mix the drink and not lose the stripey effect, you know."

"I don't know what that is, but I'll take your word for it." Kat threw another book on the stack, which was dangerously close to toppling over. How did her office always turn into such a disaster area? It was like books procreated in here.

"The bar environment isn't as bad as it used to be. The fern place is progressive. They are seeing the writing on the wall and just went non-smoking, since they're gonna have to at some point here pretty soon anyway. I'm thinking the cleaner air might improve the clientele—it might upgrade them from cigarette-stained beer guzzlers to clean-cut yuppie fancy-cocktail types. Those guys might tip better."

"It's probably better for the ferns too."

"Not to mention me. When I was bartending in Vegas, I thought I was gonna die of lung cancer right there on the spot. They'd do an autopsy and find big, black holes in my organs."

"Eww." That was not an image Kat wanted to dwell upon.

"Yeah, but I'm sure my lungs are all pink again after years of plying the secretarial trade. The good thing is that working at night means I can still continue the quest for a new job during the day. If I ever get an interview, I'll be at the ready."

Kat held up a book on database theory. Definitely not hers. How did *that* get in here? Now Joel's books were multiplying too. "If you're not seeing your family, what are you doing for Thanksgiving?"

"Everyone I know has something to do, so my holiday is going to consist of checking out the Thanksgiving episode of that new TV show everybody is watching with all those 20-somethings who drink coffee. They live in huge fancy apartments in New York City, even though they have crappy entry-level jobs. Have you seen it? It's like this fantasy city life where you don't have to pay outrageous rent and there aren't any roaches. Plus, some of them have really good hair. I plan to enhance my viewing experience by dining on a fine Swanson TV dinner with turkey, gravy, mashed potatoes, and the itty-bitty chocolate square that is supposed to be cake. But I may need to augment that pathetic little excuse for a dessert with a Twinkie. It's important to keep up my strength for the job hunt."

"True. It sounds quiet, anyway. Here, it is not quiet and it's snowing like crazy—to the point that Joel's sister and nephew can't leave. It's possible I may slowly go insane. I mean the kid is kind of cute, but too much time with him and I want to gobble down that entire pink package of pills I got from the gynecologist."

"I think that would be bad for your lady parts. But I'm glad to hear you took action after the kitten scare."

"Lady parts? Really? Since when did you start talking like you walked out of 1954? But yes, I don't think this Kat is ready for a kitten right now. I don't know how Cindy does it. Or Joel for that matter. He's really sweet and patient with his nephew."

"Well that's good information to have anyway. Just in case."

"Yeah. I know. But I think my already cautious nature has reached a new level of vigilance. And I have a calendar that I'm using to keep track, so I'm paying a little more attention." Kat thumped a book down on the desk. She'd discovered pregnancy scares were extremely bad for her mental health. "I really wish you were here instead of Cindy. Joel is like a different person around her. And now, there's something wrong with his leg. So I'm worried about that too. Nobody tells me *anything*."

"Sorry, girlfriend. Although I know that my hot date with Mr. Swanson sounds like a lot of fun, it is a little lonely. I wish I could come up there too. But unless there's a Miata-snowmobile conversion kit I don't know about, you're on your own for the winter."

"I know. Uh-oh, I think I hear different yelling upstairs. I gotta go. Happy Thanksgiving. I'll talk to you soon." Kat hung up the phone. It was time to venture back into the fray.

Chapter 2

Into the Wilderness

Becca squinted at her windshield and wiped a tear of frustration from the corner of her eye. She'd already *been* on this road. Maybe twice. Where was Alpine Grove? How could she lose an entire town? She thought she'd turned the right way out of the driveway of the kennel, but all she'd seen were masses of trees for what seemed like forever. And snow, which was falling so fast she could barely see the road anymore.

After driving in circles for what seemed like hours, Becca hunched over the steering wheel as the car inched along through the snow. What should she do? Maybe if she kept going this way, she'd end up back in Alpine Grove. But she'd thought that before and had turned back. And then made the left on the other road with the mailboxes. Now, who could say? She wasn't sure about anything. Whatever she did, it was going to happen slowly because the road was slippery. Except for that one ski trip with her ex-boyfriend Tony years ago, Becca had never driven in snow. And on that trip, in the end, she'd just stopped the car and made Tony drive the rest of the way home because she had been so stressed by the road conditions. That experience was nothing compared to this. If she didn't find the town soon, she might never get out of here. By the time anyone found her, she'd be a Popsicle.

Becca pulled the car over next to a row of mailboxes and spread her maps out across the passenger seat again. It was getting late. Although the sun was completely obscured by the thick clouds, it was obvious that it was also sinking low in the sky. The only thing worse than getting lost in the snow was getting lost in the snow in the dark. Getting to the assessor's office today wasn't going to happen. She really was going to be stuck here over Thanksgiving. This trip just kept getting worse and worse. Pat had told her not to give up Joanne's motel reservations for Thanksgiving weekend. Good thing. Even the rather nasty-looking motel would be a welcome sight at this point.

Becca leaned over the seat, studying the maps in an effort to figure out where she was. On the standardized tests she'd taken when she was a kid, she got great marks in vocabulary and math and alarmingly bad numbers for map-reading skills. It was the thing she was most worried about as far as going into appraisal work. Pat seemed to shrug it off as a non-issue, but Becca knew how frequently she got lost a lot better than he did. A poor sense of direction couldn't be fixed with a better organizational system or to-do list.

"Okay Becca, focus," she said out loud, in an effort to bolster her confidence. It didn't work. The only sound was the flap, flap noise of the windshield wipers going back and forth. And now she was talking to herself like an idiot. What she really needed was a "you are here" arrow on the map. Sadly, it was sorely lacking. There were no landmarks. Trees didn't count. What was the last road sign she'd seen? Misty something or other?

She jabbed her finger at the map. "Misty Meadow Lane! I saw that road." If she turned around and went back, she could make a left there, then go back past the kennel and get back to town from there. How had she gotten so far north? What a disaster. Once she got back to the H12 motel, she was going to take an incredibly long hot shower. Maybe there was a nice place to eat somewhere too. Her stomach growled in agreement.

At least it was a plan. And any plan was better than no plan. Becca pulled away from the mailboxes and made possibly the slowest three-point turn on record through the snow. The tires spun briefly and then gripped again, lurching the car forward. The jolt of terror in Becca's chest was almost as alarming as what the car was doing. She was not good at this winter driving thing at all. If she didn't have a nervous breakdown or freeze to death first, she was going to treat herself to something fabulous like a shoe-shopping spree. But the first item on the to-do list was to get out of here and get back home.

Tony used to tease her about being a fast-talking city girl who had never even seen a wilderness area. Of course, he wasn't exactly Mr. Mountain Man either. Sitting in a hot tub in a ski chalet in Vail didn't count as camping or as even a remotely outdoorsy activity. When it came to skiing, Becca had been more of a fan of the après-ski aspect of the experience. The ski outfit she'd bought for the trip to Vail was cute, but the actual skiing part of the trip was mostly just cold and humiliating. She had spent most of her skiing time on the bunny slope, sliding around on her backside. It was way more fun to just stand around and look cool next to the huge stone fireplace in the lodge.

She smiled at the memory of being with Tony in Vail. What a fantastic trip that had been. A lot better than being here, that was for sure. In that situation, the snow had been charming and picturesque. Here, it was a slippery, treacherous, road hazard.

But snow certainly wasn't the worst hurdle she'd ever overcome. So she'd deal with the weather just like everything else. In retrospect, the Vail trip had been one of the last good experiences with Tony. After everything that had happened, Tony had lost interest in her and suggested that she see a psychiatrist—"a really good shrink," as he had so eloquently phrased it. It wasn't like she hadn't tried to pull herself together. Counseling, self-defense classes, self-help books— she'd tried them all and worked hard on getting her life back. But when Tony called her a "head case," that had been just plain mean. Becca had lost a lot of respect for him then. The final breakup had been horrible, but she still missed his easy sense of humor. When was the last time she'd even laughed? Was she doomed to turn into some bitter, man-hating crone?

Something leaped onto the road on the passenger side of the car and Becca yanked the steering wheel to the left. Out of the corner of her eye, she realized a small deer or moose was running alongside her car. A *moose*! *Well, there's some real wilderness for ya, Tony!* The car fishtailed slightly, but because she was going so slowly, she managed to get the vehicle back under control.

The animal jumped back off the road and into the trees. Good thing there were no other cars and she hadn't hit the thing. It must have been a baby. The poor little guy was probably lost too! Becca straightened her shoulders and leaned forward. Time to stop thinking about the past and focus on the road. Concentrate!

A green road sign appeared out of the foggy whiteness. Misty Meadow Lane! At last, she'd found it. Maybe she was finally, *finally* going to get back to town. Becca gripped her hands more tightly on the steering wheel. Just a little bit farther. No problem.

~

As Becca turned onto Misty Meadow Lane, the dull ache in her shoulders from clenching the steering wheel transitioned into a sharp muscle twinge. She stretched out her fingers on each hand, one after the other. *Relax.* By the time she got to the motel, she'd probably burst into tears. *Breathe deeply.* It was all going to be okay. Becca had been through far worse than a stupid little snow storm. Time to put on her big girl panties and deal with it. It couldn't be much farther. Maybe some music would help. She glanced down at the radio and turned the knob.

When she looked back at the road, she gasped. A huge brown vehicle seemed to fill the entire windshield in front of her. Where had *that* come from? Becca turned the steering wheel sharply, which sent her car into a slide. Shrieking, she slammed her foot on the brake and a huge plume of snow sprayed up from the back wheels as the car skidded. When she opened her eyes again, the brown vehicle was gone. The only thing visible through the windshield was a lot of white. Becca turned her head to look around. What had just happened? The car was at a sharp angle and had apparently gone nose-down into a ditch. She moved to try to open the driver's side door, but it was wedged closed. The passenger side might be a better exit route.

Becca jerked her head back to the left at a loud knock on her window. Her heart thumped wildly in her chest. A scruffy-looking hooded man waved his gloved hand at her. Becca covered her mouth with her hand, trying not to scream. *No! Not again.*

He pointed to the other side of the car. Biting her lip, Becca realized she was shivering and crying. She grabbed her coat and moved across to the passenger seat while trying to pull her skirt down. The man had waded down into the ditch and was yanking at the passenger door. He smacked his gloved hand on the window and yelled, "Unlock it!"

Becca did as he suggested and the door opened with a whoosh. Snow swirled around and into the car. She wrapped the coat around herself and blinked the snow out of her eyes as she struggled to get out of the car.

He pushed the hood of his coat back and said, "Are you okay?" Taking her hand, he helped her out. "You look okay. That's a relief."

Becca looked into his eyes, which were a startling shade of blue. They reminded her of the color of Lake Tahoe and another fun vacation. The guy's dark brown hair was long enough that it was falling into his eyes and curling around his collar. And the scruffy factor wasn't actually razor stubble as she had assumed, but an extremely short beard.

Becca snuffled and her teeth began to chatter as her pumps sank into the snow. The frigid sensation hit her legs in an icy blast of cold pain. She turned back around to the car and reached to grab a tissue out of the glove compartment, so she could wipe her nose. She probably looked frightening from all the crying.

The man pulled her forward and said, "Come on. Let's get out of the ditch." As they moved around the front of the car, a sharp cracking noise rattled through the muffled silence of the snowfall. Cringing, Becca crouched involuntarily. "What was that?"

"A tree broke. This is some heavy snow."

With the man's help, Becca stumbled up the hill onto the road. Her teeth were chattering so hard they were starting to ache. Kat was right—these were not the right shoes for winter. Her toes were going to freeze off. The man pulled her up the last bit of the incline and turned to face her. "Are you sure you're okay?"

Becca put her shoulders back, stood up straight, and attempted to look like a professional again. "Yes, I'm fine. Where did you come from?"

He indicated a brown truck with its hood facing down into the ditch on the other side of the road. "Over there. You ran me off the road. It was either hit you or bail out into the ditch."

Becca crossed her arms across her chest and stamped her feet, trying to get circulation back into her toes. "I did not! You ran *me* off the road!"

"I don't think so. Look which way your car is facing. I watched you spin out. It was an impressive performance. Mostly, I was just trying to get out of the way."

Becca turned back to look at her car in the ditch. Maybe he was right. But still. "It's not my fault. You were hogging the whole road!"

"Listen, it doesn't matter. We need to get out of this weather. I can see you shivering, and you're not dressed for this snow. There's a driveway right up there. Let's go see if they can call us a tow truck or something."

"You can't just go barge in on someone like that without calling!"

"Would you prefer to die of hypothermia? It's almost dark, which isn't going to make it any warmer out here."

Becca's shoulders slumped. Suddenly, she was completely exhausted. All she wanted was to just go home. "I could just sit here in the snow and wait here for a while until someone comes by."

He gripped her arm and looked into her eyes. "No. Do *not* sit down! Let me go get my dog out of the truck. You stay here. And I mean it, don't sit down. Stay right there."

Becca stood and shivered while he walked across the road to the truck and opened the door. A huge black and brown dog leaped out joyfully, whirling about amid the snowflakes. Becca knees were cold and wobbly. She slowly started to sink down toward the snow, which looked really soft and inviting. Just for a minute.

The man ran back across the road to her, reached out, and grabbed Becca around her shoulders before she hit the ground. "Don't you do that. Keep moving. You're coming with me." He pointed down the road. "See that driveway? We're going right down there."

"I'm so tired. You go. I'll just stay here and wait. I don't even know who you are. What's your name?"

Without releasing his grip on her shoulders, he started walking her down the road. "I'm Jack Sheridan. That's my dog Frank. Nice to meet you."

"I'm Rebecca Mackenzie." She tripped on something in the snow. Maybe her feet. "I'm not normally this klutzy."

"It's okay. I get the impression you don't do much walking in the snow."

"I think I need different shoes."

"I'm sure of it." Jack stopped and pulled off the plaid wool scarf he had around his neck. "Here. Wrap this around your head and neck to keep the snow off."

Becca fumbled with the scarf and dropped it in the snow. "Can't we just sit down for a minute?"

"No. Here, let me do it." He swept the snow off her hair, shook the snow off the scarf, and wrapped it around her head.

"Thank you. I hope these people have a bathroom." She really needed to pee. It felt like a lifetime since she'd seen civilization and experienced the joys of indoor plumbing.

"Put your hands under your armpits to keep them warm. And follow the path Frank's making in the snow. It will be easier."

"He seems so happy. Don't dogs get cold?"

"Frank's a Bernese Mountain Dog. They're bred for this sort of weather. He loves winter."

"That's because he doesn't have to drive."

Jack brushed snow off her shoulders. "That's true."

"My dog Mona would be so scared now. I'm glad she's not here."

"Me too. Keep walking."

~

Mona was not scared. In fact, she seemed downright happy. Kat smiled at the dog, who had heartily enjoyed her dinner, along with the rest of the pack. Mona now was now enjoying a post-meal nap under the table next to her new doggie best friend, Chelsey.

Satisfied that all was well in the canine realm, Kat opened the gate and walked back up the stairs. The cats were another story. After Cindy and Johnny arrived, they'd all disappeared to their various feline hidey-holes to pout, but apparently they came out long enough to eat, because their cat food had been consumed. After the loud, obnoxious house guests finally left, the feline residents would undoubtedly reappear.

Back upstairs, Cindy and Joel were arguing. Again. Still. They had an infinite ability to snipe at each other, which was exhausting to be around. Kat wanted to crawl into bed and pull the covers over her head so she couldn't hear them anymore.

It was hard to believe Joel was the same rational human being she lived with and loved so much. Something about his sister really brought out the worst in him. After commenting about other aspects of Joel's lifestyle, it seemed Cindy had circled back to the topic of his broken leg. Kat was still not clear about when or how his leg had been broken, but according to Cindy, it had been some type of serious injury. One that Joel obviously *really* didn't want to talk about.

Joel said quietly, "Would you please, please just leave me alone?"

Kat walked into the kitchen. She knew that tone. When Joel got seriously angry or upset, his voice got eerily quiet. Cindy had to know this too. Maybe. She couldn't be that clueless, could she? Picking up a knife, Kat said overly brightly, "Dogs are all fed. So, what should I chop next?"

Joel turned to her. "The bread is toasted. Could you cut that up into cubes?"

"Sure." Maybe if they looked busy, Cindy would shut up.

Cindy waved her glass of wine at Joel. "Remember when you pulled Mabel out of the ditch two years ago? You said you'd be more careful in the winter."

Joel stood in stony silence, chopping onions. Apparently, he was done talking.

Kat pointed her knife toward the window. Time to change the subject. "I don't think I'm ready for winter. And looking at the snow outside, I'm sure my car isn't."

"We can take the truck wherever you need to go," Joel said.

"I know. I'll miss driving my Toyota, though. I think it's done for the season." Kat leaned over the counter to peek out the window. "At this rate, I may never find my car again. The snow is really coming down out there."

Johnny, who had moved under the table for his coloring project, emerged and announced, "I'm bored. I don't want to color anymore. And you guys talking all the time is boring. Can't we do something? I want to build a snowman. I want it to be a space man snowman!"

Cindy bent down and rubbed his upper arm, "It's almost dark, honey. We can do it tomorrow. Mommy wants some more wine now. Let me get that and then we can read your fireman book, okay? Go sit on the sofa and I'll be right over."

"That's a baby book! I want something different! I want to *be* the fireman, not read pretend baby stories about a fireman. Can we make a fire?"

Joel and Kat both said, "No!" simultaneously.

"But your stove has a fire," Johnny said. "How does it work? Our stove at home has metal things, but I'm not allowed to touch them."

Kat said, "No fires. And you need to stay away from the stove. We do not want any other fires here. None. I mean it." The poor stove had seen enough fires in its day. Kat's aunt

Abigail had apparently had a few cooking issues when she'd lived here. It was a miracle the house hadn't burned down.

Johnny stood up and walked into the kitchen. "I want a flamethrower for Christmas, but Mommy says I can't have one. Santa doesn't care what Mommy says, though. I sent him a letter and asked."

Cindy gulped down the last of her wine and followed him. "Santa doesn't always give you what you ask for, honey."

Johnny whined, "But he *has* to. That's why he's Santa."

Cindy walked into the kitchen and got the wine bottle out of the refrigerator. She tilted the tip of it at Kat and said in a stern voice, "Don't you let Joel do anything stupid again." Joel thwacked the cutting board loudly with the knife.

Kat shrugged. "I'll, uh, see what I can do." It was beyond time to find out what had happened to Joel's leg. They were going to have *such* a conversation after Cindy left tomorrow.

Cindy took Johnny's hand and walked him back to the sofa in the living room. She sat down and started reading the book out loud to him. Unimpressed, Johnny sat and glared at her with an irritated expression, his arms firmly crossed over his chest.

The celery, carrots, and onions were simmering in the pot and the scent of sage and thyme wafted through the kitchen. Joel threw some more spices into the pot. Kat touched his arm and whispered, "Please don't kill your sister on a national holiday, okay?"

The stern expression on his face relaxed and a corner of his mouth turned up, "I'll try."

Kat leaned her head on his arm and rubbed his back. "She'll be gone tomorrow. Look at the bright side—at least my mother isn't here."

He put down the knife and wrapped his arms around her. "You have no idea how thankful I am for that."

Kat stood on her tiptoes, put her arms around his neck, and kissed him. "Me too."

Johnny bellowed from the living room, "Eww, stop that! No kissing! Gross."

Kat jumped away from Joel and whispered. "Wow, that's a mood killer if ever there was one."

Joel picked up the knife again and began chopping some leafy herbs. "Six-year olds are like that. As a girl, you have cooties, you know."

Johnny called out from the living room. "You guys are boring. There's nothing to do here."

As she threw the bread cubes into the pot, Kat could hear Cindy giggling quietly. Turning to Joel, she said, "Is it bedtime yet?"

"I think it's still a little early."

"Maybe I should go find some sheets for the guest bed in my office. I'd like to be really, really prepared for bedtime when it arrives."

He smiled. "That's not a bad idea."

~

Becca was sick of walking. She couldn't remember ever being this tired. Exhaustion was even trumping the cold. This had to be the longest driveway in the world. And whoever owned it certainly wasn't out here plowing. She could practically see the snow piling up deeper and deeper as they trudged on. Her feet and ankles no longer felt connected to her body. But Jack kept dragging her along. What a grumpy taskmaster he was.

Finally a small log cabin appeared out of the whiteness. It was the only thing that wasn't white. The sky was white, the ground was white. Even the dog was covered with white now, the snow swirling around him as he leaped forward. Thank goodness for Frank. What did Jack say he was? A Saint Bernard? Maybe he had one of those kegs of cognac around his neck. She could really use a drink.

Becca tugged against Jack's sleeve. "Can't we stop and rest?"

"Nope. Almost there."

The only sound in the clearing was the rustle of Jack's huge coat as they approached the house and the sound of her own breathing into the scarf. The dwelling was dark and looked abandoned. Becca wanted to cry in frustration and despair, except that she was too tired to even muster up a tear. They got up to the entry and Jack finally let go of her so he could pound on the door. Not surprisingly, the knocking was greeted with nothing but silence. He yanked at the knob, but the door was locked.

Becca pulled at the arm of his coat. "Please, can I sit down now?"

"No. I need to break this glass so we can get in."

She shook his sleeve again. "Wait! You can't break into this place! It's not yours." Who *was* this guy?

He turned and gave her a hard look. "Remember what I said about hypothermia? You're not looking too good. I'm breaking in." He looked up at the sky. "This storm is not going to get better for a while."

The hard look in those icy blue eyes indicated he wasn't taking no for an answer. Fine. Becca let go of his coat and waved weakly. "Do whatever you want." She was way too tired to argue anymore.

Jack pulled a roll of duct tape out of one of the many pockets in his coat. "I'm going to put tape on this pane to see if I can keep it from shattering too badly. Don't sit down."

"I'm leaning, not sitting. You carry tape in your coat? How many pockets does that thing have?" Who needed that many pockets?

"A lot."

"It's good to be out of the snow anyway." She looked up. "Thank you to whoever put up this little overhang over the door. I love you, wherever you are." Maybe Jack was right. The idea of being indoors was blissful.

Jack busied himself with trying to tape over the pane of glass at the bottom right corner of the door. The tape didn't want to stick very well, but once he was satisfied, he started digging around in the snow near the doorway.

Becca turned her head to look at him. "What are you doing?"

"Looking for a rock. This area has extremely rocky soil, so there's bound to be a piece of granite nearby, if these folks have ever planted anything at all in the yard." He pawed at the ground, "C'mon Frank, do some digging."

Frank was enthusiastic about the new game and started pawing the snow. His rear was in the air and snow started flying everywhere. He hit bottom and pulled his head out of the hole, looking proud of himself.

Jack bent down and pulled a rock out of the hole. "Good boy." He went back to the door and smashed the pane of glass with the rock. Carefully reaching in through the opening, he felt around and flipped the deadbolt. He opened the door and turned to Becca. Grabbing her sleeve, he shoved her through the doorway. "Watch out for the glass." Following her inside, he pushed the glass aside with his boot. "Okay Frank, let's go."

Frank bounded into the dwelling and stood in front of an old mission-style sofa, sniffing the air and looking somewhat confused. He snuffled at the rug a few times, and apparently determining it was okay, he spun around and laid down. Grabbing a back paw in his mouth, he began chewing at the ice chunks that had collected between his toes.

Becca looked up at the ceiling. "What's wrong with this place? It smells like smoke." They certainly hadn't broken into the Ritz. If the place was filled with toxic chemicals, that might be a problem.

Jack closed the front door, walked into the small kitchen area, and started opening cabinet doors. "I don't care. It's not outside, which is an improvement. Get out of those wet clothes. I'm going to look for blankets and something to cover up the hole in the door."

Becca sat down on the sofa and shook her pumps off her feet. She curled her toes in agony as the movement caused her circulation to move blood back into her feet. It was like 700 straight pins were being jammed under her toenails and into the skin on her feet. She shook her hands and the pins started jabbing her fingers too.

Flexing her hands first, she tried to remove the scarf, but her clumsy pain-riddled fingers had other ideas. Finally, she pulled enough on the wool fabric that she was able to shake her head and get it off. Her teeth started chattering and she tucked her hands under her armpits again.

At a thump from above, Becca looked up. Jack was climbing the ladder up to a loft that jutted out above the kitchen area. He threw a blanket over the railing, which landed on the floor behind the sofa.

He called down to her, "Take off your coat and wrap that around you."

Becca stood up and squealed like a little girl. She almost fell down as her feet hit the floor. It felt like the thousands of pins were jabbing into her sole. She plopped back onto the sofa. "My feet hurt!"

Jack came back down the ladder, picked up the blanket, and handed it to her. "Take off that coat. It's soaked."

Becca flexed her fingers in front of her face and cringed. "My fingers hurt too. Could you just stop for a minute? I can't undo the buttons."

He turned and their gazes locked. "Are you okay?"

"Stop asking me that! Thawing out really hurts."

Sitting down on the couch next to her, Jack pulled off his gloves and unbuttoned her coat. He said in a softer voice, "You really didn't dress for this weather. Don't you have gloves?"

"When I got up this morning, I didn't think I'd have to dress like an Eskimo to go take pictures of houses."

"Take pictures?"

"I have an appraisal assignment. It's a home appraisal for a bank." She sighed heavily. "But then I got lost."

He pulled the wet coat off, dumped it on the floor, and grabbed the blanket, wrapping it around her shoulders. "Better?"

Becca gripped the edge of the blanket in her hand. "Yes. Thanks."

"I need to find something to cover that hole in the door. Tuck your feet up under the blanket too."

Becca curled up into a fetal ball on the sofa. "That does feel better. I think I love this blanket now too." She looked up at the ceiling. "Thank you, whoever owns this stinky place."

~

Jack continued rummaging around the house while Becca tried to warm herself on the sofa. She pulled a hand out from under the blanket and examined it. The skin was beet red. It looked strange, but her fingers were finally feeling better.

Jack leaned over the back of the couch. "Are there any white areas on your hands?"

"No. They're red." She popped a hand out from under the blanket again. "See?"

"Good. Check your feet too." He continued toward the doorway.

"Did you find something for the hole in the door?" Becca tried to covertly remove her pantyhose under the blanket without letting any cold air into her cocoon of warmth or giving Jack a free peep show. It was a complicated maneuver, but finally she yanked off the shredded L'eggs and threw them on the floor. She looked up and noticed that Jack appeared to be amused by her under-blanket machinations. The twinkle in his deep blue eyes was unmistakably humor.

He said, "There was a case of Twinkies in the cabinet. I'm going to use the cardboard for the time being. Soon I won't be able to see what I'm doing, and this is better than nothing."

"Twinkies?"

He waved the orange cardboard toward the kitchen area. "I know Twinkies last for thousands of years, so maybe they're some type of experiment. It's almost the only food here that I can find. Twinkies and a few cans of soup."

"That sounds appetizing." Becca snuggled down into the sofa and her stomach growled. "It's getting dark—could you turn on a light?"

Jack ripped a piece of duct tape off the roll. "The power has been turned off. And the water has been drained from the pipes."

"You mean no water in the bathroom? No *toilet?*" Becca's dreams of indoor plumbing vaporized into nasty potty nightmares. She still needed to pee badly. Her feet were almost at the point where she could consider walking on them again and her bladder was not going to wait around forever.

"There is a toilet. But it won't flush without water."

Becca curled herself up more tightly in the blanket. "I can't tell you how depressing that is."

"It's better than being outside. Have you looked out the window? I haven't seen a storm like this in years." He tore another piece of duct tape and placed it across the cardboard. "We've got a wood stove here, but I've gotta go outside and see if there's any wood."

"What about all the trees? There's wood everywhere."

"It isn't dry."

"Oh." Wood covered with snow probably *was* more difficult to burn.

"I'll be back." Jack grabbed his coat. "C'mon, Frank. Let's go."

The dog eagerly leaped up from his nap. Jack opened the door with a whoosh and they were gone. Becca clutched the blanket. She was alone. Without the large man and dog, it was like all the life had been sapped from the little cabin. The last bit of twilight coming through the windows gave the house an antique patina, like an old sepia-tone photograph.

She sat up and tentatively touched her feet to the floor. The scuffed wooden floorboards were freezing. But at least it didn't feel like she was walking on a bed of nails anymore. She might not die of hypothermia, but she could die of dehydration and malnutrition. They had no water and the only things to eat were Twinkies and soup? This trip just got worse and worse. If she lived through this experience, she was going to kill Uncle Pat for making her come here.

The door opened and a blast of frigid air entered the room along with Jack and Frank. The dog returned to his spot on the rug and began the snow-removal process on his toes again. Jack had found a few sticks of wood that definitely were not completely dry, since they were covered with snow. He whacked the wood on the floor to shake the snow off and then began examining the wood stove.

"Is the wood okay?"

He brushed the snow off his shoulders and removed his coat. "It's almost the bottom row of what was obviously once a huge wood pile. Apparently, someone took the rest of it away or used it up at some point. I guess they left these because they were close to the ground."

"Is that bad?"

"Well, it's not great, but the wood will probably burn." He opened the door of the stove and looked inside. "At least

I don't think that smoky smell came from the stove. It looks okay."

"I didn't think about that. We're not going to die in a fire now, are we? Or get carbon-monoxide poisoning?"

"No. I examined the chimney. It looks like it was cleaned before they shut this place down for the winter. I don't think it has been used in quite a while."

Becca sat up straighter on the sofa. Her brain was returning. "Wait! This is a summer cabin. That makes sense. That's why they drained the water." Of course, knowing this didn't make the whole potty situation any less bleak.

Jack looked over his shoulder. "You seem to be feeling better."

"I was supposed to appraise a summer house. There are lots of summer houses in the Alpine Grove area. But I know it wasn't this one. I don't know how I ended up on Misty Meadow Lane. I was going to go to town then to the place I was supposed to look at, which is on Edgewater Road."

"That's down by the lake. You were about 30 miles off." He started ripping pages out of an old magazine and crumpling them up. He turned the magazine over and looked the cover. "Computers? Humph."

Becca bent her head and rested her forehead on her knees. "I missed it by 30 *miles*? That's pathetic." Her map-reading skills had reached a new low.

"I don't know where you thought you were going. Misty Meadow Lane dead-ends into a private quarter section of land that connects to national forest."

"I was supposed to be going back to town." Becca gripped the blanket more tightly.

"Not that way, you weren't." Jack struck a match and the flame lit the room, casting shadows on his face, emphasizing his angular features.

"But that's what the map said. I needed to turn, then connect to the road with the mailboxes and get back to the kennel place. From there I had directions to get back to town. Well, if I reversed them, anyway." Except it didn't work.

"I think I know why you didn't make it."

"Why?"

"Those are the worst directions I've ever heard." He held his hands in front of the flame. "It should be warmer in here soon."

"Good. The floor is freezing. I don't suppose you have any socks in those pockets of yours."

Jack grinned at her, which completely transformed the serious expression he'd had on his face. "Sorry, no socks. There is a dresser in the loft. I'll go look." He stood and Becca noted that underneath all the Eskimo attire was a startlingly attractive male form. Who would have guessed?

Becca was not a fan of beards or long hair, although Jack's dark brown hair did curl in a kind of sexy way. But the guy was definitely scruffy. And she did not find the scruffy look attractive. Maybe he was a farmer or something. What did people in Alpine Grove do? He was clearly in extremely good shape, with broad shoulders and not an ounce of extra weight. What was this guy doing out here in the middle of nowhere?

Jack descended the ladder and threw a pair of wool socks and a well-worn flannel shirt over the back of the sofa. "Here you go."

Becca grabbed the socks, pulled them under the blanket and onto her feet. The heavy knit of the socks was like a little slice of heaven. Thick, warm, and wonderful. Shucking the blanket off her back, she put on the flannel shirt, which was obviously made for a man who shopped at the big-and-tall store. But the flannel was warm. And it was beyond time to face the bathroom situation before she couldn't see a thing. Darkness was falling fast.

She padded across the floor and stood next to Jack, who had returned to crouching in front of the wood stove. Holding her hands out in front of her toward the stove, she said. "Thank you."

He looked up and smiled. "You're welcome."

"Thanks to Frank too, for helping. He's a great dog."

"Yeah, he's my buddy."

"I'm missing my dog too. Even though she wouldn't be happy here, I still miss her."

Jack stood up. "Where is she?"

"At the boarding kennel somewhere around here. As I mentioned, I'm not exactly sure where it's located."

"There's a kennel in Alpine Grove? I didn't know that."

"Sort of, I guess. It's this woman with a bunch of dogs. Mona is staying in her house. There's an outbuilding where Mona was supposed to stay, but I was worried she'd be scared. Mona is really sensitive."

"I see." The flicker of the light from the wood stove reflected in Jack's eyes.

Becca dropped her hands to her sides, "Oh no, I forgot! I should call Kat. I don't know how long it's going to take them to pull my car out of that ditch. I'm going to have to stay in Alpine Grove a lot longer than I thought." She scuttled back to the couch, grabbed the receiver off the phone sitting on the end table, and put it to her ear. There was no dial tone. She sat down heavily on the sofa. "The phone doesn't work, either." This took isolation to a disturbing new level.

"Didn't you see that tree that fell across the road? It's sitting on power lines and probably phone lines, too. Even if the power weren't turned off here, I doubt we'd have electricity."

Becca put her face in her hands. "This is awful. I hope Mona is okay." Poor little scared Mona.

Chapter 3

Lights Out

Kat finished making up the guest bed in her office and was checking on the dogs, who were happily napping in their favorite spots in the hallway. Mona was certainly an easy dog to care for, once she'd decided she was part of the pack. Joel came downstairs and checked on the state of the wood stove. The warmth from the stove probably added to the soporific effect in the downstairs hallway. At least the dogs were going to be well-rested this winter.

Kat stood next to him as he bent to prod the logs in the wood stove with a long metal poker, which sent brilliant orange sparks swirling around the inside of the metal box. "Thanks for all your efforts to keep us warm."

He turned and put down the poker. "Having your mother here increased my wood-chopping motivation."

"Understandable. Too bad I didn't have any excuse to escape off into the forest." Her mother's presence tended to cause Kat to want to run far away.

"I'm guessing you aren't going to go home to see your mom for Christmas."

Kat wrapped her arms around his waist and placed her head on his chest. The beat of his heart was comforting. "What? And leave you here? No way." She leaned back so she could look into his eyes. "I've had enough family time.

Speaking of which, you do know that you're going to have to tell me what happened with your leg."

Suddenly, all the lights went out in the house and they were enveloped in velvety blackness except for the flickering orange light of the flames in the wood stove. Joel extricated himself from Kat. "I was afraid that was going to happen."

"Did the power go out? It's so quiet. I can't see a thing."

Johnny started shrieking upstairs. "Mommy, I can't see!"

At the cry of the unhappy child, all the dogs stood up and started milling around anxiously. Joel walked toward his office, reaching out to find the wall. "Let me go find a flashlight."

Kat stumbled behind him. "Linus, please get out of the way! I think Abigail had some lanterns packed away in that storage room across from my office."

Cindy stood at the top of the stairs, holding Johnny's hand. "What is going on?"

"We lost power. Joel is looking for a flashlight. I'll be right up. I think there are some lanterns down here," Kat said. Maybe Cindy could keep Johnny from completely losing it until they got up there.

Joel emerged from his office and turned on the flashlight, shining it toward Kat. "Let's see if we can find those lanterns."

Kat dug through the boxes in the storage room as the six dogs looked on. She found two kerosene lanterns and turned to Joel. "Do we have fuel for these things?"

"Yes, it's outside on the shelf in the shed." He took the lanterns from her and started toward the stairs.

"Wait! Don't run away with the light." She turned to the dogs. "I guess you guys can come up."

Kat opened the gate and all of the dogs thundered up the stairs. As part of her new role as pack mate, Mona followed the resident dogs without any hesitation.

While Joel went outside looking for fuel, Kat and Cindy sat at the table. Cindy had Johnny in her lap with her arm around his waist. The boy was still upset and making an obvious effort not to cry. Cindy tilted her head down toward his face and wiped away a stray tear with her fingers. "It's like camping out, honey. You love flashlights! When Joel comes back, we'll have more light and then you can play with the flashlight." Mona came over and put her head on the little boy's thigh. He stroked her head. "I like this dog."

"See what happens when you're quiet and treat her nicely? She's a very sweet girl," Kat said. Mona was good with him. Maybe she liked kids.

Johnny smiled weakly. "Nice doggie."

Mona wagged and wiggled her body, trying to absorb more affection. Realizing that there was petting to be had from the humans, Linus came over to Kat and placed his big muzzle on her leg. "Hi Big Guy. I know it's dark. We're working on it."

The door opened and Joel came back inside. He shined the flashlight around in the kitchen, found some matches, and lit one of the lanterns. The kitchen was illuminated with a golden yellow glow. He lit the other one and walked toward the dining area. Weaving his way through the dogs, he placed it on the table. "Let there be light."

Kat pushed Linus's head away and stood up. She glanced into Joel's eyes briefly, raised her eyebrows, and took the flashlight from him. "Hey Johnny, I have an idea. Have you ever made a pillow fort?"

He crawled down off his mother's lap dubiously. "I don't think so."

"It's really fun. I'll be right back."

Kat went into the bathroom and grabbed a sheet out of the linen closet. She went across the small hallway, took the pillows off her bed, and returned to the dining room. "Okay, let's set up over here." She handed Johnny a pillow and pointed to the back of the couch. "Here is the impenetrable fortress that you need to defend. There is a moat, so no one can get across. But you need to make some fortification over there on that side."

Johnny carefully set up his pillow at a strategic location on the floor. Kat opened up the sheet, floated it over the back of the couch, and tucked it in under the secondary pillow wall. She crawled in and gave Johnny the flashlight. "You need to stand guard. Do you require assistance?"

"I think I need Joey to be my second in command."

"Okay. I'll go get him." Kat crawled back out and Cindy handed her a stuffed dinosaur, crayons, and a stack of coloring books. Kat placed the supplies in the fort. "Here you go."

After Kat had backed out of the fort, Mona poked her nose inside and wagged her tail. Johnny said, "Mona, you can stand guard too." He brandished the dinosaur at her. "But you have to take your orders from Joey." Mona laid down in the entryway to the fort, apparently figuring out that it could be quite a while until Joey had something to say.

Now that Johnny was busy explaining the details of fort management and hierarchy to Mona, Kat stood up and walked back to the dining room. Cindy waved her glass of wine at her. "Thank you. You could make some kid a good mom someday."

"Since that's not happening in the immediate future, I think I'll join you in some wine. The refrigerator isn't working, so I think I'd better do my part to use it up." Kat quickly opened the refrigerator, grabbed the wine, and closed the door. It was best to keep the cold air in there for as long as possible.

"Do you know if there are any coolers around here somewhere?" Joel asked.

Kat poured her wine into a glass. "Maybe downstairs in the storage room? That seems to be where Abigail kept her camping-type stuff."

Joel took the kitchen lantern by the handle and went down the stairs, leaving Kat and Cindy sitting in the glow of the other lantern.

The light from the lantern flame flickered and danced across the wine in Cindy's glass. She twirled the liquid and gazed at it thoughtfully. "It's so weird that this is your house, but it's not really your house."

Kat took a sip of her wine. "I'm getting used to it. A lot of times it feels like I know Abigail better now than I did when I was a kid. I just wish I could talk to her again." So many questions had come up since she'd inherited the house, but they weren't answerable anymore.

"Yeah, I feel that way about my parents." Cindy leaned forward and wrapped her hands around her wine glass. "I barely remember them now."

"I'm sorry." Kat looked down at her glass. Joel never talked about his parents.

"I try not to think about it too much." Cindy shrugged. "It's just sad that Johnny will never know his grandparents, you know?"

"What about his dad?" Kat knew nothing about him, either.

Cindy looked at Kat sharply. "I don't *want* him to know that guy."

"Oh." Kat sighed. Oops. She'd really walked into that one. Talking to Cindy was always tricky. "At least you have Joel. Johnny seems to like him."

"Yeah, Joel is really sweet with him." Cindy peered down into her glass. "But since most of the time Joel and I tend to fight, that's probably not the greatest influence either."

Kat set down her glass. Cindy actually realized that? Hmm. "That's true. You should sign a peace treaty or something."

"I have tried not to fight with him, but he makes me insane. I suppose it's not unusual. Everyone's parents drive them nuts."

"Well, my mother certainly drives me nuts. But he's your brother."

"It's the next-best thing."

Joel came back upstairs with the lantern and placed it on the kitchen counter. He sat down at the table. "I found a big cooler. If the power doesn't come back for a while, we can put snow in it and put the frozen stuff in there. Then throw the whole thing into a snow bank."

Kat looked at him. "Snow *bank*? Exactly how much snow is out there."

"You don't want to know."

⌒

Jack lit another candle and placed it on the kitchen counter. The place was starting to look like a small shrine, with candles flickering from their spots on most of the flat surfaces throughout the small cabin. He looked over his shoulder. "Would you like a Twinkie?"

Becca stood up and walked into the tiny kitchen area. The wood stove was doing its job and she had finally faced the terror of the bathroom. Warmth and bladder relief did a lot to improve her mood. She opened the tall door to the pantry. Thirty or forty individually wrapped snack cakes were stacked on one of the shelves. "When they ask you the question, 'if you were stranded on a desert island, what would you bring?' Twinkies are never on that list." She looked around the door at Jack. "There's a reason for that, you know."

He turned to look at her. "We're not on a desert island."

"Same idea. You know what I mean. Twinkies are not on the list of key survival supplies. Or they shouldn't be."

"I suppose not. We could heat up some soup on the wood stove. I think there are some Chef Boyardee pasta things in there too."

Becca looked back into the cabinet. "Is the owner of this place twelve years old? Who eats like that?" What was *in* stuff like Twinkies or canned pasta anyway? Gross. It was probably better not to know.

Jack shrugged. "At least we're warm. And crummy food is better than no food. I'm not sure what I'm going to give Frank. He's starting to look anxious about dinnertime."

At the mention of his name, Frank got up and stood next to Becca, gazing into the cabinet forlornly. Becca reached in, pulled out a can, and held it in front of the dog. "How do you feel about SpaghettiOs, Frank?"

Frank wagged and hopped backward a few times. Becca smiled at his enthusiasm. "Yeah, a can is a can, right? It could be Alpo." Frank didn't exactly seem to be a picky eater.

Jack took the can from her and held it up to the candle. "I suppose we can all eat it for dinner. Just don't read the ingredients list." He handed the can back to her and bent down to open a lower cabinet. "I'm going to use this pot to melt some snow."

"I suppose this is part of the not dying of dehydration program?"

"Yes. And the plumbing improvement program. Be right back." He put on his coat and went outside.

Becca looked down at Frank and stroked his huge head. "You are the most awesome dog. Jack is lucky to have you." Frank wagged in agreement.

Jack returned with the pot, which was overflowing with huge hunks of snow. He placed it on the wood stove. "This is some heavy snow. It should have a high water content."

Becca looked at the pot. "Great. Now I'm thirsty. I wasn't before. And if I drink something, then I'll need to use the bathroom again."

"Well, melting the snow could take some time, so you don't have to worry for a while. By the time there's enough water for a flush, you'll be ready for it."

"I guess I'll just hang out. It's not like I have anything else to do." She settled onto the sofa and inspected her fingernails. It didn't seem like she'd done much today, but the polish was thrashed and chipping off. "What I would give for a spa treatment right about now. A little time in the whirlpool, massage, manicure, pedicure. The whole nine yards. But that's sure not going to happen until I finish this appraisal." She chipped a fleck of nail polish off her thumb with her index finger and looked over at Jack. "You know why I was here. So what are you doing out here in the middle of nowhere?"

"I was out at the property at the end of the road. They are trying to get a conservation easement, so they need a management plan."

"Managing what?"

Jack was staring down at the snow in the pot. Becca said, "I don't think you need to watch the snow melt, do you? Aren't you tired?" She was certainly exhausted.

"I suppose it has been a long day." He walked over and perched on the edge of the couch. "I'm working on a forestry management plan."

"You mean trees?" There certainly were enough of them around here.

He looked down and picked at something on the faded fabric of the sofa. "Yes, trees. I'm a forester."

Becca tried to act cool like she knew what that meant. "Oh. That's interesting." What did a forester do exactly? Look at trees?

"It is to me." He got up, walked into the kitchen, and started rummaging around in the cabinets again. "Did you see a can opener?"

"No. I was admiring the Twinkies." She tapped her foot and wiggled her toes in the big wool sock. Happy toes were a marvelous thing.

"Hmm."

"Hmm?" Becca put both feet on the floor and turned to look at him. "What do you mean, 'hmm?' Are you telling me we can't get into the SpaghettiOs? Because Frank's going to be upset. I promised him SpaghettiOs."

"No, it's okay. I have a Swiss army knife in my coat."

"That coat is amazing." Becca leaned her elbows on her knees. Did he have everything he owned in there?

"It's good to be prepared."

"Do you think the tall twelve-year old that lives here would mind if I look through his dresser? My legs are still freezing and my pantyhose are shredded. I don't think they can be resurrected at this point."

"I doubt they were warm either." Jack turned from a cabinet and pointed toward the loft. "There's a bunch of old clothes up there."

Becca climbed up the ladder, hoping that Jack wasn't looking up her skirt. She was definitely not wearing her sexiest pair of panties. Why hadn't she done laundry earlier this week? If she'd known, she would have opted for a lacy Victoria's Secret bikini, not this utilitarian cotton J.C. Penney model. Mom was right about wearing good underwear when you go out. Because you never knew when you might be in a car accident out in the middle of nowhere. With some scruffy forester looking up your skirt. It was hard to imagine how this day could get any more bizarre.

Becca found some old sweatpants in the dresser, put them on, and rolled up the bottom of the legs, so she didn't trip all over them. She was going for the full-on serious bag-lady look now, but at least she was warm. She bent over the railing and called down. "Hey, I like it up here. I feel like I'm in a bird's nest. And it's warm!"

Jack looked up at her from the living room. "You can sleep up there then."

Becca turned and descended the ladder again. "Where are you going to sleep?"

He patted the back of the couch. "This is fine."

"That's very chivalrous of you, but you're taller than I am. You'll be uncomfortable." Cramming those broad shoulders onto that narrow sofa would have to be unpleasant.

Jack gestured toward the wood stove. "I can watch the fire more easily from there."

"I could do that!"

"What if it goes out? Have you ever built a fire in a wood stove before?"

"No." Becca tugged the sweatpants up and tightened the drawstring. "But I'm sure I could." How hard could it be?

"I'll deal with it. Are you hungry? I can heat up one of the canned things."

"I can do that, if you want." The fact that by this point he probably thought she was an incompetent moron was starting to bug her. Plus, she really needed something to *do*.

Jack walked to the front of the cabin and pulled his coat down from the hook next to the door. He pulled the Swiss army knife out of a pocket and handed it to her. "The can opener requires some patience."

She pulled out the various blades and held one up to show him. "This is it, right?"

"Yes. Go for it. I'm going to go get some more wood. Tomorrow, once we have light again, I need to dig the chain saw out of the truck and see if I can find some downed trees that aren't too wet."

Becca walked over to the kitchen. "You drive around with a chain saw?" This wasn't going to turn into a horror movie, was it?

"I told you, I'm a forester. I spend a lot of time in the woods."

"Oh." She looked down at the can. Opening it could take forever, given the stupid way the Swiss army knife worked. This was like some type of martial-arts master patience exercise. Wax on. Wax off. She was not the Karate Kid. What were those Swiss people thinking with this design?

Looking up from the tedious can-opening process, she said, "Wait a minute, this is great! If you have a chain saw, you can cut up the tree that fell across the road." She put down the Swiss army knife and clapped her hands together. "That would be fantastic! We can call someone to get us out of here."

Jack shook his head. "I don't think so."

"Why not?" He never liked her ideas. What a grump.

"I'm not getting near an electric line with a chain saw." He leveled a stern look at her. "I don't have a death wish."

"Maybe the tree isn't on the line. How do you even know?"

"There used to be a wire crossing the road. It wasn't up there anymore after the tree was down."

Becca picked up the can opener again. "Oh. Okay." Logic could be so irritating. At this rate, she wasn't going to get out of this place until the spring thaw.

~

Becca dumped the contents of the can into a pot. The revolting smell of soggy pasta and heavily sweetened fake tomato sauce accosted her nostrils. Even little kids didn't eat canned pasta like this anymore, did they? She turned away from the counter toward Jack, who was crouched in front of the wood stove again. "I'd like to give Frank the SpaghettiOs, if it's okay with you. I don't think I can stand to eat something that smells like that." She looked down at the dog. "Frank seems pretty excited about the idea though."

"I'm sure he'd enjoy it."

"He probably doesn't need them heated up, right?"

Jack stood up and walked into the kitchen area. "No. Just put it in a bowl. Frank will be your best friend."

Becca poured the nasty contents of the pot into a bowl. It landed with a slurpy *glop*, and she put the bowl on the floor for the dog. "Here you go, Frank. Eat up."

Frank wolfed down the contents in approximately four bites. He looked up at Becca expectantly. She shook her head at the dog. "Sorry. That's it." A dog that size was probably used to getting a whole lot more food.

Jack said, "There was some soup in the cabinet that didn't look as bad."

"I think I'm going for this rice and vegetable one." She held up a can. "The picture on the label looks less disgusting than the pasta stuff." Becca went through the laborious can-opening process again and poured the thin soup into the pot. Grabbing a spoon, she went over to the wood stove, and placed the soup on it. She peered into the large pot that had been filled with snow. The giant stack of snow had melted down to only about four cups of water. It could take a long time to get enough water for even one flush.

Jack joined her in front of the stove and they stood and stared down at the soup in silence as Becca stirred for what seemed like ages. Apparently not satisfied with his SpaghettiOs, Frank was closely supervising the cooking operation and drooling on the floor. Becca had to admit that the soup did smell good. When was the last time she'd eaten anything? No wonder she was hungry.

At last, the soup started bubbling and Becca brought the pot back to the kitchen. She set two bowls of soup on the tiny table and sat down. Jack sat across from her, looking somewhat morose. The flickering of the candlelight reflected in his eyes, so they flashed a deep sapphire blue. Now that she wasn't about to die from hypothermia, she wasn't sure what to say to the guy beyond "thank you for not leaving me out in the frozen tundra and letting me turn into an icy corpse." She'd already thanked him, so now what? She cleared her throat. "So I guess you live in Alpine Grove somewhere?"

He looked up from his soup. "Yes. Right now, I'm renting a place near town."

"That must be convenient. They might even deliver pizza. I would so love a pizza now. I'm guessing this place is out of the delivery area. Even if they could get here. Which they can't, unless they want to use a snowmobile or a team of sled dogs."

Jack sipped his soup and put down the spoon. "You probably don't want to think too much about food, given how little we have here."

"Oh, come on. I think some fabulous crusty bread would go so well with this soup. I'd love to have one of those long sourdough flutes with seeds all over the top. Lightly toasted with some melted brie? Oh, and some creamy roasted garlic too. That would be fantastic." Her stomach growled loudly and she looked down at the bowl. "Oh. I see what you mean."

"One little can of soup doesn't make much of a meal."

"You're right." Becca set down her spoon in an effort to prolong the dining experience. Best not to dwell on decadent dinner fantasies. "Clearly, I need to think about something other than our lack of food. What do you do other than wander around in the woods? What do you do for fun?"

"Sometimes Frank and I go out hiking."

"So, you go walking around in the woods when you're not walking around in the woods?"

He shrugged. "I guess so. What do you do when you aren't trying to find houses?"

"I like going out to eat with friends." She glanced at her spoon. "Never mind. What else? Okay, I like to go shopping. I used to go out more at night, but not as much anymore." Why did she say that?

Jack peered over his spoon with a half-smile. "So are you afraid of the dark or something? I hope not, because we're going to have to put out all these candles at some point."

"No. That's not what I meant." Becca waved her hand toward the window. "If we ever get out of here, is there anything fun to do in town? I mean, you aren't going to be hiking all winter in the snow, are you?"

"I have snowshoes."

Becca put her spoon in the bowl with a clink. "You're kidding, right?" Was this guy, Grizzly Adams or something?

Jack nodded. "I do have snowshoes. And cross-country skis."

"Don't you ever do anything inside? Where it's warm?"

"I read sometimes."

She leaned forward. "So are you a hermit or something? Wait, you're not associated with the Unabomber, are you?" Did the Unabomber have a chain saw?

He chuckled. "No. I don't have any secret agenda. It's just we…I…haven't lived here that long and I haven't met a lot of people because I spend so much time out in the forest working."

"That sounds lonely."

"Most of my family is in Colorado. I have a bunch of friends there too."

"Didn't you want to spend Thanksgiving with them?" Becca stirred her soup. "This is shaping up to be the worst Thanksgiving ever for me. Tomorrow, I was supposed to be drinking wine and making mashed potatoes with my mom and the rest of my family. I had a whole list of things I was going to be doing. And I'd be doing them in a house with functional plumbing and heat that just turns on when you flip a switch. Instead, I'm eating soup of dubious vintage with you."

"Thanks."

"I didn't mean it like that. You did save me from freezing to death, and I appreciate that. But didn't you have plans? What were you going to be doing tomorrow?"

Jack crossed his arms across his chest. "Well, I had plans, but they didn't work out, so Frank and I were going to watch some TV."

"Alone? How depressing. What plans?" Becca rested her forearms on the table. No wonder he looked sad.

He leaned forward, the candle flame illuminating his eyes. "You sure ask a lot of questions."

"I have nothing else to do. Have you seen any books, playing cards, *anything*?"

"Not really."

"So what were your plans?"

Jack placed his crossed arms on the table. "I was supposed to be going to a huge dinner with my wife's family. The whole thing had been planned for months at a resort south of here. But that didn't work out."

Becca leaned back away from the table. "You're married?" Was he wearing a ring? She hadn't noticed.

"Not exactly." He scowled and sipped a spoonful of soup.

Becca glanced down, but she couldn't see his left hand. "Um, okay." Given his expression, the not-exactly-wife probably was not a popular topic to pursue. "At least you get to hang out with Frank, the super-cool dog. How long have you had him?" The dog sat up and turned his head to see if the mention of his name meant food was forthcoming. Seeing no evidence of feeding, he sighed loudly and collapsed back down onto the rug.

"I got him about six months ago. I did a timber cruise and some consulting for a family. They didn't have enough money to pay me, so they gave me Frank instead."

Becca's eyes widened. "You got paid in dog?" Alpine Grove was a seriously odd place.

"Yes. They needed someone to evaluate the forest to see if they could harvest sustainably. If they didn't do some logging to get some cash fast, they were probably going to lose their property. But they were worried a logging company might strip the land, so they wanted my opinion."

Becca looked over at the dog, who was snoring quietly. "Frank, do you feel cheap?"

The dog lifted his head and cocked his ears. Clearly, there still was no food to be had. He placed his head back on the floor with a thud.

Jack looked down at Frank. "I doubt it. Mostly he rides around with me in the truck and gets to run around in the woods. He was a terrible farm dog anyway."

"Frank was a farm dog?"

"Yes, he was supposed to guard chickens, but he wasn't very good at it after he ate one and discovered they were tasty."

"Eww. Oh Frank, bad dog!"

Chapter 4

Kung Fu

After finishing the soup, Jack got up and started blowing out some of the candles. "We should probably save these."

"We're not going to be here for another night." Becca peered into the darkness, trying to see where he was. "Are we? Please say no."

"It's still snowing."

Becca slumped in her chair. "I can't believe this. It's so dark I can't even see my hand in front of my face." She held up her hand and wiggled her fingers. In the light of the one last candle and the flickering of the flame behind the glass door of the wood stove, her hand was only a dim outline with blackness behind it. How did anyone read by candlelight? In the days before electricity, everyone must have endured serious eye strain. "Is there a flashlight anywhere?"

"I found one in a drawer, but the batteries are dead. I have one out in the truck that I can get tomorrow when I go dig out the chain saw."

Becca got up, carried the candle in front of her over to the sofa, and put it on the coffee table. She sat down and wrapped herself in the blanket again, not because she was cold anymore, but because she wanted the feel of something

67

around her. It was so quiet and something about the blackness emphasized every tiny strange noise. "Where are you?"

Jack walked in front of the wood stove so she could see the outline of his body. "I'm right here. Where would I go?"

"I don't know. It's just really dark."

He sat down on the sofa next to her and leaned closer to see her face. "You really are afraid of the dark, aren't you?"

"No, I'm not! I go out at night all the time. A bunch of friends and I like to go out dancing at clubs." Well, they used to anyway. Her "club buddies" as she thought of them, had finally given up and stopped asking. Even before everything happened, the last few times they went out had felt strained. Trying to relive college party-girl days just seemed a little sad after a certain point. And all the scantily clad nubile youngsters at the clubs made her feel like a crabby old crank.

"Why are you huddled up in the blanket like that? You can't be cold anymore."

"There are weird noises." A log clunked in the wood stove and she jumped, clutching the blanket closer. Her heart was hammering in her chest. This was so stupid. Why couldn't she just get over this?

"That was the firewood breaking down into ash. And Frank is snoring. Sorry about that. He is kind of loud."

"Actually, I like the snoring. I'm used to hearing traffic noise. People noise. Any noise. Not this weird, creepy silence."

"You're afraid of the quiet?"

"I'm not afraid!" Becca fingered the blanket. Yes, she was.

"Okay. Whatever you say." Jack got up and disappeared into the darkness.

Intellectually, Becca knew her fears were completely irrational. But it didn't change how she felt. Maybe Jack wouldn't notice how nervous she really was. At this point, she was worried she might have a full-blown panic attack again. Even the idea of a panic attack made her more anxious. That was an experience she never wanted to have again. Maybe it would be better if she went up to the loft. She picked up the candle from the table and held it in front of her, trying to will her hand not to shake. Jack's shadowy form moved in the kitchen. She held out the candle toward him. "Could you hold this candle so I can see the ladder? I'm going to go up there and lie down."

He took the candle from her. "Sweet dreams."

Becca crawled up the ladder and stretched out her hands to feel her way to the bed. Crawling under the covers, she closed her eyes and breathed deeply, trying to focus on Frank's reassuring snoring. When she'd let Tony talk her into watching *The Shining*, she'd never dreamed she'd be stuck in the middle of nowhere in a snowstorm with a guy named Jack. That was a train of thought she needed to derail *right now*. Time to focus on her breathing like they taught her in yoga class. It was unfortunate that she was essentially lying here in corpse pose, however. Best not to dwell on that idea either.

~

Becca jolted awake and sat up. Where was she? Utter blackness surrounded her. She moved her hands in front of her face. Had she gone blind? Her heart thundered in her chest and she laid back down, trying to relax. A canine groan rose from below and she remembered. Everything. Frank. Jack. The cabin. The whole awful thing.

Apparently, she had been more tired than she'd realized and had finally fallen asleep. And then had some seriously bizarre dreams. There was swirling snow and Frank was typing on an old typewriter about Jack being a dull boy. But typing would be really hard with those gigantic paws. It didn't make sense. Then Frank went and got a drink of water from the soup pot. *Slurp, splash*—water was everywhere in her dream. That made a little more sense anyway. He was a nice dog, but definitely a bit of a drooler. Of course, now she really needed to pee again. And that meant crawling down the ladder and feeling her way around to the tiny bathroom. Oh, no.

Huddling back down in the covers, Becca tried to forget about her bladder and go back to sleep. No, she did not need to go to the bathroom. No, she did *not*! She tossed and turned a few times. It was no use. She sighed. There was no way she could hold out until morning. Flipping back the covers, she sat up and put her feet on the floor. Looking over toward the railing, there was a tiny bit of flickering light from the wood stove. That helped a little. It was like she was a moth, desperate to fly toward any tiny bit of illumination.

She padded across the floor and carefully turned around to descend the ladder. At the bottom, she turned toward the deep inky darkness where the bathroom was located. Holding her hands out in front of her, she shuffled slowly along the floor. It had to be here somewhere.

Something touched her shoulder and she whirled her fist around, slamming it into something solid. There was a loud crash and then an outburst of energetic male swearing. After exhausting his supply of creative expletives, Jack shouted from below her, "What is *wrong* with you?" At all the commotion,

Frank toddled over to offer his assistance. Jack pushed the dog away from him. "Frank, stop that. Go lie down."

Becca bent down and reached out a hand to try to help Jack up off the floor. "Are you hurt? I didn't know it was you."

He pushed her hand away and put his own hand to his face gingerly. "Who *else* would it be?"

"I'm so sorry! Are you okay? I hope so, because right now I've really, really got to go to the bathroom." Being startled was not a good thing for her bladder. The urgency factor was officially extreme. Thank goodness she hadn't wet her panties.

She scuttled off to the bathroom and could hear Jack mumbling as he got back to his feet. Maybe she'd learned more in those self-defense classes than she'd thought. She smiled at herself in the darkness. Kung Fu Becca.

After appeasing her oppressive needs, Becca carefully shuffled her way back out into the living area. Jack had lit the candle again and was sitting on the sofa, a plastic bag filled with snow pressed to the side of his face. She sat down next to him. "Are you okay?"

He turned his head to glare at her. In the dim light, the flickering flames from the stove made his eyes flash like icy blue daggers. "I've been better. Good thing we have all this snow, since there's a shortage of ice packs—or anything else—in the freezer."

Becca pulled a corner of the blanket up over her legs. "Why did you sneak up on me?"

"I didn't. I was just standing there. I thought you saw me."

"I couldn't see anything. Then you touched my shoulder." She clutched the blanket. "Why would you sneak up and scare me like that?"

He rearranged the plastic bag on his cheek. "I didn't touch you."

"Yes you did!"

"No I didn't. Maybe it was a spider."

"Yeah, right. What spider is out crawling around in the snow?" Becca peered at her shoulder and brushed it with her hand, just in case.

"They aren't outside; they're inside now. Sometimes they hang out in wood piles."

"I didn't need to know that." Becca moved her hands around the sofa pillows, looking for wayward arachnids. "I hate spiders. Now I'm really creeped out."

"Don't worry about it. You're sitting on my bed. They probably all crawled up off the sofa onto me."

Becca giggled. "True. You can keep them." She leaned back on the sofa, pulled her feet up and snuggled herself into the blanket with her arms wrapped around her legs. "I'm really sorry I hit you. I took self-defense classes, after, I… um…took classes. Never mind."

Jack looked up from the bag of snow he was rejiggering in his hands. "After what? Since you just hit me, I think you can tell me."

Becca moved her head farther away from the candle, so he couldn't see her face. "After everything that happened today, you probably already think I'm an incompetent moron. At a minimum, I'm sure you think I can't drive."

"I'll admit, I have seen better drivers."

"I can drive fine. Or I can when it's not snowing. And I'm really not a helpless idiot, either. I wasn't, anyway." She waved her hands in front of her. "I had a fantastic career—everyone loved me. I was managing seventy-five properties. I kept track of thousands of details about tenants, rooms, inspections, repairs, utilities—you name it. The folks in the office called me Becca the Efficient. Work was my whole life. I loved it."

Jack moved the plastic bag off his cheek and examined it again. "I thought you were an appraiser? What does any of that have to do with hitting me?"

"I took self-defense classes after I was attacked." She paused and took a deep breath. Even after all this time, talking about it was still awful. "After it happened, I couldn't go to work anymore. I went to counseling, took yoga and the self-defense classes. I tried to fix it—or fix myself—I guess. I really did. But everything still fell apart."

"You were attacked?"

Becca sighed. "Yes. I hate talking about this. And now I've had to tell so many people, you'd think it would be easier. Really, the whole thing could have been a lot worse. I was lucky."

"What happened?"

"I was going home—just walking to my car outside the office like I always did. When I was leaving the building, two drunk guys said they wanted to "get to know" me. I've lived in the city my whole life—I always thought I was kind of street smart and all that. So I ignored them and just walked faster. But they wouldn't let up. They kept saying they wanted to know me. Finally, I said I didn't want to know *them*. They got closer and then one of them hit me. I started screaming and I think I kicked one guy, but then a third guy came out of nowhere and grabbed my purse."

Jack touched her arm gently. "I'm sorry that happened to you."

Becca shook her head. "Someone called the police. There's a warrant out for one guy who ran away. I guess it's felony aggravated assault, officially. The other two were arrested for misdemeanors. But it bothers me that that guy is still out there, you know?"

"I can see why."

Becca leaned her cheek on her knees. "In some ways, that's not even the worst of it. I couldn't go back to work. Every time I tried to go into that parking lot, I got so anxious. I'd see something out of the corner of my eye. And the smells from the Indian restaurant down the street or the sounds of someone clattering a trash can lid would just bring everything back, so I'd just sit there in the car. I tried taking some sick days, hoping it would go away. But it kept getting worse, and finally I had a full-on panic attack at work. I thought I was dying and I couldn't breathe. I passed out and they took me to the hospital. It was all so embarrassing. In the end, everyone was really nice about it, but it wasn't like they could move the office. I had to quit."

"That must have been hard."

"It was one of the hardest things I've ever done. I've always been so good at my job. It was a huge part of my life. Then there was just *nothing*. I didn't know what to do with myself. I looked for another job. Sort of. But mostly I just sat in my apartment feeling sorry for myself. I didn't want another job. I wanted *my* job. The one I loved and where everyone loved me. My mom was actually the one who suggested I get into property appraisal work because of my uncle. He owns an appraisal company. So I'm training with him. I like the work for the most part. Well, until he made me come here anyway."

Jack squished the plastic bag of snow. "I agree that today was not a good day."

"No. You seemed to handle it a lot better than I did though."

"I think you were just busy trying not to freeze to death. It wasn't particularly enjoyable for me either." He pointed at the dog who was, once again, flat on his side snoring on the rug. "I think Frank had a good time though."

Becca wrinkled her nose. "What is that horrible smell?"

"It's possible the SpaghettiOs didn't agree with Frank."

"That's disgusting. Just when you think your day can't get any worse, the gigantic dog gets a case of the farts."

Jack laughed. He had a wonderful hearty, warm laugh and Becca couldn't help but smile in response. He said, "Well, Frank is a big dog and this is a small cabin. It could be bad." Jack got up and shook water off his hand. "I think my snow has melted."

Frank jumped up and followed Jack toward the kitchen area, wagging his tail. Becca waved her hands at the dog. "Don't you be sending that stink over here." Suddenly exhausted again, she leaned back on the sofa. How was Mona doing? Maybe they lost power there too, with all this snow. Poor scared Mona. She hoped her little dog was okay.

~

After eating stuffing for dinner, Johnny had collapsed in his fort, so Mona spent most of her evening curled up next to her canine buddy Chelsey. It was clearly time to give up on the long, tiring day, so Kat led all the dogs, Cindy, and Johnny downstairs with the flashlight and returned upstairs to go to bed herself. Joel appeared to be asleep already. Kat turned off the flashlight and crawled under the covers next to him. He rolled over and reached out to find her. "Hi."

Kat took his hand and stretched out her legs to figure out where the rest of him was situated. "I want my nightlight back. If I have to go to the bathroom tonight, I might seriously damage myself. This is the darkest dark ever. It's like someone coated the world in black construction paper."

He squeezed her hand. "So did you explain the water conservation measures?"

"Yes. Talking about anything related to the bathroom with a six-year old is complicated, and the conversation degenerated quickly. It took forever for Johnny to get through every possible question related to flushing protocol and bodily functions. I think he's on board with the program now though. And he liked the idea of making some yellow snow tomorrow."

Joel chuckled. "I'm glad I missed it."

"The no-water thing is arguably worse than the no-electricity thing." Kat snuggled up closer, enjoying the warmth.

"No electricity means no well pump, you know."

"I know. I understand it, but I don't have to like it. I hope the power comes back tomorrow, or I'm going to start looking really bad. The long, stringy, greasy hair look is not attractive. And the kitchen is a disaster. Lori was starting to look way too interested in all the stuff on the counters. Why is it that the dog that is hardest to see in the dark is also the most sneaky?"

"I'm sure it will be fine." Joel rolled over on his back and groaned. "I'm more worried about plowing. I just couldn't face digging out the truck in the dark. But that was probably a mistake."

Kat put her head in the hollow below Joel's collarbone. "The truck isn't going anywhere."

"If I wait too long to plow and it keeps snowing like this, there will be too much snow, and the truck won't be able to move it."

"But it's got that huge plow blade."

"We'll see. I was just too tired."

Kat stroked the soft short beard on his cheek. "There are lots of shovels. The rest of us can help too, you know. If Cindy ever wants to get out of here, she can help shovel."

"Ugh. You can tell her that."

"Are you feeling okay? How is your leg? Cindy really gave you a hard time about that."

"Spending half the day fighting with her is why I'm so tired. She wears me out."

"I can't believe she was mad we ate 'her' stuffing. You made it. I'm afraid severe weather delays may affect her big Thanksgiving party."

Joel groaned again. "I don't want to think about that."

"Did you really have eight surgeries?"

"Nine." He gently moved Kat's head and rolled over. "That's another thing I'd rather not think about right now."

"What happened?" Kat ran her fingertips across his arm, tracing the contours of the sinewy muscles. Joel had always seemed so healthy and invincible. It was hard to imagine him in the hospital.

"Car accident. Cindy is overreacting, as usual. I'm fine. It was all years ago."

Kat put her arm around his waist and laid her cheek on his back. "I'm sorry. That sounds awful."

"It was."

"From what Cindy said, I guess running is bad. If Swoosie comes back, we'll figure out some other way to tire her out." Joel didn't respond and from the regular sound of his breathing, it seemed he had fallen asleep again. Kat stared into the darkness as questions swirled in her mind. *Nine surgeries?*

~

The back door slammed downstairs and Kat jolted awake. She rolled over and realized Joel had left the bed at some point. She had planned to ask him about the car accident this morning while they were alone. Oh well. Feeble light was peeking through the curtains. Maybe he was taking the dogs out. Or maybe it was Johnny randomly letting dogs out that were supposed to be on a leash. Uh-oh.

Kat jumped out of bed and pulled on her jeans under her nightshirt. She scuttled down the stairs and looked around the hall. The door to her office was still closed. That was a relief. She opened the back door and peered outside. Many canine prints and one large set of human footprints trailed off into the forest. The snow had stopped, but the sky was still white. It looked like this was just a small break in the wintery action. There had to be almost two feet of snow on the ground already. Wow. Crossing her arms across her chest, Kat turned around and went back inside. It was freezing out there. The calendar might say it was still fall, but winter had definitely arrived.

Cindy emerged from Kat's office and stood in the hallway looking tousled and dazed. Kat waved. "Good morning."

Cindy rubbed her face with both hands. "I feel awful. How much wine did I drink?"

"I'm not sure, but the bottle was empty. I had half a glass. I'm not sure if Joel drank anything. He doesn't drink wine very often."

"Ugh. That was a mistake."

Johnny ran out of the office and yanked on Cindy's pant leg. "I want to watch cartoons! Where did Mona go? I told her she could watch too."

"Mona is outside with Joel going for a walk," Kat said. "The electricity is still out and we don't have a TV. Even if we had power, you couldn't watch cartoons."

Johnny's eyes widened as he processed this important bit of information. "No TV? *No TV!* But I want to watch *Rocky and Bullwinkle.*"

Cindy moaned. "I forgot about that."

Kat turned her palms upward. "Sorry. My aunt didn't have a TV. I sold mine, and I think Joel's was thrown out a window along with his computer. Its final resting place is probably at the dump somewhere."

Johnny said in an exasperated voice, "What are we going to do?"

"I'm going to make breakfast," Kat said. "The stove still works." It was a good thing the stove ran on propane, or there could have been a major mutiny last night. "We should use up the eggs anyway, since the refrigerator is still off. There's a lot of snow out there. I don't think the power will be back any time soon."

"Mommy, there's no TV!" Johnny whined. "*Moooommmmmmmy!*"

Cindy slowly started stumbling toward the stairs. "C'mon Johnny, let's go see what we can scrounge up. I'm not sure I can handle eggs yet. Maybe crackers. Or one cracker." She looked back at Kat. "Do you have any aspirin?"

"Yes, I'll go get it." Kat followed them toward the stairs. "Oh, and happy Thanksgiving!"

Cindy gripped the handrail with both hands, dragging herself up the stairs. "Yeah, happy, real happy. I'll be thankful when I can finally get outta here."

Kat sighed. At least, being hung over had slowed Cindy down. Kat would be extra thankful if Cindy left before she got enough strength back to start fighting with her brother again.

~

Since no one seemed interested in her breakfast suggestions, Kat left Cindy and Johnny to figure out food for themselves. The messy condition of the kitchen was depressing, and given the lack of water, it was going to stay that way. She put on her coat and boots and went outside, where Joel was standing with the dogs and considering the state of the truck. Although Kat knew the truck was green, no part of the old Ford was visible under its blanket of snow.

Joel handed her the leashes for Mona and Chelsey, who were panting happily. "Here, have some dogs." The other dogs were romping through the snow, looking like porpoises, leaping joyfully through the vast expanse of white.

Kat took the leashes. "Gee, thanks." She pointed at the truck. "This could take a while." Linus cavorted over to her through the snow along with Tessa, who was attached to him using the harness and leash arrangement Kat had devised. She rubbed Linus's ears. "You guys sure are excited about the snow." Linus and Tessa wagged and ran off to join the other dogs in some power snow wrestling.

Joel looked up at the sky, which was a monochromatic grayish white color. "I think it's going to start snowing again soon."

"Maybe we should have breakfast and fill up the coolers with snow like you suggested. Soon the refrigerator is not going to be useful as a cooling device anymore."

After dealing with the food situation, Kat convinced Cindy that if she ever wanted to leave, she needed to help dig out the truck. Grudgingly acquiescing, Cindy bundled up Johnny and they all went outside. Although most of the dogs were content to sleep away the rest of the morning, Linus made it clear he wanted more time in the snow, so he was allowed to join them.

Johnny followed the paths the dogs had created earlier in the snow and found a good spot where he could begin working on his snowman project. Linus sat down nearby to supervise. Johnny explained to the dog, "I'm making a snowman with a time machine, so he'll never melt." Linus swished his tail, creating a snow-angel wing.

Cindy took the shovel Kat handed to her. "How come I have to use the big heavy metal shovel?"

"It's a grain shovel," Joel said.

Kat said, "I'm smaller, so I get the half-broken plastic shovel." She flung some snow away from the truck, toward Cindy. "Oopsie."

Cindy shook her shovel threateningly. "Hey, stop it! That's not funny."

Kat giggled. "Oh, you're so wrong about that."

"Start shoveling," Joel said.

Cindy dug her shovel into the snow. "Fine." She picked up a clump of snow and lifted it. "Yuck, this is so heavy. We're going to be doing this forever! Where am I supposed to put it?"

"Somewhere away from the truck," Joel said.

"There's just more snow over there!"

Joel winged some snow over the side of the truck and onto Cindy's head. "Oops."

"Nice shot," Kat said.

Cindy stamped her foot in the snow. "Stop that!" Throwing the shovel aside, she bent down, picked up some snow in her hands, packed it together, and hurled it at Kat.

"That's cooold," Kat shrieked as snow slid down her neck. She charged around to the other side of the truck, away from Cindy, and stuck out her tongue at her. "You're gonna pay for that."

Cindy stuck out her tongue back at Kat. "Go ahead, shorty, make my day."

"Watch me, you giant galumphing Amazon!"

"Shut up, you little shrimp!"

Joel turned, jabbed his shovel in the snow, and glared at Kat. "You are really not helping here."

She picked up some snow and threw it at him, beaning him in the shoulder. "You're no fun," she said over her shoulder as she ran in the oppose direction.

Cindy lobbed a big clumpy snowball, which landed on Joel's other shoulder. She raised both arms in the air in a show of victory. "Direct hit! Score!"

Johnny peered around the large snowball he was pushing around. "Hey, how come you're playing without me?"

Cindy turned around and said, "We're not playing, honey. We're trying to shovel out the truck, so Joel can plow and we can go home."

"Don't you need a shovel for that, Mommy?"

Cindy picked up her shovel again. "I'm shoveling." She picked up some snow and hurled it away from the truck. "It's just going to take a while, that's all. Be patient."

While Cindy was distracted, Joel had moved around to the other side of the truck. Hoisting his shovel high, he heaved a gigantic pile of snow, which exploded all over Cindy's head and shoulders. She whirled around and charged toward him. "I'm going to get you for that!"

Joel laughed, dropped his shovel, and ran behind the truck next to Kat again, "Good luck! You know you're too slow."

"Not anymore—I'm going to get you." Cindy heaved herself onto her brother, throwing them both down into the snow, their long flailing arms and legs swirling everywhere. Linus galloped over to help, then stopped and stood cocking his head, trying to figure out what was going on.

Kat giggled and yanked on the sleeve of Joel's coat. "Would you guys cut it out? You're making a huge snow crater."

Cindy sat up first, breathless from the exertion. She pointed at Joel. "He started it."

"Did not." Joel sat up and pointed at Kat. "She did."

Kat backed away from them and picked up her shovel. "I have no idea what you're talking about."

Johnny walked over and sat on his mother's lap. "Are you done yet? I have to go to the bathroom."

Cindy smirked at Joel and Kat, "I have to help my son go find a tree now. Have fun shoveling, you two." She threw a small clump of snow in Joel's face to emphasize her point, stuck her tongue out at him, and got up. Taking Johnny's mittened hand, she led him through the snow pathways toward the back of the house.

Kat stood in front of Joel and held out her hand to help him up. "You are such a problem child."

"Me?" He pulled on her hand, dragging her down on top of him. "You started it."

"Did not."

"Did too." Joel wrapped his arms around her and gave her a fiery kiss that ignited her senses, melting the Arctic cold out of her, right down to her toenails.

"Okay maybe I did start it a little." Kat brushed her lips across his again. Who knew snow could be so sexy? "You're very persuasive."

"Good thing." He reached behind him and handed her the shovel. "Have fun."

Chapter 5

Bigfoot & Lodgepole

A dog barked, startling Becca. She sat up in bed and looked around, momentarily disoriented. The dog was Frank and she was in the loft. Oh yeah. In the morning light, it was easier to see what the little cabin actually looked like. She gazed up at the ceiling, which was made of old tongue-and-groove boards that had aged to a golden yellow color. She got up, walked over to the railing, and looked down at the living area below. Jack was sitting on the sofa in the center of the room and Frank was parked in front of him, staring intently. They both looked up and Becca waved. "Good morning."

She descended the ladder and Frank rushed up to her expectantly. "Hi Frank, I'm not sure what you think is happening here, but I doubt it involves me."

Jack put his arm over the back of the sofa. "He's thinking food thoughts."

Becca walked over and bent to look at Jack's face. He had a huge purple bruise on his cheekbone. "Wow, I really nailed you."

"Thanks for noticing."

"I'm pretty sure everyone is going to notice that." She reached out to touch his cheek. "Does it hurt?"

Jack moved his face away from her hand. "It's fine."

"Sorry." She turned and walked toward the windows. Her jaw dropped at the view. Everything was white. "I've never seen that much snow in my life."

"It's about two feet."

"Two *feet?*" She turned to face him. "We're never going to get out of here. What are we going to do?"

Jack stood up and walked over next to her. "Well, it could be a while."

"I need to get my knitting." Becca gestured toward the window. "It's still in my car."

"Knitting? As in sweaters?"

"Yes. I'll go stir crazy in this place. Knitting calms me down." The counselor she'd talked to had recommended knitting after her panic attack and oddly, it did seem to help. The simple act seemed to quiet her mind, or "internal dialogue," as the counselor had called it. Becca thought of it as the little chatterbox in her head, which almost never shut up. The reason she'd been such a great property manager was because she had a running to-do list in her mind all the time. It hadn't seemed like she was anxious back then, and Becca had argued that she had just liked being busy. The counselor had been unimpressed by her career accomplishments and said she needed to work on controlling her "generalized anxiety."

Becca didn't really buy into the diagnosis, but she would do almost anything to avoid having another panic attack. The whole hospital experience was not something she *ever* wanted to repeat. So at this point, everyone in her family was getting a scarf for Christmas, which might not be the most practical gift for those living in Los Angeles, but oh well.

Jack touched the bruise on his face gingerly. "If knitting keeps you from smacking me again, I'm all for it."

"Very funny." Becca stole a glace at his face. His expression was impassive and it was impossible to tell what he was thinking. Why had she told him all about her attack last night? The whole thing was just awkward and embarrassing in the light of day.

"I have to go out and get the chain saw. I can get that too."

"I'll come with you."

He shook his head. "Not unless you find some better footwear. Those heels you were wearing aren't going to work."

"I'll find something." Becca turned and went back up to the loft. The tall guy with poor eating habits might have left some shoes here somewhere, although they probably were enormous. It was still worth a try. Rummaging through drawers and looking under the bed yielded nothing. She called over the railing, "I don't suppose you found coffee, did you?"

"No."

"I was afraid of that." Becca hung her head. No coffee. How utterly bleak.

"Have a Twinkie."

"Absolutely not." She descended the ladder again and faced Jack. "There are no shoes up there."

Jack was staring into the tall pantry cabinet. He looked over his shoulder and pointed at some old rubber boots sitting under the coat hooks next to the door. "How about those?"

"Those are mud boots, not snow boots."

"They're better than heels."

"Fine." Becca grabbed the boots and dirt eddied from them, swirling like a dust devil in the desert. "Eww. I hate to think what Mr. Tall Guy was walking through the last time he wore these things." She slipped one on and it dropped off her foot onto the floor. "I think I need more socks—a lot more socks."

Three pairs of socks later, Becca was suited up in boots, the ugly sweatpants, oversized flannel shirt, and her coat. "Okay, I'm ready. I look like some sort of demented refugee from the Ringling Brothers clown school, but I'm ready."

Jack looked at her appraisingly and grinned. "P.T. Barnum would be proud of you."

"Very funny." She shuffled toward the door. "Let's do this thing. I need to knit something before I go insane."

Jack opened the door and Frank bounded outside with glee. Becca scuffed along behind the dog in the path he created through the snow, trying not to trip over the huge boots and fall on her face. She looked up at the pale sky. "That does not look promising. Please don't snow again. Please."

Jack disappeared behind the house and then followed behind her holding a shovel. "Finding my chain saw in this is not going to be fun."

They walked down the driveway in silence. Frank followed the trail they had created the previous day, which was now only a slight depression in the deep snow. "Why does anyone need such a long driveway?" Becca said.

"No road noise or dust."

"Noise? From all the traffic on this road? Are you kidding me?"

"People move out here to get away."

Becca was breathing heavily by the time they finally made it out to the road, which was filled with completely untouched snow. She looked toward the right. Two bumps in the whiteness off each side of the road represented Jack's truck and her car. Beyond that, the fallen evergreen lay across the road, a few branches poking up through the whiteness.

She unbuttoned a couple of buttons on her coat. "I think I need to get more exercise."

"Shoveling snow is good exercise."

"I didn't mean that. Maybe I'll take up jogging, if we don't die from starvation first. I'm not too excited about the soup and snack-cake diet so far." Her stomach growled in agreement.

They walked to Jack's truck first, which was off the right side of the road. He slid down the ditch and began digging at the rack mounted in the truck bed.

Becca crossed her arms over her chest, tucking her hands under her arms, and leaned toward him from the road above. "I don't suppose you have any other gloves in there, do you? Oh, and don't forget the flashlight—please find the flashlight!"

He paused in his digging to look up at her with an irritated scowl. "I'm working on it. Why don't you go get whatever you want out of *your* car?"

Becca straightened. "Fine. C'mon Frank, let's go over there." Frank began bounding toward her car. "Good boy!"

She slid down the indentation Jack had dragged her out of the day before and yanked her sleeves down over her hands, so she could dig out the passenger door handle without freezing her fingers off. After a lot of swearing, pushing, and yanking, at last she opened the door. A clump of snow landed on the floor of the car. Nice. She crawled in and reached over into the back-seat to grab her bag of knitting. She'd been so annoyed with herself when she realized she'd forgotten to take it into the motel when she checked in. But now she was glad. She sat in the passenger seat and stroked the soft teal-colored wool. It was definitely time for some serious yarn therapy.

Jack called down from the road, "What are you doing down there?"

Becca jammed the yarn down into the bag and got out of the car. "Nothing." She hung the bag over her shoulder and tried to climb up out of the ditch, but the gigantic boots were not cooperating. One boot started falling off her foot and she let herself slide back down to the bottom of the ditch. After yesterday, she did not want to deal with the whole frozen toes situation again.

Jack leaned over. "Is there a problem?"

"I'm working on it." She jerked the boot back onto her foot and started scrabbling up the side of the ditch again. Near the top, she felt Jack grab her arm. He yanked her up onto the road and she stumbled to her feet. Becca was not going to let him know how relieved she was to be back on level ground. She started brushing snow off herself. "I was getting there."

He picked up the chain saw and proffered a pair of old gloves to her. "You're welcome."

Becca snatched the gloves from his hand and put them on. "Thank you."

Jack turned and started walking down the trail they had created, back toward the cabin. "Let's go, Frank. Time for breakfast." The dog bounded out in front of them, clearly eager for food, no matter what it might be.

~

Becca trudged along the snow path behind Jack and Frank. She looked up at the sky. It had begun to snow again. By the time they got back to the cabin, Becca's coat and scarf were covered with a layer of snowflakes. She wanted to shake her fist at the clouds in frustration, even though it wouldn't do any good.

Stumbling through the door, she dropped her bag of knitting on the floor and shook off one of the huge boots, which landed with a thud. "This is déjà vu all over again."

Jack turned to look at her. "Except you haven't almost frozen to death."

"I may be a fashion disaster, but I'm warm. Good thing there's no one to see me, except you and Frank."

"Frank is very accepting."

"What about you?"

"I'll just avert my eyes."

"Ha, ha. You're hilarious." Becca shook off the other boot. "We can't be the only ones out here in the middle of nowhere. Aren't there neighbors?"

"I suppose so. Maybe. After I feed Frank, I need to go back out and cut some wood before the snow gets any worse."

"More canned pasta?"

"Yeah, either you get to eat it or he does."

Becca bent and shook snow out of her hair. "Given what it did to his digestion, I'm nominating the dog." Running her fingers through the light brown strands, she tried not to think about what her hair looked like. Seeing her reflection in the tiny bathroom mirror this morning had been discouraging. At this point, her hair was greasy, filthy, and stringy. The hot rollers she used to add body seemed like a distant memory. After two days of snowed-in rural life, the gel and hair spray she'd used certainly were not doing much for her hairstyle, either.

Straightening, Becca looked around the cabin. It was definitely getting that "lived in" look, with dirty dishes in the kitchen sink, soot and dirt surrounding the wood stove, and blankets strewn all over the couch. Jack was standing at the kitchen counter working the can opener as Frank sat and looked on with great interest. A rivulet of drool dropped from his mouth onto the linoleum.

"I think your dog is hungry." Her stomach growled loudly and she put her hand to her stomach. "I know I'm hungry. How much food is left here?"

Jack shook his head. "Not much. We've got a couple cans of soup."

Becca sat down on the sofa. "I don't want to starve. We need to find help. There have to be neighbors down the road."

"I'm not sure how far and it might just be more summer places like this one. I think it's more important to keep the wood stove here going."

"I could go look. I'm going to go insane if I just sit around here doing nothing."

Jack put down the Swiss army knife and leaned back on the counter. "That's not a good idea. Wandering around in the snow in an area you don't know could be dangerous."

"Oh please, spare me your safety lecture. I've got better clothes now."

"No, you don't." He gestured toward the windows. "Look at it. The snow is really coming down again. You do not want to get out of view of this cabin. People get turned around in weather like this. And we already know your sense of direction is, well, perhaps not one of your greatest strengths."

"So I have to sit around here?"

"I thought you were going to knit?"

"Fine." Becca got up and snatched her knitting bag from the floor. "What are you giving Frank? It smells horrible."

"Today's delight is Beefaroni." Jack picked the bowl up off the floor and dumped in the contents of the can, which landed with a *slurp*. Frank wagged his tail eagerly as Jack placed the bowl in front of him.

Becca settled back onto the sofa, pulled the scarf out of the bag, and held it in her hands. The teal yarn was soft, warm, and soothing. It had been expensive, but so worth it.

Jack walked over and pointed at the blue-green blob of wool in her lap. "What is it?"

"A scarf."

"You almost froze to death and you had a scarf all this time?"

"It's not done." She held up the needles and a long rectangle of knitting cascaded into her lap.

"It's huge. Who is it for? Bigfoot?"

She looked up at him. "Probably my uncle Pat. And he wouldn't appreciate you calling him Bigfoot."

"How do you know when it's done?"

"When I run out of yarn." Becca began knitting, the metal needles clacking together rhythmically.

Jack went toward the door and began suiting up for a return to the cold outdoors. Becca looked over at him as he yanked on his coat. "Where are you going to be? You just told me I can't get too far away, so you'd better not disappear into a snow drift."

"Out behind the house. There's a tree that must have been felled a long time ago but never cut up. It was under a tarp."

"I guess Mr. Tall Guy was saving it. Kind of like a squirrel storing things away for winter."

Jack grinned. "Yeah, just like that." He looked at Frank. "Sorry, you need to stay here too, buddy." Frank sat down with a thud and glared at Jack for a few moments. Seeing that the human was clearly not going to change his mind, the dog opted to settle on a rug for his post-breakfast nap.

"Good boy, Frank." Jack pulled on his gloves and waved toward the dog. "Frank will keep you company."

"Be careful." Becca looked down at her row of stitches, examining it carefully. Did she just drop one? "Maybe I've seen too many slasher movies, but chain saws are scary."

"I'll stick to cutting up the tree and avoid body parts." He opened the door and a gust of wind whooshed in, covering Frank with a light dusting of snowflakes. "Sorry Frank."

The dog put his head back down on his paws with a disconsolate look on his face. Becca smiled in sympathy at his expression. She could relate. It was so frustrating not being able to do all the things she should be doing. Uncle Pat probably thought she was busily working on the appraisal. He would be furious when he discovered it wasn't done.

Plus, she was on her last skein of yarn. If the snow didn't let up soon, she'd face the ugly prospect of ripping out her knitting and starting over. It was either that or lose her marbles from all this quiet. How could people stand to live like this?

~

Becca knit furiously, her knitting needles clattering together as she worked. She was diligently trying to shut out the nagging chatterbox voice in her head that was conscientiously listing all the things she needed to do for the appraisal she couldn't work on. In addition to not even visiting—or finding—the house, she hadn't seen comparable properties, talked to real estate agents, or even visited the county offices yet. Not even one item had been crossed off the to-do list yet. How was she going to get this done?

Pausing mid-row, Becca put her knitting down in her lap. The drone of the chain saw outside had stopped. She got up and ran around the cabin, looking out the windows, but wherever Jack was, he wasn't visible from inside the house. What if he had hurt himself? Frank got up from his nap and followed her around.

Taking a few deep breaths in an effort to not completely come unhinged, Becca waved at Frank, who was giving her a quizzical look. "Come on Frank, we need to go see if Jack's okay."

She bundled up in her coat and the horrible boots and opened the door. Frank rushed out and ran toward the back of the cabin. Becca slowly made her way around the house, following the trail Frank had blazed through the snow. Jack was standing with a portly older man with a white beard who was wearing snowshoes. Although Becca wasn't close enough to hear what they were saying, their body language indicated that the two men were not having a pleasant conversation. It looked like Jack was getting into a fight with Santa Claus.

Jack bent to corral Frank's enthusiasm at meeting the new human. "Settle down, Frank." The dog was largely undaunted by the chastisement and continued to cavort through the snow around Jack and the other man.

As Becca shuffled up to them, the older man thrust his index finger toward Jack and shouted, "You're trespassing. If I could call the cops, I'd do it right now!"

"I think the folks in the sheriff's office are probably busy dealing with a lot of pretty serious emergencies related to this storm." Jack put his hand on Frank's collar. "Frank, sit."

The other man shook his finger. "I know the owner and he isn't going to be happy that you just went and broke into his place."

"Who is the owner? I told you that I'll pay him for the damage to the window. We really had no other choice."

Becca said, "I didn't want to break in. I told Jack that."

Jack turned to look at her. "Thanks. You're a big help. I didn't hear any other suggestions from you at the time. What would you have preferred we do?"

"I...I didn't mean it that way," Becca said. "I mean, I didn't want to break in, but we had to. I was freezing! I didn't have warm clothes. Or gloves or anything." She waggled Jack's oversized glove on her hand at the older man and went for her most charming smile, "I'm Rebecca Mackenzie, by the way. Nice to meet you."

"I'm Cliff Dearning," the man said gruffly. "I live down the road a ways."

Jack said, "Okay, so we all know each other now." He pointed in the general direction of the neighbor's house. "If you get me the owner's phone number, I'd be happy to give him a call when we get the phone back and we can get out of here."

Cliff scowled. "Fine."

"I don't suppose you have any food, do you?" Becca said in the sweetest tone she could muster. "I know it's Thanksgiving, but if you end up with any leftovers, we'd really appreciate it. There were a couple of cans of soup here and that's it. I think the owner isn't much of a cook." That was certainly putting it diplomatically.

"Actually, Joel invited me over here a couple times. My wife will be the first one to tell you, I sure don't cook anything myself, but Joel does. Maybe the soup is from some of the other people who stayed here." Cliff shook his head. "Joel was kinda using the cabin as a guest place or something. I don't know. He moved in with that woman and I haven't heard much from him."

"What's the owner's last name?" Jack asked.

"Ross. Now he lives about five or ten miles away, I think. I went out there once to help with a roof problem they had. I've got the number." Cliff said, looking down at his feet in the snow. "I'll ask the wife about the food. She's pissed at me though. I haven't been able to get our generator to keep running. It starts, then quits, so the refrigerator's out, and we had to throw a bunch of food out in the snow. She told me to go outside and fix 'that fool machine' as she calls it, so I'd better get back before she gets even more mad."

"Thank you." Becca said. "And Happy Thanksgiving too!"

Cliff turned and started clomping back toward the forest, his snowshoes leaving heavy tracks behind him in the virgin snow. Becca turned to Jack. "See, I told you there had to be neighbors!"

"Cliff knows where this place is. We do not know where his place is. That was my point." Jack reached out and brushed snow off Becca's head. "And you're covered with snow. In a few minutes, you'll be wet and cold again."

Becca bent over, grabbed a handful of snow, and threw it up in the air, so that it drifted down on their heads. "You are really kind of a stick-in-the-mud, aren't you?"

"Why don't you go back inside? And take Frank with you. I'll be done here in a few minutes."

Becca turned, "Come on Frank. Let's go." Jack was such a grouch. It was a good thing she'd heard him laugh or she'd think the guy had absolutely no sense of humor at all. What was his problem anyway? Just by smiling and being nice, she'd managed to break up a potentially nasty neighborhood squabble and even get Cliff to consider giving them real food. That was more than Jack had done. He was so crabby all the time. She refused to look behind her as the sound of the chain saw firing up again rumbled through the silence of the snow-laden forest. Those sound effects in chain-saw massacre movies certainly were realistic.

Later, Jack came back inside holding a clump of whitish strips in his hand. Frank greeted him joyfully, racing around the room as Jack removed his layers of outerwear.

Becca looked up from her knitting. "Those are pretty small pieces of wood. Little bitty things like that aren't going to keep us warm."

"I stacked the firewood right outside the front door under the overhang so it would stay dry. These aren't for heating; they're for eating."

Becca put her knitting down in her lap. "You want me to eat wood? Yuck. All of a sudden, the Twinkies are starting to look better."

"It's not wood. This is the cambium layer from a lodgepole pine, or *Pinus contorta.* It's rich in sugar and starch. You chop it up into little strips and fry them. If you add a little salt, they kinda taste like French fries." He walked to the kitchen and got a frying pan out of a cabinet. "I saw some olive oil behind the Twinkies. That's not really the best oil for frying, but it should work."

"I know you're a forester and all that, but you've got to be kidding me, right? What's a camb—uh—whatever you said? This is like that old commercial with the guy who eats trees."

Jack turned and flashed a smile at her. "Yeah! That was Euell Gibbons. He was known for his foraging skills. The cambium layer of a tree is right under the bark. Lodgepole needles are useful too. They are high in vitamins C and A, and the tea isn't bad. Sailors used to drink pine tea to avoid getting scurvy."

Becca strolled into the kitchen and watched as Jack chopped up the strips. She leaned back on the counter so she could look at his face. Was he serious? "You're really going to fry up some tree?"

He nodded. "I'm hungry and I want to save the soup for dinner."

Becca returned to the couch. "This is truly the weirdest Thanksgiving ever. What I would do for some of my delectable mashed potatoes right now."

"If it weren't for all the snow on the ground, you might be able to find some wild Jerusalem artichokes. They're not bad."

"I'll take your word for it."

Jack dumped the slivers of cambium into the pan and took it over to the wood stove. "Could you keep an eye on this while I get some more wood?"

Becca got up off the couch and stood next to the stove. She gazed down at the pan as the little strips sizzled merrily. They did smell kind of tasty actually.

Jack returned with an armload of wood and crouched in front of the stove to stoke the fire. "Keep stirring. Don't let them burn."

"Because we wouldn't want to have the world's tiniest forest fire here in the pan, right?"

He closed the door of the wood stove, stood up, and took the spatula from her. "Thank you, Smokey Bear. If you don't want them, no problem. That just leaves more for me."

"I didn't say that. I'm starving and now you made this place smell like a giant fast-food deep fryer."

Walking back to the kitchen, he said over his shoulder. "Sorry, but McDonaldland never smelled this good." He dumped the strips onto a plate, sprinkled some salt on them, and walked to the table. "Eat up."

Becca sat down, waving both hands in front of her with a flourish. "And the tree fries are served!"

"Don't knock it until you try it. I saw some ponderosa pine cones that I could harvest for pine nuts too. Those are tasty."

Becca popped a tree fry into her mouth. "Maybe later, if the lodgepole isn't too filling." She chewed thoughtfully. "Hey, these are actually good. Maybe squirrels are on to something."

Jack grinned. "They're smarter than you might think."

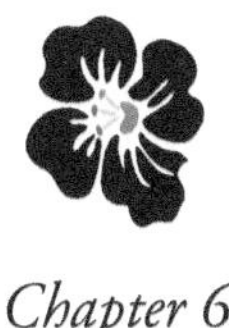

Right Now

Joel stood up and leaned on the side of the truck. "Well, that was fun. But at least the chains are finally on there."

From the other side of the truck, Kat waved her ice scraper at the sky emphatically. "It can stop snowing now. I mean it!" She looked over at Joel as he brushed snow off his coat. His face was pale, so his lashes seemed to cast shadows on his cheeks as he blinked away snowflakes. The tiny smile lines radiating from the corners of his eyes were more pronounced than usual and Kat had a strange flash of what Joel would look like as he got older. Would she still be with him 20 or 40 years from now? The Beatles song about being 64 rattled through her consciousness. Would she still love him in the year 2031? Hmm.

He looked over at her. "Are you done berating the snow gods?"

"I think so." She thumped the hood of the truck with her hand. "Let's plow, baby."

"You're sure you want to do this? I mean, driving this old thing is not like driving your little Toyota."

"Hey, I know how to drive a manual. No big deal."

"Yeah, but you haven't driven a crappy old Ford lately, have you?"

Kat gave him a playful nudge. "No, but thanks. Now I'm gonna have that stupid jingle stuck in my head."

"Plowing is boring. Singing will give you something to do, since the radio doesn't work."

Kat walked around to the driver's side and opened the door. "No one wants to hear me sing. I don't want to hear me sing. It's much better for everyone if songs just stay in my head." She got into the driver's seat and stared at the floor. Joel was almost a foot taller than she was, so the pedals were far, far away from her feet. "Um, I'm going to have to pull the seat forward. Way forward."

Joel leaned into the cab from the passenger side and pointed toward the floor. "The seat adjustment is under there."

Kat pulled on the lever and tried to jerk the seat forward. "This could take a few tries."

"It could be rusty I guess."

She continued to yank on the seat. "Vehicles aren't supposed to rust on the *inside*."

"Tell that to the truck."

At last the seat moved and Kat was able to grind it forward. The creaky thing acted like it was being dragged through sedimentary rock. "That was quite a workout. Can you still get in? It's unfortunate that Ford did not see fit to embrace the concept of bucket seats on this truck."

Joel struggled to fold himself into the cab. "This would be easier if I were one of the seven dwarves."

"The correct term is little people. And I'm not *that* short." She looked over at him. "Are you okay?"

"Kneeling in the snow putting on the chains was uncomfortable. Twisting myself into a pretzel is worse."

She glanced at his face. "What you're not saying is that your leg hurts."

"Yes." He struggled to rearrange himself, stretching out his legs across the cab toward the passenger door so most of his upper body was sprawled into Kat's lap.

Kat moved, trying to readjust herself around him. "Well, that's creative."

He enveloped her in his arms and wiggled his eyebrows lasciviously. "Wanna make out? This is like high school."

"I beg your pardon. I was not that kind of girl." More like man-free, dateless, and alone. She gave him a quick kiss and pushed his arm out of the way so she could get at the steering wheel. "I think you're losing focus here. No fogging up the windows."

"I suppose that would be bad." He sat up straighter. "The defroster doesn't work that great either."

She tapped the dashboard. "Is that thingie for the plow?"

He twisted in the seat to look. "Yes. That controls the hydraulics. And that's for the lights."

"I hope you're not suggesting that I plow in the dark. That's just asking for trouble."

"I'm just explaining. When the plow is attached, it blocks the headlights. It's good to be able to see."

"If I'm still out here plowing by nightfall, you'd better come out and check to make sure I haven't frozen to death." Kat reached to grasp the key in the ignition. "I think you need to move a little." She started the truck and the engine coughed to life with a rumbly snort. "I'm so glad you put the plow on before it snowed."

"Yeah, if it were still sitting under a tarp ten miles away, we'd be in trouble." He directed her attention to the shifters on the floor. "When you plow, you want to make sure it's in four-wheel drive. There's a low and a high. I locked the hubs already, so it's good to go. Always press in the clutch when you put it into four-wheel drive. And if you need to put it into four low, the truck shouldn't be moving."

Kat pushed in the clutch and put the truck in gear. It lurched forward and stalled out. "Oops." She restarted it and tried first gear again. The truck slowly moved forward in the hole they'd dug out around it. "Yay!"

"Okay, use that toggle to put down the blade. See the down arrow?"

Kat followed his instructions. As the blade thudded to the ground and hit the wall of snow, the truck strained to move. "Uh-oh. This is bad, isn't it?"

"No. Let the truck push the snow. If you want to get fancy, you can raise the blade to push the snow up into a pile. Put it into reverse and try again."

Kat grabbed the gearshift and looked down to see where reverse was on the diagram. She manhandled the knob with both hands, forcing it down and around. The gears screeched. "I don't think that's it."

Joel put his hand on her shoulder. "No. And you might want to lift up the blade."

"Sorry if I'm killing your truck."

"It's old and stubborn. You have to be firm with it."

Kat hauled on the gearshift again, got the truck into reverse, and the truck slowly moved backward. "Reverse is not for the faint of heart."

He smiled. "You'll figure it out. Fortunately, the driveway is flat and there aren't any ditches, so you don't have to worry about falling off the road."

"That's reassuring."

He nodded. "You never want to try plowing uphill, and sliding down into a ditch is bad, unless you happen to have a tow truck or winch handy. When you're plowing, you need to go fast enough that you retain your momentum and don't get stuck. Create push-out spots along the driveway. You want to push the snow back as far as you can, but don't hit anything." He pointed toward a group of trees. "See over there, next to that clump of cedars, how there's a big break in the trees? That's a good spot for a push-out."

Kat sighed. "This driveway is so long, it's going to take a while."

"I told you plowing was boring."

She put down the blade, pushed some snow around, put the truck in reverse, and then moved forward again, enlarging the clear spot where the truck had been sitting. After she'd created a cleared-out area in front of the outbuildings, she stopped the truck and turned to Joel. "I think I get it now."

"You're sure?"

"Yeah. You look a little tired." Kat looked into his eyes. Tired was a nice way to put it. She probably wasn't looking too good either. "Maybe you could go inside and check on the dogs. We've been out here for quite a while." She cleared her throat. "Also maybe see what your sister and nephew are up to."

Joel wrapped her in a bear hug. "Thanks for doing this. My leg really didn't want to deal with hours of the clutch on this thing."

"I can see why. After all the things you've done to help me, I think it's the least I can do. If you have any clout with the snow gods, please feel free to tell them we've had enough now."

"I'll see what I can do."

~

Many hours later, a tired and cold Kat finally parked the truck, got out, and went back inside the house. She opened the door and Linus ran up to her, wagging with glee. "Hey Big Guy, how's it going? It's suspiciously quiet in here." She stroked his large head and then went through the process of removing her coat and boots.

Walking into the living room, she found Joel sitting on the sofa reading a magazine. She flopped down next to him. "Where did everyone go?"

"Cindy got pissed off at me and took Johnny downstairs. She's in your office calling all the people who aren't attending her Thanksgiving party tonight."

Kat snuggled her head on Joel's chest and said quietly, "I'm happy to report that the driveway is clear and I didn't break anything. The bad news is that no county plows have been anywhere near this place, as far as I can tell. The road is a winter wonderland."

He put his arms around her and looked into her eyes. "Why are you whispering?"

"My throat hurts. I think I spent too much time yelling at your truck."

"Did it help?"

"Not really. There was a little bit of a stuck situation where I had to put it into four low to get out. It was kind of a mess and I may have said some bad words. Loudly and repeatedly."

"I promise I won't tell." He hugged her more tightly. "Do you want some tea?"

"As long as I don't have to get up. If you're offering, I'm drinking."

Joel extracted himself and went to the kitchen. Kat slumped down on the sofa and closed her eyes. She really needed to call the motel and let Becca know that Mona wasn't going anywhere. If Becca tried to come out here, she'd inevitably get her little car stuck somewhere. She should stay where she was, which had to be better than here. The idea of being at a motel with lovely hot running water sounded so decadent and wonderful. Being clean again…warm…mmm.

Kat started awake and looked up into Joel's face. He was leaning over her smiling and holding a mug of tea out to her. "Did you hear anything I said?"

She took the mug. "Um, I may have dozed off. I was dreaming of a hot shower. It was so good to wash my hair. And now back here in real life, I just feel disgusting again."

He sat down next to her. "Sorry to kill the mood."

"I'm tired. But I'm trying to muster myself up to call the H12 and tell Becca to stay there until such time as a plow decides to visit our remote little corner of the world. Is Mona still okay?"

"She and Chelsey are napping under their table in the hall."

Kat smiled. "That's so cute that they're friends now." All Becca's cautions had been worrisome, but Mona was easy to care for after all.

"Do you want me to call the motel?" Joel stroked her cheek. "This quiet, raspy voice you've got going, while kind of sexy, is difficult to hear."

"I'm trying to speak up." She coughed and took a sip of tea. "But it hurts."

"I'll go downstairs and see if Cindy is done with the phone. Before she stalked off in a snit, she said that half the kids in Johnny's class have some horrible cold or flu thing."

Kat leaned her head on Joel's chest. "So what you're telling me is that Typhoid Johnny has infected me with some first-grader plague?"

"Well, probably not him, since he's fine now. But maybe some child who drooled on a shopping cart at the grocery store. You haven't spent enough time with little kids to be resistant to all those evil diseases that get transferred around the germ exchange."

She tilted her head up to look at him. "What's the germ exchange?"

"School."

"I'm doomed."

Joel got up and Kat leaned her head back on the sofa again. She closed her eyes and evaluated her physical state. Her muscles ached, she was inexplicably hot, and her throat hurt. Now that she'd thawed out somewhat, she was starting to feel seriously cruddy.

Kat opened her eyes at the sound of shrieking and clattering canine claws. It was starting to get dark and the living room was bathed in twilight. How long had she been lying here? Rubbing her neck, she sat up and looked toward the stairs just as Johnny leaped up onto the couch next to her. Lori jumped up on the other side and gave her cheek a sociable slurp. Linus, Mona, and Chelsey put their muzzles in her lap as Tessa ran around the room.

Johnny yelled. "I'm a fire engine. That's my siren noise! Did you hear me?" He jumped around on the cushions next to her. "Kat! Where were you? Mommy called Joel a bad word. I'm not supposed to say it, but it means butt!"

"I was outside plowing the driveway," Kat whispered.

"What? I can't hear you." He paused in his jumping. "Oh. This is your inside voice, right?"

"Yes."

He sat down next to her and looked up at her with a sincere expression. "I built the best snowman ever! But then there was a war and he was demolished. I rode Linus into battle. But he got tired and had to lie down, so I fell off into the snow a lot. It was fun!"

Kat gazed at Linus's muzzle, which was resting in her lap. She ruffled his ears. "Good boy."

Joel and Cindy were in the kitchen apparently discussing food. Kat looked over Johnny's head and heard Joel say "whatever" before turning around and heading into the living room. He leaned over the couch, lifted Johnny over the back, and put him on the floor. "Why don't you go tell your mom what you'd like to eat."

Johnny ran toward the kitchen. "I want another Twinkie!"

Kat closed her eyes. Oh perfect. The kid was riding a sugar high. No wonder he was screaming. Thousands of creepy chemicals were probably coursing through his tiny body right now. The couch cushion moved and she opened her eyes again. Joel was sitting next to her, gazing at her face intently. "Are you feeling okay?"

"No. I feel like dirt."

"What?"

Kat contorted her expression into a 'yuck' face.

He leaned closer to her and cupped her cheek with his hand. "You're really hot."

"I think you're pretty cute too."

"Okay, I heard that. Thanks." He laid the back of his hand on her forehead. "I think you have a fever."

Kat shrugged and moved her head away from his hand so she could lean on him. Closing her eyes, she heard his voice call to Cindy through his chest, which was sort of bizarre when you got right down to it. He gently moved her head, and Kat looked up at Cindy, who was leaning over the sofa.

Cindy raised an eyebrow at her. "You look like crap. Yup, that's the creeping crud."

"What did the doctor say when Johnny had it?" Joel said. "We can't really get to a doctor. Is she going to be all right?"

Cindy waved her hand dismissively. "Don't be a Nervous Nellie. It's a virus. The doctor pretty much said the typical 'get lots of rest and drink lots of fluids' thing. The fever burns it out, so it comes and goes pretty quick."

Kat tried to say, "Stop talking about me like I'm not here," but it ended up more like, "Stphmmfntblurphf" mumbled into Joel's chest.

Johnny poked at Kat's leg with his finger. "The doctor has one of those beeping thermometers. He put it in my butt! I can say butt, since it's not a bad word like what Mommy said."

Cindy said, "You've told us about the thermometer many, many times, honey."

"I'm glad you have the other kind of thermometer, Mommy. I didn't like the butt one. But I like saying butt!" Johnny sat down on the floor next to Mona and pointed at her tail. "Mona, look, it's your butt!"

"The glass thermometers are supposed to be more accurate," Joel said.

"Johnny, stop that. The dog knows where her butt is." Cindy turned to Joel. "Yes, you used that old mercury thermometer of Mom's for years. And I'm not dead, even after the chicken-pox episode."

Joel said, "That was unpleasant."

Kat pushed herself away from Joel and sat up straight again. She got up and went toward the bedroom. Joel followed her and closed the door behind him as she crawled into bed and under the covers. He sat down on the edge of the bed and stroked her hair, pushing it back from her face. "I'm sorry you feel so bad."

Kat stuck out her tongue. "Ugh."

"I talked to the folks at the H12. Rebecca Mackenzie checked in and her stuff is still there, but she isn't."

Kat sat up in bed and squawked, "What?" Where was she?

Joel put his hand on her arm. "After the storm hit, the motel was overrun with people wanting rooms. Becca had told them she was going to check out this morning, so they knocked on the door and there was no answer. Nothing had been unpacked, and the bed hadn't been slept in. They needed the room, so Becca's luggage is in a storage closet. If we hear from her, they want us to call them."

Pulling her arm out from under his hand, Kat rasped, "Becca!" She curled her fist in frustration. "Mona!"

"Mona is fine. You saw her; she's sleeping on the rug."

Kat mimed the action of writing. Then shook both hands, encouraging him to move. *Don't just sit there!*

"Okay fine. Calm down. I think there's a pad in the nightstand." He rummaged around and handed her paper and pencil.

She wrote, "Where is Becca? What if she had an accident? Did you call the hospital?"

"No. Do you think I should?"

Kat nodded furiously. She scribbled, "What if something happened to her?"

Joel put his hand on hers, pushing the pencil down. "I'll call if you want, but I'm sure she's fine. If she slid off the road or something, someone probably pulled her out. That happens a lot around here in the winter. Don't worry."

Kat yanked her hand and the pencil out from under his and scrawled. "I am a worrier. It's what I do."

"So I've heard."

~

Becca was tired of knitting. Her last skein of yarn was looking like a deflated balloon and it was only a matter of time before she had nothing at all to do. Except think about all the things she couldn't do because she was trapped in this stupid cabin. The reality was that she hadn't even started the appraisal and she had way, way too many things on her to-do list. She needed comps, legal descriptions, and every other form of data to finish the project. Not to mention the fact that she hadn't even seen the house yet. Pat was going to kill her when he found out she hadn't done the inspection, much less taken pictures.

At the familiar sensation of her pulse starting to race, she took a deep breath and plopped the knitting down in her lap. She glared at Jack, who was sitting at the table with a stack of pine cones. He'd been sitting there for ages. "What on earth are you doing with those things?"

"Sorting. And eating. I can get seeds out of some of them without heating them."

Becca got up and walked over to the table to get a closer look. "You mean the pine nuts? At least that's a food I've heard of. I think you use them in pesto, right?"

He looked up from the tiny pile of seeds. "Yes, although I doubt we'll find any fresh basil lying around here at this time of year."

"How many did you eat?" She pointed at the pile. "That's it? After all this time?"

"I ate a few. This is most of them though. It's kind of slow going."

Becca stalked back over to the couch and flopped down onto it. "You must have the patience of a saint. I'm losing my mind here. Isn't there anything we can do to get out of here? I have so much work to do."

"Not really. Just relax. Think of it as a vacation."

"Relax? I can't relax! I have to work. There are so many things on my list I have to do. And I have a deadline. Today is Thanksgiving, November twenty-third. I only have until December first to get this entire appraisal together. Pages and pages of stuff. And I haven't even seen the house. It might be buried under twelve feet of snow by now for all I know."

Jack waved a pine cone at her merrily. "I'm sure it will work out."

"No it won't. I know it won't!" Becca put her hand on her chest, trying to will the vise-like tightness to go away. Her heart was thundering and she gasped, trying to breathe, but it wasn't working. Not again. *Please no.* As her vision began to blur, she whimpered slightly, then slumped down on the sofa, raising her hand to her throat. It was closing up. What if she couldn't breathe at all? She was going to die out here in the middle of nowhere. She'd never finish this stupid appraisal. Pat would be so disappointed. And she'd never fall in love, never have kids, never have anyone love her. She couldn't die! There were too many things she hadn't done yet.

There was a distant thump as a chair moved across the floor, but it seemed strangely far away to Becca. Maybe dying was like a tunnel. Wasn't she supposed to go to a light? Where was the light? What did it mean if there was no light? Uh-oh.

The couch cushions moved and there was pressure on her upper arms. Becca opened her eyes, but everything was blurry. Jack was pulling her up to look into her face. "What is going on?" He shook her gently. "Look at me, Becca!"

Becca took a deep breath. Then another. Her vision cleared and she threw her arms around Jack, squeezing her eyes shut and hugging him as hard as she could. He smelled like Christmas. Happy memories of sitting around the tree on Christmas morning, opening presents and laughing with her family flashed through her mind.

He pushed her away and looked into her eyes. "What just happened? You were talking even faster than usual. Then I heard you make this horrible little squeaky noise and you disappeared behind the back of the couch."

"I was thinking about everything I have to do and then it felt like I might be having another anxiety attack. That completely freaked me out because I can't get to a hospital this time. I started to think I might die. Everything kind of went downhill from there."

Jack shook his head. "Stop. Just stop."

"Stop what?"

He gently placed his hands on her shoulders. "Stop thinking about the future. Or the past, for that matter. Close your eyes and just listen to my voice. Now tell me, what is happening right this second?"

"What? Nothing. I'm just sitting here with you. That's the whole problem. I have so much to do!" Becca's eyes widened and she put her hand to her chest again.

"You're thinking about the future again. Stop it. Close your eyes and take a deep breath. What is happening here right now?" He glanced down at Frank. "For example, from my perspective, I can tell you that right now Frank is falling asleep because he's starting to snore. The cabin is warm, smells like roasted lodgepole, and I'm still hungry. That's what I'm feeling and noticing right this second in this tiny cabin twenty miles north of Alpine Grove. How about you?"

She looked into his eyes, which were an especially dark blue. This was stupid. But he really seemed to mean it. "Okay, fine. I'm closing my eyes. And I guess, um, I suppose I'm hungry, too. And I noticed that you smell like a Christmas tree."

"It's an occupational hazard. What else?"

Becca shrugged slightly, her shoulders moving under his hands. They were warm and comforting. "You have large hands."

"Okay. What else?"

"I need something to do."

He squeezed her shoulders gently. "That's the future. Stay in the present. Right now."

"Ugh. I don't know. Okay, I love these socks. They make my toes happy. And there's a little crumbly noise that the wood in the wood stove sometimes makes. It reminds me of standing around a fire pit at the beach." She opened her eyes. "I'm stuck. I can't think of anything else."

"That's fine." He dropped his hands from her shoulders. "How do you feel?"

She took an experimental breath. The tightness in her chest was almost gone. "Better. But it doesn't change anything."

"No. But you can't do anything about the past or the future. We're here right now. We can heat up some soup to deal with the hunger problem we both have. But that's pretty much it. All those other things are just a bunch of stuff you can't do anything about."

Becca didn't know what to say. It was true. Annoyingly true. "But I *want* to do something about it!"

The serious look in his eyes softened. "Everybody does. I have so many things I wish I could change, but I can't." He dropped his hands into his lap. "And certainly not right now when I'm stuck in a cabin miles from anywhere."

Becca leaned back on the sofa, suddenly exhausted. "Are you saying I have to meditate or something? Because I tried that and I'm really, really bad at it." The other people lying on the floor in yoga class didn't need to know she was calculating property valuations when she was supposed to be clearing her mind.

"I'm just saying it helps to pay attention to what you're thinking. What you think affects how you feel."

"So I should just get all Zen and pretend that I'm all happy and cheerful all the time?" She made a sardonic face at him. "Give me a break. I'm not going to turn into Miss Inner Peace all of a sudden."

"No doubt. But if you stop letting your thoughts get out of control, you might stay out of the hospital." Jack got up and started back toward the kitchen. "It's just a suggestion. I'm going to heat up some soup."

Becca sighed and picked up her knitting, noting the sensation of the soft wool under her fingertips. He did have a point. The hospital experience was definitely not one she wanted to relive.

~

It was a quiet afternoon as Becca knit and tried not to focus on how embarrassed she was about melting down in front of someone she barely knew. Now, in addition to thinking she was incompetent, Jack also probably thought she was completely nuts. At this point, her ex Tony wouldn't be the only one who considered her a head case. In the unlikely event they ever met, the two men could compare notes. Wonderful.

Although her ego was battered, Becca had to admit that Jack had been so kind to her, it was difficult not to start to like the guy. Talk about seeing her at her worst. She was unwashed, poorly dressed, mentally unstable, and hungry. This was really not the way to impress a man.

Later, Jack brought the soup to the table as Frank bounded around next to him. "Sorry Frank, you got what you're getting already. The mini-raviolis were it."

Outside, the light had almost disappeared behind the trees. Soon it would be completely dark again. Becca got up from the couch with a sigh and tried not to think about facing another long night of pitch blackness. She sat down and made an effort to focus on the soup. "This smells way better than it should. Canned soup was never so good."

Jack took a sip of soup. "I know. Live it up."

They ate quietly and the meal ended all too quickly. Becca stared down at the empty bowl. It was amazing how ravenously you could consume hot soup when you hadn't eaten much all day.

Jack put down his spoon and looked across the table at her. "It's getting dark. Are you okay?"

"Yes. I'm trying to run with the whole inner peace, live in the moment thing. Even when the moment kind of stinks."

He laughed. "Good. But I'll light the candles, just in case."

She watched as he moved to the kitchen and got the matches. He lit the candles on the table and the light reflected in his eyes as he sat down.

Becca leaned forward, crossed her arms, and rested them on the table. "So you know every bad thing about me, including what I look like after not showering for way too long. My hair is a disaster and I'm pretty sure I smell bad now, too. So now tell me about your life. How did you get all Zen?"

"I don't know that I'm 'all Zen.' But I suppose that given the big lack of Zen in my life lately, I've been thinking more about finding ways to be happy." He looked down as he turned the spoon in his fingers. "But that's way more than you want to know."

"Try me." She put her elbow on the table and rested her chin on her palm. "Does the lack of Zen have something to do with your 'not-exactly' wife?"

He looked up. "You really don't miss much do you?"

"I'm all about details. That's why Pat thinks I'll be a good appraiser." She tilted her head. "Another detail is that you aren't wearing a wedding ring."

"No. I took it off."

Becca raised her eyebrows and waggled her fingertips, encouraging him to elaborate. This was like pulling teeth. "Aaaand, when was that?"

"After the separation. It seemed stupid to wear it anymore. And it was kind of a pain when I was working in the woods anyway."

"Stupid? Why?" Becca sighed. It was time to suck it up and ask the obvious question. "So are you actually married or not? I mean *exactly*." She was surprised to discover that she really wanted to know the answer.

"Legally, we're separated." He bowed his head. "The divorce becomes final in a couple weeks. Thursday, December seventh. Pearl Harbor Day."

The despairing expression on his face was heart-rending. Becca reached her hand across the table to touch his arm. "I'm really sorry."

At the contact, he looked up. "It's for the best. She was unhappy for a while I guess. Then, I was really unhappy."

Becca squeezed his arm. "I'm guessing that was the 'not Zen' part."

Smiling he said, "Definitely not Zen at all." He pulled his arm away from her and gestured in exasperation. "I know I'm not the easiest person to live with. I get that. But she cheated on me with a drywall salesman. I mean, sure, I know maybe trees are kind of boring to other people. But *drywall?* What do you even talk about with a guy who sells drywall?"

Becca just shook her head, not wanting to suggest that perhaps they hadn't been talking. "I don't know."

"FYI, you don't want to have a cheating wife when you live in a small town." He put his elbows on the table and leaned his forehead on his palms. "Everyone knows *everything*. Everywhere you go."

"I think having your wife cheat on you with a drywall salesman is probably bad no matter where you live. But I see what you mean. How did she meet this guy?"

He put his hands on the table. "I guess he spent a lot of time up here because he was going out with the librarian for a long time."

"The librarian?"

"Yeah, I don't know." He gestured toward the windows. "That's what people told me anyway. Did I mention it's a small town?"

"You mean people gossip here? Say it isn't so!"

"Trust me, it wasn't funny at the time."

Becca's eyes widened. "I'm sorry. That was more a criticism of the town. As you may have noticed, I'm not a big fan of Alpine Grove. But that was insensitive of me to say. I've never been married, but when my ex, Tony, broke up with me, it was pretty horrible. I can't imagine how bad it would be to have a marriage implode like that. How long were you married?"

He picked up his soup spoon and spent some time examining it before saying, "Almost five years. We moved out here so she could be closer to her family."

"Oh. It seems like you like it here anyway." Becca raised her brows slightly. "Well, except for all the gossipy people, that is."

"The forests here are amazing. It's an unusual habitat type, and the tree diversity is remarkable. It makes the work I do so much more interesting. What I was doing in Colorado was nowhere near as much fun. So I do like that."

Becca grinned. "I like the fact that some parts of the forest are edible."

Jack folded his hands in front of him. "You might want to consider spending more time out there in the forest."

"Spoken like a true forester. You may have noticed I'm not exactly what you'd call an *outdoorsy* person." That was putting it mildly.

"I know, but I'm serious." He leaned back in the chair. "You probably think I'm some kind of nature nut, but it can be relaxing. Over the last six months, I've been thankful that so much of my job involves being out in the woods. It sounds odd, but some foresters spend a lot of time sitting in cubicles. I think that would have made everything even worse. After my marriage fell apart, I think I needed that time out there in the trees."

Becca leaned toward the candle and wiggled her eyebrows. "You're not getting all woo-woo on me, are you?"

"No. But you wanted to know how I got 'all Zen.' That's how. A little quiet time by yourself with no noise except the wind in the trees and a few chattering squirrels isn't such a bad thing."

"I'll take your word for it. There are also bears and mountain lions out there that might eat me. Oh, and moose. They're supposed to be dangerous. I don't want to meet a moose out in the woods. It was bad enough seeing one on the road. Or a deer. Whatever it was, it was big."

"They don't want to meet you either. If you don't bother them, it's unlikely they'll bother you. You should think about doing something to relax though. Aren't you worried about your health?"

Becca crossed her arms across her chest. "I'm fine. Well, maybe once I have a shower. *Then* I'll be fine."

"No. You're not."

She dropped her arms and leaned forward. He was one to talk. "You don't exactly seem to be Mr. Cheerful after all that time in the forest. Half the time you're a total grump."

"Maybe so. But it was worse before. A lot worse." He pointed at her. "And I'm not the one having panic attacks."

"I have a disorder."

Jack smirked. "That's obvious."

"No, I mean it's official. I have generalized anxiety disorder. G-A-D. That's what they said anyway."

"Didn't they make suggestions for what you could do about it?"

Becca picked up her spoon and tilted it toward him. "I did all that! I went to yoga. And counseling. I did what they said to do!"

"Did it help?"

"Sort of." She placed the spoon back on the table and looked down at it. "Yoga was okay. And most of the time the breathing exercises do work. Today I just got a little too wound up. Why are we talking about me again?" Becca looked up at him. "We're supposed to be talking about you. What's your not-exactly wife like?"

He turned his head to look out the window. "Do we really have to talk about this? I just finished saying how terrible the last six months have been."

"Yes." Becca leaned forward and looked at him intently. "It's time to work through *your* issues for a change. And we all know that I need something to think about other than not being able to do my job. How did you meet her?"

"All right. We met at a biker bar in Colorado."

Becca raised her eyebrows. "Gee, how romantic. Details?"

Jack locked his gaze to hers. "Fine. You really want to know? She was the most beautiful woman I'd ever seen. Long, honey blonde hair and she was—what do they call it? Dressed to kill? Long legs and she was wearing some red slinky thing that didn't leave much to the imagination. Annie always wears red."

Becca glanced away at the window. It was officially dark, and she felt fine. Plus, this was getting interesting. "So, what were you doing at a biker bar anyway? That doesn't strike me as the type of place tree-huggers hang out."

"I rode my motorcycle there. What do you think?"

"*You* have a motorcycle?" A corner of Becca's mouth turned up. Okay, the thought of Jack on a motorcycle *was* kind of sexy.

"Why should that be such a surprise?"

"No reason. It's just hard to imagine you without your Eskimo garb and seventeen layers of flannel."

He crossed his arms across his chest. "Well, the bike is in storage at the moment. I don't ride in the winter for obvious reasons."

Becca tapped her fingers on the table. "So you married a biker chick. I definitely would *not* have guessed that."

"Well, Annie doesn't ride, but she liked spending time at that bar. She likes excitement." He leaned forward and picked at some dried candle wax on the table with his fingernail. "In the end, I wasn't exciting enough, I suppose."

"How were you supposed to be more exciting?"

"I don't know. We moved here because she said she didn't have enough friends in Colorado and all her family is here." He shook his head. "We had great times with her family. Her brothers and I got along really well. It was fun going over to their places for barbecues and things like that. There were lots of family get-togethers. But then at some point that wasn't enough either. I'm not sure what she wanted. Maybe she found it at the H12 with the drywall guy. I don't know. I haven't talked to her in quite some time."

"The H12?" Becca sat up straight. If only she were there. "That's where I'm staying. Or was supposed to be staying. I wonder what happened to my stuff. Not to mention my dog. Poor Mona. Everyone probably thinks I'm dead or something."

Jack looked up. "But no. Thanks to Mr. Tall Guy and his collection of old clothes and canned goods, you're just fine."

Becca reached out and placed her hand on the back of his. "I think it's more like thanks to Mr. Tall Guy and *you*."

Looking startled, Jack pulled his hand out from under hers and off the table. "I think the stove needs more wood."

Becca watched as Jack crouched in front of the stove, loading logs onto the red coals. A flame sparked around a piece of wood, lighting up his face. His expression was definitely not Zen. Becca wondered if Annie, the legendary gorgeous woman in red, knew that she'd broken his heart.

Chapter 7

Dreams

Kat tossed in bed, throwing off the covers with her leg. Her black-and-white cat Murphee stood up on the bed, glared at her, and resettled her furry body in a new spot. When was last time she'd been this sick? Years? Decades? It was like she'd been run over by a steamroller. Everything ached, particularly her throat. She paused before attempting to swallow again. Ouch. That really hurt. And now she was freezing again. Yanking the comforter back over her body, Kat dimly remembered what woke her up. It was shouting. Was everything okay out there? She closed her eyes and flopped onto her back again. Ugh. Not her problem.

Later, she started awake at a loud crashing noise. What was that? There was an eerie silence. Not even purring. Murphee must have given up and left. Maybe the noise was just part of a dream. Her fitful dreams had been beyond bizarre. In one of them, Joel was talking to Cindy about chicken pox. Or maybe that really happened. In another one, they were talking about blood and Cindy was sobbing. Joel said something about being seventeen years old. And Stanford. But he didn't go to Stanford, so that didn't make sense. Then in another dream, Linus came up to her and said she had to follow the Yellow Brick Road. She told him he couldn't talk, but he looked so sad about it that she felt bad and went with him anyway. Then they were walking down the Yellow Brick

Road, but Linus wanted to take a nap in a field of poppies. She couldn't get him to get up and she wanted to get to the Emerald City because it was the same color as Joel's eyes.

Kat stared at the ceiling. What a panorama of weirdness. Now she had an idea what it must be like for people who did way too many drugs. Flying high on the creeping crud was probably better than LSD. Too bad she felt so awful. Otherwise she could have some fun with this. Sleeping was becoming quite the spectator sport. But now she was hot again. Alternating between roasting and freezing was getting old. Kat pushed the covers off her body and closed her eyes.

Later, sensing warmth on her eyelids, Kat opened her eyes and squinted as sun streamed through the window. Was it actually not snowing? Oh please, please, let that be true. She staggered out of bed and looked out the window. One small blue hole appeared in the blanket of clouds, letting a stream of sunlight through. It was like a Monty Python movie. Which she realized she'd also dreamed about. The Black Knight from the *Holy Grail* spurting blood was seriously gross. Dreams that included blood were not a good idea. Her subconscious needed to just move on from that topic. Yuck. No wonder she was dizzy. Returning to the bed, she crawled back under the covers and pulled them over her head.

Through the door and the sheets, she heard Cindy shout, "Why do you always do this? Just when I start to think you're a normal human being, you stop talking again. What is *wrong* with you?"

Kat sat up in bed and put her hand to her throbbing temple. That was mean, even for Cindy. She could hear the low undertone of Joel's response, but not what he was saying. He probably had moved into the overly calm voice he only used when he was furious. Uh-oh. Was Cindy completely brain dead? Why did they continually antagonize each other?

Cindy shrieked, "Everyone else had cool parents. But mine were dead!"

Kat shook her head to try to clear her fuzzy mind. All these dreams were so strange, she wasn't sure if what she'd heard before was real. Okay, the Yellow Brick Road definitely was *not* real. But maybe some of what she'd heard Joel and Cindy say was true. It didn't matter. They needed to stop. Now.

She pushed herself up out of bed, shuffled into her slippers, and opened the door. The glare of sunlight was worse in here, and the pain in her temple intensified. Joel was in the kitchen facing the counter. He was gripping it with both hands and his head was bowed.

Cindy had retired to the sofa with a look of smug fury on her face. As Kat shuffled into the room, Cindy said, "Oh look, the sleeper has finally awakened."

Kat cringed as she swallowed painfully and whispered, "Could you please stop fighting?"

Joel walked over to her and put his arm around her shoulders. "Are you all right? What did you say?"

She reached up and yanked on his collar, pulling his head down so she could whisper in his ear. "Where is Johnny?"

"He's outside."

Kat rasped, "Good. But you still need to stop fighting."

He straightened and glared at Cindy. "I'm not doing anything."

Cindy put her arm on the back of the sofa, "You never do. That's the whole problem."

Joel waved toward the sofa. "Maybe I don't *want* to talk to you. Did you ever think of that?"

Kat turned around and went back into the bedroom. This needed to stop. Grabbing the pad of paper off the nightstand, she marched back out into the living room. She wrote on a piece of paper, "Don't clam up when Cindy wants to talk to you. It makes her nuts," and handed it to Joel, who looked down at it.

On another piece of paper she wrote, "When Joel starts speaking quietly, for heaven's sake just shut up and leave him alone for a while." Kat walked over to the sofa, tore the note off the pad, and handed it to Cindy, who looked at Joel and shrugged.

Scowling, Kat shook her notepad forcefully at both of them and stomped her foot to emphasize her point. A dog barked downstairs with a vote of support and she turned to leave. At least they were quiet now. She went back into the bedroom, closed the door, and crawled back into bed, exhausted. Having to deal with someone else's family stuff was way over the line for someone as sick as she was. She closed her eyes and tried to get back to sleep.

The door opened and Joel entered the room, closing the door behind him quietly. He laid down on the bed next to Kat and collected her into his embrace. He kissed the top of her head. "That was the quietest tongue-lashing I've ever received. I'm sorry. Feel better, okay? I miss you."

Kat closed her eyes and hugged him, hoping he knew that it meant 'thanks.'

~

The next morning, Becca woke up slowly. She sprawled out on her back with her arms and legs stretched out in the bed, reveling in the snuggly warm comforter. The lack of electricity certainly was helping her get a lot of rest. Staying up late was virtually impossible in the dark, which led to the whole 'early to bed' thing.

Before they retired for the evening, Jack had pointed out that it was snowing. Becca made an effort not to think about the ramifications of more snow, instead recalling the feel of his hands on her shoulders and his deep soothing voice advising her to think about only what was happening right now.

Here in the loft, it was nice and warm, and it certainly wasn't like she had to rush off and do something. She stared at the wood ceiling. Some of the knots in the wood looked like friendly gnome faces smiling down at her. The realization came slowly, but as Becca catalogued the state of her muscles, she determined she was, in fact, completely relaxed. The last time she'd felt this way was at the spa. Of course, then she had smelled a lot better. When she got home, she was going to take the longest bubble bath ever.

Becca's stomach growled. Maybe Jack had found some more tree parts to eat. She rolled over, got up out of bed, and looked out over the railing, down at the room. Jack was sitting at the table quietly sorting through pine cones again as Frank stared at him intently. The dog really had a one-track mind. He'd probably go into paroxysms of joy if Jack accidentally dropped a pine nut on the floor.

She descended the ladder and joined Jack at the table. "Morning."

He smiled at her. "You slept late. All this mountain air is probably good for you."

"Maybe. There could be less smog in my lungs by now. They're probably getting all healthy even as we speak. Plus, I'm losing weight. I'll be willowy by the time I get home. I've never been willowy before. People won't recognize me."

Jack looked at her appraisingly. "I think you might be a little too…uh…curvy to get to willowy."

Becca held the flannel shirt out in front of her. "Underneath all these baggy layers of flannel and fleece, there could be a delicate willow just waiting to emerge."

Jack laughed. "Yeah, I guess you'll find out. Have a pine nut. I heated up the cones to get them to open, but it's still sort of a process to get the pine nuts out."

Becca leaned over the table to count the small pile of seeds. "You have twenty-seven here. How long have you been at this?"

"I don't know. It's been a while."

"I'll eat slowly."

Later, there was pounding on the door and Becca shot up off the sofa, dropping her knitting on the floor. Frank started barking furiously and she looked over at Jack, who seemed equally startled by the noise. They both looked at the door, where Cliff's outline was visible through the dirty panes of glass.

Jack quieted Frank and opened the door. Cliff walked in and looked around the cabin. "You people sure aren't neat, are you?"

Becca said, "Housekeeping is more challenging with no water." She pointed at the pot they'd been melting snow in, which sat on the wood stove. "That's our water supply right there."

Cliff shook his head, causing his white beard to bob back and forth. He walked over to the table, depositing a brown grocery bag on it. "My wife packed up some food for you that doesn't need refrigeration, so you don't die before the plow gets out here."

Becca ran to the table and began rummaging through the contents of the bag. "Oh thank you, thank you! Thank your wife, too." She pulled out a jar of tomato sauce and held it out, along with a bag of pasta. "Look, Jack, real pasta! Real tomato sauce. Be still my heart."

Jack nodded and turned to Cliff. "We really appreciate this. Do you know when the road will be plowed?"

Becca bent down and showed Frank a can of dog food. "Look Frank, home-style prime cuts!" Frank wagged his tail, looking pleased at the prospect of a meatier meal.

Cliff said, "Well, I slapped on my snowshoes and went over to Ron's house down the road. His place is beyond that white pine that took out the phone and electric lines. I'm sick of not knowing what's going on out there, and the wife was nagging me because the batteries are dead in our radio. I sure heard about that, lemme tell you. So I went down to Ron's, had a coupla beers, and called the power company to see what's what."

"Do they know when they'll be able to get up here?" Jack gestured toward the wintery scene outside the windows. "Is *anything* plowed yet?"

"Yeah, it's the same as always," Cliff said. "Everything's just dandy in town. But power's out all over the county.

They're saying it will be tomorrow before they get the phone and power back out here."

"But what about the road?" Becca asked.

Cliff shrugged. "They say that the plows are getting closer, but it keeps snowing and they haven't been able to keep up with it. Here we've got that damn tree across the road, so they bumped us down the plowing priority list. Until the electric guys come out and get rid of that tree, the plows aren't touchin' it."

Jack said, "Thank you for letting us know. I don't know if the phone is turned on in this cabin, but when you get your phone back, could you try giving us a call?"

Cliff shook his finger at Jack. "Well, the first thing I'm gonna do is call Joel and tell him you've been here. He's got a right to know."

"I know," Jack said. "I want to talk to him too. I'd like to ask him if he'd be willing to turn the electricity back on temporarily. Then I can come back and clean everything up for him and fix the window."

Cliff glanced down and patted his jeans pockets, looking annoyed. "Goddang it, I forgot to bring the number. The wife was throwing more stuff in that bag and I hadta get outta there before I couldn't lift it. I'm gettin' too old for this."

Becca made little noises of glee as she opened a box of crackers. She popped one in her mouth. "Ritz! I love these things." She snuggled a small jar to her chest. "Peanut butter. Mmm."

Cliff said to Jack. "Well, I'd better go. You should calm down your wife before she eats everything and makes herself sick."

"She's not my wife." Jack said, "Thank you for the care package. Please thank your wife too. We were getting pretty hungry."

Becca waved at Cliff. "Mmmftt…me too!"

Cliff left and Jack walked over to the table to survey the bounty. After pawing through the items, he looked over at Becca as she was stuffing another cracker into her mouth. "It's nice to see you enjoying your food."

She wiped the crumbs off her mouth. "The pine nuts were good, but I've decided the willowy look isn't for me. How do you feel about peanut butter and crackers for lunch?"

Jack grinned. "I feel *really* good about that."

~

The next day, Becca and Jack were sitting at the table eating again. Becca had spent much of the last twenty-four hours reveling in the joy of packaged food. Although Jack hadn't whined about starvation like she had, the increase in the amount of food they had available had obviously improved his mood, as well. He was a surprisingly easy person to be around. She already knew he was incredibly self-sufficient, but over the last day or so, she'd discovered that he also didn't need to be constantly entertained.

Although Becca had enjoyed her whirlwind trips with Tony to fun places like Vail, she often came home exhausted. All the excursions, shows, talking, socializing, and drinking had been fun, but when she'd returned to her regular life, she found she needed some time to decompress. Becca used to think of it as 'post-Tony personal time,' and she'd always assumed it was because she just needed a little time alone. But in reality it may have been that she just needed time away from Tony. If she were really honest with herself, she knew that the persona she adopted when she had been around Tony was a bit of an act. And all that performance time was tiring.

Given the lack of anything much to do in the cabin, it was impressive that Jack had been able to keep busy for so many days. At least Becca had her knitting. She had unraveled the scarf and rewrapped the yarn into a new ball. There was too much wool for a scarf anyway. This time, it was going to be an afghan.

Jack took a bite of pasta and looked out the window. He stopped chewing and swallowed quickly. "It stopped snowing. Look, the sun is coming out. Over there, the sky is blue!"

Becca turned to look. "Blue? After the world has looked like a black-and-white movie for days, a crystal clear blue sky is the most beautiful thing in the world."

"How about checking out the great Technicolor outdoors after we finish lunch?"

She grinned widely. "You're on."

Later, Becca bundled up in her extra socks and Tall-Guy boots and followed Frank and Jack outside. She lifted her face toward the sky and squinted at the brilliant sunlight, which was reflecting off the snow. The sun was streaming through the trees and crystalline snow seemed to shimmer everywhere. After the silence of the past few days, it seemed almost odd to hear the sounds of squirrels chattering and birds twittering. Becca laughed, "This is like *Snow White* with all the little forest animals having a party."

Jack looked back at her, "I think everyone is glad the snowstorm is over. We weren't the only ones cooped up."

"The sun feels so good!" Becca flopped down on her back. "I need to make a snow angel right now."

Jack turned around and smiled down at her as she moved her arms and legs back and forth in the snow. "Feel better?" He waved at Frank, "You're not helping, Frank. Come back over here."

"That was great." She sat up and looked around her at the swirls in the snow. "But there's a real issue with stepping on your angel and squishing the design with a big fat boot print."

"That's how you can tell yours apart from a real one." Jack gestured toward the sky. "A real angel would just fly off."

Becca got up and brushed the snow off her coat. "Oops, I didn't think about that. You're not religious or something, are you?"

"Nope. Just seen a lot of birds. Many things are simpler if you can fly."

Carefully stepping out of her angel, Becca stood in front of Frank and bent to pet his head. "So where are we going?"

Jack pointed toward the road. "I thought we could go for a walk down the road and see what we can see."

Becca put her hands on her hips. "I can tell you what I'd like to see. I'd like to see a plow. Or a big repair truck from the electric company. And lots of burly men with really big chain saws."

The sound of a chain saw motor starting in the distance echoed through the trees. Her wish had come true! Becca locked her gaze with Jack's, clenched her fists, and jumped up and down in the snow excitedly. "Just one burly guy with a chain saw would work too. We might finally get out of here!" She opened her arms wide and charged toward Jack, wrapping her arms around his huge jacket and shoving him backward in an exuberant hug.

At the impact, Jack staggered a few steps back and ran into Frank, who bolted forward out of the way with a yelp. Jack lost his balance and fell backward into the snow with a giant whoosh. Becca landed on top of him, so they were nose-to-nose, snowflakes fluttering down around them.

"Ow." Jack kissed the end of Becca's nose playfully. "Okay, you can get off me now. We should go back to the cabin and try to clean it up." He squirmed, trying to push her off into the snow, but Becca didn't let go.

She didn't want to let go. Gripping Jack's jacket more tightly, she said. "That's the future. I'm focusing on right now." She looked into his blue eyes, bent her head, and pressed her lips to his. After all this time, she just had to know what it would feel like. And it was better than she ever could have imagined. Warm, soft, and utterly inviting. Becca closed her eyes, enjoying his response, slow at first, then increasing in intensity. As he enveloped her in his arms, Becca forgot about the snow, cold, and pretty much everything else.

Suddenly Jack stopped and moved to sit up, pushing Becca away successfully this time. Frank peered down at them with curiosity. Shaking the snow off his hair, Jack said, "We really need to go."

Becca sat in the snow and watched as Jack stood up and brushed snow off himself. He reached his hand out to her to help her up. "Well, come on."

She grabbed his hand and he yanked her upright. Becca tried to meet his gaze, but he wouldn't look at her. The expression on his face was difficult to read, but he did seem to be unreasonably irritated for a guy who had just kissed her like *that*. Her lips still tingled. It was remarkable that the snow hadn't melted into a puddle around them.

Turning away from her, he said, "Let's go, Frank." The snow swirled around the big dog as he galloped back toward the cabin.

Becca took a deep breath and tried to will her pulse rate to drop back down to a reasonable rate. For a change, this time the racing of her heart had been a good thing. A very good thing. She sighed. Even unwashed and bundled up like an Eskimo, Jack sure knew how to make a girl swoon. That was some kiss. It had left her breathless and wanting more. Too bad it didn't seem like the feelings were mutual. Because she really wanted to do that again. But maybe after she brushed her teeth. She wasn't exactly looking or smelling her best right now either.

~

After following Jack and Frank to the cabin and unbundling herself, Becca started gathering the various articles of garbage strewn around the room and throwing them into a big black trash bag Jack was hauling behind him. Frank was following after Jack, making sure nothing fell out of the bag. Becca grabbed the edge of the black plastic and chucked a Ritz cracker wrapper in. "Would you slow down? It's not like we're leaving this second."

Jack stopped and the harsh jangling noise of the telephone ringing reverberated through the small space. Becca jumped and pressed her hand to her chest. "Answer it, Jack! That thing almost gave me a heart attack."

Handing her the bag, he said, "Keep this away from Frank. He's a pro dumpster diver."

Jack picked up the phone. "Hi Cliff. Thanks for calling and letting us know. I'm going to call a tow truck and see if they can pull out our rigs. Yeah, the food was great. Thanks again."

As he hung up the phone, Becca looked at him, clasping her hands together around the bag expectantly. "So the road is clear?"

"They're working on it. The plow is out there and we'll probably hear it in a few minutes." He walked over to the sofa, sat down, and pulled the phone book out from under the old olive green telephone.

Becca waved toward the phone on the end table. "Utilities. What a concept. I feel so modern."

He looked up from the phone book. "I hope you didn't hit anything when you spun out your car."

"I don't think so. I didn't feel anything. But that's all kind of a blur." She sat down next to him, holding the garbage bag closed, away from Frank's large head. "It feels like a long time ago."

"Four days is a long time without a shower."

Becca stood up, suddenly self-conscious. "Thanks." She looked down at the phone. "I need to call the H12. And Kat. I hope Mona is okay. My poor little dog probably thinks I dumped her there for good." Handing the bag back to Jack, she said, "You are officially responsible for this again. I need to go find Kat's number."

Jack took the bag from her as Frank wagged a tentative, hopeful wag. "It's not happening, Frank."

Becca called down from the loft. "How come he didn't just eat everything off the counters and every other flat surface? He's certainly big enough to jump up and get it. There's trash and dirty dishes everywhere."

"Frank knows better. He had a learning experience about taking things he's not supposed to off counters."

At last, Becca found the number in her bag. She collected her possessions and stripped the sheets off the bed, folding them in a pile.

She came down from the loft and stood in front of Jack, clutching the pile of sheets to her chest. "So what should I do about all these clothes and the sheets? Personally, I'd like to burn them at this point. Should we leave them here?"

"I can wash everything at my place." Jack looked thoughtful for a moment. "Cliff *still* didn't give me Mr. Tall Guy's number. After we finally get out of here, I'll come back out here tomorrow, stop by Cliff's, get the number, and sort everything out with the tall guy."

Becca ran through the to-do list for her appraisal in her head and groaned. "I have to get home. I have so much to do."

Jack glanced at her. "I'm calling the towing company now."

"What day is it?"

"Saturday."

"I mean the date."

"November twenty-fifth, I think."

"I have to get this appraisal done by December first. Next week, I have so much work to do. I still haven't even seen the house! Or the comparables. I don't know how I'm going to get this done. Pat is going to kill me."

He gave her a quick assessing look. "Please don't think about that now, okay? Let's just focus on getting out of here first."

Becca looked down at the pile of sheets she was holding. Going back to real life meant meeting her deadlines. She couldn't melt down again. "Okay," she said softly.

After making the necessary phone calls and cleaning up as much as they could, Jack and Becca sat at the table. Becca's knitting needles clacked together as she worked on the afghan. She looked up at Jack. "I can't believe we have to wait so long."

"The tow trucks have been busy. We aren't the only ones who slid off roads."

"I know, but still. At least the people at the H12 were nice. I'm glad they didn't auction off my stuff. I brought some shoes that I really like." She looked down at the baggy sweatpants she was wearing. "It will be nice to wear clothes that fit again."

Jack got up and went over to the wood stove. "I'm letting this go out now."

"I hope they show up soon." Becca laid her knitting in her lap. "I just want to go home."

"Me too."

A few hours later, Becca was curled up in a blanket, dozing on the couch, when something shoved against her shoulder. She opened her eyes and Jack was bending over her. "Get your stuff. They're finally here."

Becca hurriedly gathered her things and bundled up in her coat and the huge boots. She looped her handbag and her knitting bag over her shoulder and they went outside. Frank leaped ahead of them through the snow, thrilled to be outside cavorting again.

She followed Jack down the driveway toward the road. Turning her head, she looked back at the snow-covered log cabin. *Thanks for saving us, little house.* It was hard to believe, but she was actually going to miss the place.

The tow truck laboriously dragged Becca's car up out of the ditch as they watched. It was interesting to witness all the cables and motors in action. Becca looked up at the waning sunlight and turned to Jack. "It's getting late. I know we went over this, but can you tell me again where the kennel is? I'm really worried that I couldn't get in touch with Kat. I left six messages on her answering machine. I hope Mona is okay. I hope she's okay too. Maybe something happened there."

"We're on Misty Meadow. At the bottom of the hill, you go left on Aspen. Then you take the first right onto Hemlock. Then take that down to the big red barn and you'll see the turn for Cedar Glen. I'm not sure where the kennel is exactly, but that road should be familiar, right?"

Becca's eyes widened. "Maybe. That's a lot of tree streets."

"Do you want me to follow you?"

"Would you?"

"I suppose I can do that. I've waited this long. My shower can wait for a little while longer, I guess."

"That would be great." She stepped forward and at the alarmed look on his face stopped before she got any closer. "Thank you."

Jack turned and surveyed the automotive proceedings. "I'm going to go find out how long it will take to get my truck out."

Chapter 8

Light & Simplicity

Kat rolled over in bed at the sound of the phone ringing. The answering machine clicked on and she groaned. She felt like she'd been sleeping forever. Risking a tentatively swallow, she found that it no longer resulted in scorching pain. *Please let this be over.* She almost never got sick and she wasn't good at it. Now she wasn't even sleepy anymore. At this rate, she'd start getting bedsores. Kat stretched out her arms and legs in the bed and was pleased to note that the dull ache that had plagued her muscles for days was finally gone. The house was completely quiet, except for the low hum of the refrigerator.

The refrigerator!

Kat bolted upright in bed and reached over to turn on the light on the nightstand. "*Light!*" she squawked at the empty room. Job one was to take a shower. Right now. Being clean would have to make her feel better. Warm water. Warm *running* water! She wanted to scream with joy, but settled for a tiny yip of happiness as she got out of bed, gathered some clean clothes, and went off to the bathroom.

After what had to be one of the best showers in her lifetime, Kat ventured out into the living room. She glanced toward the kitchen. It looked like a bomb had gone off. Almost every plate, pot, pan, and piece of silverware in the house was strewn across the counters. Wow. Just thinking

143

about cleaning up a dish disaster of that magnitude made her tired again. She picked up her novel off the coffee table and sat down on the sofa.

Even though it was only late afternoon, she turned on a light just because she could. To be fair, it was a little dim in the living room. Wouldn't want to get eye strain. Enjoying the sensation of being upright, clean, and well lit, she settled into her novel.

She jolted awake at the sound of the back door opening downstairs and dogs barking. Pushing herself back up into a sitting position, she picked up the book. Drat. She'd lost her place *again*.

Joel walked into the kitchen, looked at it, and turned toward the living room. He smiled at Kat. "Hey, you moved!"

Kat waved and managed to squeak, "Yes!"

He placed some papers on the coffee table and sat down next to her on the sofa. "Sorry the place is such a mess. I wanted to make sure Cindy and Johnny got home okay."

"They're gone?" she whispered.

He nodded, "I followed them in the truck. The roads are still pretty bad, but she went slowly. I told her she should really think about getting chains for her car. She won't, but I tried."

Kat shrugged. "Christmas present?"

He laughed. "Don't tempt me. Are you feeling better?"

Kat moved closer so she could whisper in his ear. "A little. I don't think I'm going to die every time I try to swallow anymore."

"That sounds like progress. You were sleeping for a long time."

"What day is it?"

"Saturday."

"I missed a whole day." She glanced at the papers on the coffee table. "Cleaning up?"

"Trying. It's going to take a while."

Kat reached over and picked up the papers, which were covered with pencil sketches. "These are amazing."

"Cindy tends to sketch things while Johnny is coloring. It helps keep him quiet longer."

Kat leafed through them. "Colored pencil, huh?" There was a sketch in red pencil of Joel standing at the kitchen counter with his head bowed. A blue one showed Joel and Kat on the sofa. He had his arm around her and was stroking her hair. A green one was a drawing of them in the snow. She held it up. "She made me look like a troll."

"That's just because it's green. The snow is green too."

"I hate to tell you this, but a number of significant troll-like features have been added."

Joel stroked her cheek with his fingertips. "Okay, I think you *are* feeling better."

She looked into his eyes. "I had the weirdest dreams. I guess it was the fever. There was all this yelling and crying, and blood. It was kind of surreal. Oh, and you didn't go to Stanford, did you? I thought you went to the University of California."

"I did. But I got a scholarship to Stanford."

Kat's eyes widened and she whispered emphatically, "And you didn't go? Isn't that supposed to be one of the best engineering schools in the country?"

"Probably. I *couldn't* go." He sighed. "I doubt it was just dreaming. You probably heard some things Cindy and I were talking about."

"I think you mean yelling. She kept saying you never let her do anything." She shook her head. "And there was a whole *Wizard of Oz* thing too. And Monty Python's *Holy Grail*."

"Those are some cinematic dreams." He took one of her hands in his. "Do you really want to hear this? It's kind of bad. And although I tried at the time, I don't always come off as a particularly great person."

Kat's mouth curved into a slow smile. "I think you're pretty great now."

Joel squeezed her hand. "Thanks for the support. Anyway, I told you I hurt my leg a long time ago. And that my parents died."

"Yeah, I know that."

"The two are related. We were in a car accident. I'd just gotten the scholarship and my parents took me and Cindy out to dinner to celebrate. Cindy was whining about wanting to watch the *Wizard of Oz* on TV. She was nine and basically a brat. I was seventeen and wishing I could be hanging out with my girlfriend instead of having to go somewhere with my parents and my obnoxious little sister."

"What happened?"

"A drunk driver ran a red light and crashed into us. The front of the car was crushed and they say my parents were killed instantly. The car spun around and the side I was sitting on smashed into another parked car."

Kat looked at him aghast. "I don't know what to say. I can't even imagine how horrible that must have been."

"They had to use the jaws of life to get us out. Blood was everywhere. I had nightmares about it for years. So did Cindy. I think she still does actually, but she won't admit it."

Kat leaned her head on his chest and hugged him. "I'm so sorry."

"It was a long time ago. My leg was broken in three places. That's why I had all the surgeries. They had to put in plates and pins. Then replace them because I was still growing enough that they had to redo some stuff. Then the last surgery was plastic surgery with skin grafts to try to make the huge scars less scary. It worked, and you can't really see them anymore unless you really look. But I've still got some metal stuff in my leg, so I set off the detectors at airports."

Kat looked up. "I'll keep that in mind if we fly somewhere exotic."

"I'll probably also end up with arthritis at some point. And sometimes I can tell when it's going to rain or snow, because my leg aches."

"Well, I'm sure you're more accurate than the meteorologists around here. Was Cindy okay?"

"She broke her collarbone from the seatbelt. But other than that, she was okay physically. But like I said, she had nightmares. They were really bad for a long time. She'd wake up screaming about monsters. The psychiatrists said it was post-traumatic stress. I was in the hospital for six weeks, then rehabilitation for months, so I didn't see her that much right after it happened. My aunt Eileen came out to take care of her."

"I guess you graduated from high school, since I know you went to college."

"Yes. I had lots of time to study while I was in traction. In case you're wondering, traction is boring. It's no fun, particularly when you're seventeen."

Kat glanced at the window with a half-smile. "Well, I was unpleasant when I was seventeen, and I didn't have major medical issues. In my case, I was probably hiding from my mother."

"Now that I've met your mother, I understand why." He squeezed her hand again. "Anyway, after all that, the track scholarship to Stanford didn't happen. My aunt had to go back home to her life. I graduated and I went to UCLA as a commuter student. I took care of Cindy until she graduated from high school."

"What was that? Nine *years*?"

"Well eight, really. She met a guy from Alpine Grove and had Johnny. Your family isn't the only one that has issues with accidental pregnancy and runaways. I think she mostly just wanted to get away from me."

"I see." Kat looked down at her hand in his. "So you went to school and dealt with raising your little sister and she ran away?"

"I wasn't in college the whole time. After I graduated, I got the job as an engineer. You already know about that part. Insurance paid for my medical bills, which were unbelievably expensive. So that was a good thing. My aunt talked to a lawyer and after I turned eighteen, I filed a wrongful-death lawsuit, so Cindy and I could go to college and have money to live on. But Cindy didn't go to college. She used the money for her house here instead. I wasn't too excited about that."

"What happened to Johnny's dad?"

"He left not too long after Johnny was born. She bought the house here, but I think the guy took some of her money. She won't tell me exactly what happened." He shrugged. "That's one of the things we've been known to fight about."

Kat hugged him. "It sounds like you did the best you could."

"I tried. Cindy doesn't feel that way. I don't think I was a particularly good brother or stand-in father. The fact that we don't get along is nothing new. Now that I've seen you and your mother together, I think you probably know what I mean. Sometimes it's hard to get along with family."

"But you're here." Kat looked up into his face. "You bought the place up here so you'd be nearby and you do pretty much anything she asks you to do."

He shrugged. "I feel like I have to make it up to her."

"Make *what* up to her?"

"I don't know. Everything. All the stupid things I did wrong because I didn't know how to deal with a little girl who missed her mom and dad. I mean, it's just not fair to lose your parents when you're nine."

She hugged him again and put her head on his chest. "I can't argue with that." She raised her head to look at his face. "And I can tell you that she really, really loves you, even when you're being a jerk."

He laughed. "Me? I would never be a jerk."

"Right. But thanks for telling me all this. It explains a lot."

He grinned and gave her a quick kiss. "You don't have a monopoly on family stuff, you know. I'm just glad you're feeling better."

"Me too."

Becca drove slowly down the driveway to Kat's house. Although the roads were clear, they were covered with snow, so they were still slippery. Her car really needed better tires. It was like the vehicle was floating, which was not a great driving sensation. Having Jack's truck behind her was reassuring. Becca peeked at the rearview mirror. Frank's pink panting tongue was hanging out, so it looked like he was laughing. Jack was right. The dog really did like riding in the big brown pickup.

She pulled in next to an old green truck that had a plow attached to the front of it. Having something like that certainly would have been useful over the last few days. There was a decapitated snowman in the front yard with many sticks jammed into the body. The head had little stick x's for eyes, which was a little creepy.

Jack got out of his truck and walked over to her. He looked up at the trees that surrounded the clearing. "Wow, look at those *Thuja plicata*. They're incredible!"

Becca looked up. "Are you speaking Latin again? What are they in English? They are definitely big. I suppose that means they're old."

"They're Western red cedar and they might not be as old as you'd think. I'd have to count the rings to be sure." He pointed at some smaller trees growing behind the towering trunk of one of the cedars. "Those firs over there could actually be older. They might be suppressed due to lack of sunlight because of all that shade from the cedars."

Becca leveled an even gaze at him. "So what you're saying is that with trees, size really doesn't matter?"

Jack grinned. "Pretty much."

"Oh, please. Give me a break."

They both turned at the sound of a man shouting, "Hey, come back here!" from the back of the house. Two dogs came running into the front yard. Kat had told Becca about the dogs, but she couldn't remember their names. A brown collie-like dog and a black-and-white dog that had obviously been wrestling with one another in the snow bounded toward them, stopped, and shook themselves vigorously.

Jack extended his hand to the pretty brown-and-black collie mix. "Hi there. Where did you guys come from?"

Becca bent to pet the black-and-white dog. When she stood up, a tall man with sandy blonde hair and a short beard was walking toward them. Did none of the men in Alpine Grove *ever* shave?

The man was holding two sets of leashes. He seemed to be limping as he was being dragged up the hill by a gigantic dog and an outrageously happy golden retriever. In his other hand, he held leashes for a small brown-and-white dog and… Mona! Becca took a few steps forward, slipping on the snow. "Mona!"

The man dropped Mona's leash and the little dog ran to Becca, skidding to a stop in front of her. Mona was wagging so hard it made her whole body swing back and forth. Becca crouched down and let her dog lick her face. "Oh Mona, I missed you so much." Toppling Becca over in her enthusiasm, the dog yipped and cavorted with joy. Becca wrapped her arms around Mona, hugging her furry body. Finally, she collected the leash and stood up. The tall man was attempting to get the huge dog and the spastic golden to sit. Jack was standing with the other two dogs, looking amused by the canine commotion. Frank was barking loudly in the truck, and Jack turned and gave the dog a hand-gesture indicating 'down.' Frank looked chastised and his face disappeared from view.

Becca turned to the tall man, who looked almost as disheveled as she did. Apparently the power outage was as widespread as they'd been told. "Hi. I'm Rebecca Mackenzie and this is my dog. Is Kat here?"

He rearranged the leashes in his hand. "Inside. She's been sick. And worried about you. She wondered what happened. Oh, and she wanted you to know a couple things about Mona too."

Becca looked down at her dog. "Is Mona okay? Did anything bad happen? I was so worried about her."

"She's great. But Kat is pretty sure Mona is not afraid of people like you said. She just doesn't like loud noises." He scratched his beard. "My six-year-old nephew was here and he provided evidence to support Kat's theory."

Becca stroked Mona's head. "That's interesting. Hmm."

"I'm Joel Ross, by the way. It's nice to meet you."

"Joel Ross?" Becca's eyes widened and she glanced at Jack, who raised his eyebrows in response. "You're Mr. Tall Guy!" She extended her arms and ran toward Joel, clutching him in a bear hug and causing him to stagger back a few steps. "I love you. I love your house!"

Joel jolted at the impact. "Uh, thanks." He squirmed as he tried to peel her arms off him and extricate himself.

Jack's large hand tugged on her shoulder. "Becca, you need to stop tackling people. It's slippery out here."

She stepped back away from Joel. "Sorry. I'm a hugger. You saved our lives! Or your house did. I'm so grateful."

Joel raised an eyebrow. "You mean The Shack?"

Jack said, "You have a cabin on Misty Meadow Lane, right?

"Yes." Joel bent to push the golden retriever's rear end down onto the snow-covered ground. "But it's closed up for winter."

"Didn't your neighbor Cliff tell you?" Jack said. "We broke into your cabin to get out of the storm."

"You broke into *The Shack*?"

"It's not a shack. It's cute!" Becca said. "Cliff said he was going to call you. Well, once we got the phone back. He was not happy with us. But then his wife gave us food." She looked at Joel more closely. He looked a lot healthier than she expected. "Twinkies are not good for you, you know."

"I hate Twinkies. And I can tell you, giving them to a six-year old is a really bad idea. I've been out most of the day. Maybe Cliff left a message." Joel looked down at Becca's feet. "Are those my boots?"

"Yes." She opened a button on her coat to reveal the collar of the shirt. "And your flannel shirt, sweatpants, and socks. After four days, I've become very attached to them, but I promise I'll wash them and give them back to you. I talked to Kat's answering machine too. Is she really sick?"

"I think she's getting better, but it's been a long few days." Joel waved toward the house. "And cleaning up the mess in the kitchen could take a while."

Becca smiled. "Strangest Thanksgiving ever, right?"

Joel nodded. "Definitely. It may take a while to recover from the last few days."

Jack said, "Speaking of cleaning, uh, your cabin is kind of a mess too. With the lack of water, well, you can probably imagine what it's like after four days."

"All too well," Joel said.

"I also would like to fix the window in the door that I broke to get in. Could you turn on the electricity, so I can go back and clean it up? I'll take measurements and buy new glass too."

"Sure," Joel said.

"I live in town, but I work out that way. If you find anything later that we broke, I'll pay for any repairs. It's a great place," Jack said.

"Thanks. I like it." Joel said. "I'll call the electric company. I should plow the driveway too. I can meet you out there."

While Joel and Jack negotiated a time to meet, Becca rummaged around in her handbag for her checkbook and then wrote a check for Kat. She quadrupled the original amount and added in a little extra because of the unexpected additional time. Mona looked so happy. It was such a relief to find her all healthy and cheerful, instead of stressed and confused.

She handed the check to Joel. "Please say thank you to Kat. I'm so sorry she was worried about me."

Joel said, "That's okay. It's what she does."

~

They said their goodbyes and Joel retreated to the back of the house with the dogs. Becca looked at the sky. The sun was setting and pink and purple ribbons of color crisscrossed the sky above the huge trees in the clearing. She loaded Mona into the backseat and turned to Jack. "I hate to ask, but could you drive to the motel, so I can follow you? It's getting dark and I don't want to get lost. You know where the H12 is, right?"

He gave her a you've-got-to-be-kidding-me look. "Yes."

"Oh yeah. I guess you do. Sorry." She was such an idiot. Ask a favor and remind the guy about his cheating not-exactly wife. Very smooth. Turning, she got into the car and slowly backed up, so he could turn his truck around. She looked over the seat at Mona. "I hope you had a good time because we've got a long drive ahead of us."

Jack obviously was driving extra slowly for her benefit. As they wound their way back into town, Becca clutched the steering wheel, trying to focus on the tail lights ahead of her. Thank goodness there were no other cars. Driving with the layer of snow that was still on the roads was scary.

At last they reached the motel parking lot. Jack was standing outside his truck with his arms crossed, the lights of the parking lot casting shadows that hid half of his face. She got out and stood in front of him. "Thanks for letting me follow you. I really appreciate it."

"It's getting icy out there. I'm guessing you don't have studs, do you?"

"What?"

"Studded tires. Your car was sliding all over the place."

Becca flexed her fingers, trying to remove the stiffness. "At least I didn't hit anything or spin this time. I should go get my stuff." After the drive into town, Becca's stomach was a little queasy. Now she knew what the term "white-knuckle ride" really meant. At least she didn't throw up, but she still was a little shaky.

He reached out and grabbed her forearm. "You can stay at my place tonight. It's not safe for you to drive down the hill to the city on those tires."

"Are you sure?" She looked into his eyes. "And Mona too?"

Jack gestured toward her car. "Yes, Mona too. Frank is pretty mellow about other dogs."

"He's pretty mellow about everything. I'll be right back."

As she collected her belongings from the H12, Becca tried not to dwell on how horrifying she looked. Her hair was stringy and limp and she probably stunk at this point. The couple at the front desk were very understanding and thanked her for staying, even though she hadn't. Jack had to have a shower at his place anyway. It would be such a relief to no longer be embarrassed to be seen in public.

She walked back to the parking lot and stood alongside Jack's truck. He rolled down the window. "So are you good to go?"

"Yes. They were really nice about my disappearance. Where do you live?"

"Not far. Just follow me again."

"Okay. Please go slowly."

Becca followed the brown truck as Jack drove down the main street of Alpine Grove. He turned down a side street and pulled into the parking lot of a utilitarian-looking brick apartment building. Most of Alpine Grove consisted of cute little older cottages. This building had the uniquely unattractive boxy style of multi-unit dwellings built in the late sixties.

She pulled into a space alongside the truck. Jack got out and clipped a leash on Frank, who seemed thrilled to be back home. Becca leashed up Mona and walked her over to Frank. "Okay Mona, meet Frank." The two dogs wagged happily at one another, did a little sniff dance and seemed to call it good. Both dogs looked up expectantly at the humans.

"Home sweet home," Jack said, "I'm pretty sure Frank thinks it's dinner time. Come on. My place is on the second floor."

Becca got her things out of the car and followed him inside and up the stairs. Given the grotesque pattern, the hall carpet looked to be original to the building. She hoped Jack wasn't paying much for this place.

He stopped at a door, unlocked it, and dropped Frank's leash, so the dog could rush into the apartment. Jack beckoned to her, ceremoniously ushering her in. "After you."

Becca walked into the room and looked around. The studio apartment was almost completely empty. Nothing on the walls. No rugs. No knickknacks. The only furniture was a full-sized mattress lying on the floor in front of the window, a dresser with a stack of books on it, and a huge blue recliner sitting in front of a TV that sat on a wooden table. She smiled weakly at Jack. "Um, it's nice."

"No it's not. But it works for the time being."

Mona busied herself sniffing at the three pieces of furniture around the room before settling in on the mattress. Becca hurriedly bent to grab her collar and pulled the dog off the mattress. "No Mona, why don't you sleep on the floor over here." Mona looked offended, but complied.

"It's okay. Don't worry about it. Frank stomps all over it all the time." Jack pointed at a door. "That's the bathroom. Do you want to shower first?"

Becca clapped her hands together. "Oh, yes. Please!"

"Go for it. Towels are in the cabinet. I'll feed the dogs and order us a pizza."

Gathering up her suitcase, she said, "Thank you, thank you, thank you," as she rushed off to the bathroom.

After enjoying a hot, glorious shower, Becca returned to the room fully dressed, scrubbed, and combed.

Mona and Frank were asleep on the mattress and Jack was sitting in the La-Z-Boy reading a book. He glanced up at her. "You look better."

"I *feel* better." She did a small pirouette, so her floppy skirt spun out around her. "I'm not sure I have ever had a more wonderful shower."

He stood up and grabbed a pile of clothes off the dresser. "I called in the pizza. If they show up, the check's on the TV."

Becca settled into the chair, sinking down into the deep cushions. The La-Z-Boy was unspeakably ugly but incredibly cozy. There was a reason people bought these things. She picked up the book and read the back cover. Flipping to the first pages, it seemed to be a new John Grisham novel that she actually hadn't read. Cool.

She jerked awake at the sound of Jack opening the bathroom door. Maybe she was a little tired after the stressful drive. He was rubbing a towel on his wet hair and droplets of water fell on his t-shirt. Seeing Jack wearing different clothes was startling. His shoulders and arms were extremely muscular and the faded Levis were a heck of a lot sexier than the heavy work pants he'd been wearing before. It was difficult not to stare. Jack cleaned up nicely. *Really* nicely.

Walking into the room, he grinned. "Not a big fan of Grisham?"

Becca held up the paperback. "The book is good, but I was drawn into the sucking vortex of this chair. It gives the word *recliner* new meaning."

"It's really comfortable. I refused to give it up."

"Give it up?"

"I told you about this." He waved in exasperation. "The divorce? Everything else is still in the house. I told Annie she could have it all."

"Oh. I didn't know. That was—uh—generous of you. "

Jack flopped down on the mattress next to Frank and Mona. The dogs both stood up to check out their new bedmate. He pushed their noses away. "Hi guys. Move over. We have to share." The dogs turned around a few times and resettled themselves near the foot of the mattress. Jack sat up and leaned his back against the wall. "Some things are more important than, well, things."

"I suppose that's true." She looked around the barren studio apartment again. Monasteries had more decoration than this place. "But why don't you get new furniture?"

"I'm not sure if I'm going to move back to Colorado or not."

Becca tried to sit up straighter in the chair, which was no easy feat. "I thought you loved it here. Your job and the great trees and everything."

"I do. But there are some reasons to leave too."

The doorbell buzzed and both dogs launched off the mattress, barking furiously in their quest to ward off the evil interloper. Jack got up, grabbed the check off the TV, and collected the pizza. The dogs followed him into the kitchen area with their noses in the air, sniffing excitedly.

He put a slice of pizza on a plate and carried it back to Becca.

Taking it from him, she said, "Thank you. I think I'm trapped in this chair. Getting out might be tricky. It won't let me leave."

Jack shoved dogs out of the way and settled back on the mattress. "Go lie down, Frank. You too, Mona." The dogs looked distressed, but didn't move. Jack said more firmly, "I mean it, Frank. Go!" The dog apparently knew that tone of voice and curled up at the corner of the mattress. Mona glanced over at the large dog and followed suit.

Having inhaled her piece of pizza, Becca leaned over the arm of the chair, trying to lever herself out and not drop her plate on the floor. At last, she extracted herself from the chair's gaping maw, but it was not the most lady-like maneuver. She stood up and straightened her blouse. Jack was smiling as he ate his pizza, obviously amused by her struggles. She flipped a lock of hair out of her face. "Well, that was quite an adventure."

With as much dignity as she could muster, Becca strolled to the kitchen and collected another piece of pizza. Leaning on the counter, she chewed thoughtfully and gazed around the empty space. Her own apartment was filled with personal items. All the colors, textures, fabrics, and furniture made her happy when she walked in. This place was just bleak. Who lived like this?

The lack of furniture made Joel Ross's cabin, shack, or whatever he called it seem palatial by comparison. No wonder Jack said he liked it. Of course, even though the apartment might be stark and depressing, the hot running water and electricity did make up for quite a bit.

Becca didn't want to face the body-sucking recliner again, so she dropped down beside Jack on the mattress with her back against the wall. Mona tried to inch in closer to check out the pizza and Becca shooed her away. "You had your dinner."

Jack put his plate aside and closed his eyes, leaning his head back on the wall. He had his elbows on his knees with his arms crossed at the wrists. He said in a tired voice, "I think the weather should be okay for your drive back tomorrow."

"I've got to go out to the house I'm supposed to appraise first. You said Edgewater Road is near the lake, right?"

He opened his eyes and turned his head to look at her. "You're going out there?"

"I have to at least look at the house. Tomorrow is Sunday and I can't get all the legal documents I was hoping to get from the various offices I was going to go to on Wednesday. Maybe I can get them to fax the stuff I need to me at work on Monday if I ask really nicely. At a minimum, I *have* to go see the house and take pictures."

"Do you have any idea where it is?"

"I have a map." Okay, it was a really confusing map, but it was a map.

Jack crossed his arms across his chest. "Is this the same map you used before?"

"Yes. It's the only one I have."

"I was afraid of that." He sighed. "What if I take you out there? In my truck, which has four-wheel drive and studded tires."

She gripped his arm. "Would you? I mean, you probably have things to do now that you're all clean and back to your normal life."

"Not tomorrow. But Frank has to go with us. He hates being left behind."

"What about Mona?"

"It's an extended cab. I'll clear out some of the junk behind the front seat and they can ride there. But you do realize you're going to end up covered in dog hair, right?"

Becca leaned her head on his shoulder. It was strong and hard, and yet comforting somehow. "I don't care. That would be wonderful." She lifted her head and looked into his eyes. "I'm always saying thank you to you. It's getting a little embarrassing."

He put his hand over hers on his arm. "You just aren't prepared for winter. If you ever come back to Alpine Grove again, you might consider getting some snow tires put on your car first."

"It's not even winter yet. What is wrong with this place? Winter is supposed to begin in December." Becca laced her fingers in his. "By the way, I brushed my teeth."

"That's nice." He closed his eyes, leaning his head back on the wall again. "I'm glad you feel better."

"I'm clean now and there is just this one mattress here." She tugged on his hand, causing him to turn his head to look at her. "You can't really expect to kiss me like you did before and think I'm not going to notice, Jack."

He pulled his hand away. "That's not a good idea."

"Why not?" Becca looked down at herself. She was not horrifying or stinky anymore. In fact, when she looked in the mirror, she thought she was looking downright pretty, with normal clothes that actually fit. Well, all things considered. It had been a long day, after all.

Jack looked down at his hands as he rubbed his ring finger with his thumb. "Well for one thing, I'm married."

"For what? Ten more days? So what? Given what you told me about your soon-to-be-ex wife, I don't think she's pining for her long-lost forester." Becca paused at the expression on his face. He looked so miserable. "I'm sorry. That was nasty. I shouldn't have said that. But I guess I should ask—are you still pining for *her*?"

"I shouldn't be, since I'm the one who filed for divorce." He looked away from Becca at the nearly empty room. "I don't know. Maybe. It doesn't matter. You don't live here and you're leaving tomorrow. I'll never see you again. My life is complicated enough. And it sounds like yours is too."

"I think you have embraced enough simplicity here, don't you?" Becca waved at the desolate space around them. "Are you punishing yourself? Or do you think I'm such a nut job or so repulsive that you're just plain not interested?" She leaned closer to his face, looked into his eyes, then glanced at his lips. "Because I think I've made it clear that I *am* interested."

His gaze softened. "That's not it. You're definitely *not* repulsive. It's just that I don't want to get involved with anyone right now. Maybe that seems strange to you." He leaned away from her, but took her hand again, looking down at it. "You know that time between when you file for divorce and it's final? The state calls it a "cooling off period." I just don't want to deal with anything else until that's all behind me. It's one reason I haven't moved back to Colorado, even though a bunch of my friends there said I should."

Becca just sat and looked at his face for a moment. There really wasn't anything else left to say. She'd already thrown herself at him once and that certainly hadn't worked out well. "I guess that makes sense. Even though being rejected is unpleasant and a little humiliating, I've spent enough time with you to know that you're not a one-night-stand kind of guy. It's kind of honorable, I suppose." She leaned her head on his shoulder again. "But I can't say I'm not disappointed. And if you say 'it's not you; it's me' I may have to hit you again."

He chuckled. "I'll keep that in mind. Isn't it called Stockholm syndrome when someone becomes attracted to the person who held them captive?"

"I already have a disorder. The last thing I need is a syndrome." She raised her head to look at him. "You weren't exactly holding me captive."

"Maybe there's some other name for being stuck in a cabin. But you'll forget about me. I'll just become a bit player in a story you tell your family while you're eating those incredible mashed potatoes you were dreaming about. The year 1995 will go down in history as the year Becca missed Thanksgiving."

She squeezed his arm again. "I think you were more than a bit player."

"I'm sure everyone will laugh about it—all the time you spent trapped in a snowstorm with the boring forester who fed you trees."

Becca gave him a wide-eyed look of mock sincerity. "Some parts *are* edible, you know."

He laughed and shoved her shoulder gently. "You're not going to let that go, are you?"

"Nope. Never. And for the record, I don't think you're boring."

He moved to get up. "I want another slice of pizza. Do you?"

"Sure." Becca wanted way more than pizza, but if she couldn't have what she really wanted, fattening food would just have to do.

~

Later, after a slightly awkward conversation about sleeping arrangements, Becca went to the bathroom and changed into her nightgown. She crawled under the covers next to Jack, who had finally agreed that after so many nights of sleeping on the sofa, a mattress would be easier on his back. He had his arm behind his head, flexing a really nice bicep muscle. It probably felt as good as it looked. Perhaps lifting chain saws all the time was the next best thing to body-building.

She needed to plaster a do-not-touch sign on Jack. No matter how tired she was, sleeping next to him was not going to be relaxing. Seeing the expression on his face, Becca yanked the covers up to her chin and said, "Don't worry, I'm not going to jump you."

He rolled over onto his side to face her and grinned. "It's flattering that you wanted to though."

"Maybe it's just the syndrome talking, but you know every horrible thing about me. And what I look like with no makeup and incredibly bad hair because I haven't showered for way, way too long. And yet you don't seem to hate me."

"True. I don't hate you. But I was not exactly looking my best either. When my beard gets too long, I start to look a little like Charles Manson."

Becca giggled and relaxed her hold on the sheet. "It wasn't that bad, but it does look better now that you've trimmed it. I'm glad you didn't say that back at the cabin. I was already having creepy dreams related to being stuck in the middle of a snowstorm with a guy named Jack. If I'd found *redrum* written on the door, I probably would have run screaming out into the forest."

"Nope. The only thing on the door was cardboard from a box of Twinkies."

Becca put her hand under the pillow. "You could just consider shaving, you know."

"I have really sensitive skin and I spend a lot of time outside. Razors and my face don't get along. It's better to just go with a short beard and avoid looking like I have some horrible rash or disease."

"I suppose. It works for the biker look too, but I think you need more leather and fewer pockets to pull it off."

He chuckled. "What do you have to do at this house tomorrow?"

They lay facing each other as Becca explained the information she needed to get for the appraisal when she went out to the house on Edgewater Road. Jack listened and asked a few questions. He pointed out that doing a property appraisal on a house had some similarities to what he did for a timber cruise to assess the marketability of the trees on a parcel of land.

Becca laughed. "It's all about the trees for you, isn't it? You're like the Lorax."

"Trees are a renewable resource. If you cut down that last Truffula tree, it's all over."

"Aww, I loved that book." Becca nudged herself slightly closer to Jack and raised her eyebrows. "Okay, I'm giving you fair warning. I want to give you a hug again."

"It's okay. I'm already lying down." Wrapping his arms around her, he returned the hug briefly, then rolled over and said, "Go to sleep."

The next morning, Becca awoke to the rich, savory aroma of brewing coffee. Jack was in the kitchen and Frank and Mona were looking up at him with great interest. Becca got up to investigate. "Is that what I think it is?"

He handed her a mug. "You said you drink coffee, right?"

"Yes! With enthusiasm." She sniffed at the coffee and took a sip. "Oh how I've missed you, glorious elixir of awakening."

Jack turned to look at her. "Wait, with your disorder you probably shouldn't have caffeine, should you?"

Becca glared across the rim of the mug, hugging it with both hands. "I can have one cup. *One!* And it is a beautiful thing. Don't mess with me."

Jack laughed and held up his palms. "I'll just leave you two alone then. I've got to go clean out the truck anyway."

After he left, Becca returned to the mattress with her coffee and sat sipping contentedly while Frank and Mona looked on. Clearly, the dogs wanted to be sure she didn't make a move toward food without their knowledge. "Hey, you two. Are you ready for a little road trip?" Frank wagged a few times, but didn't take his eyes off the coffee mug.

Even Mona looked relaxed and happy. Maybe Kat was right. One thing Alpine Grove certainly had going for it was quiet. Although Becca had made a point of staying on her own side of the mattress last night, as she had predicted, knowing Jack was there, feeling his warmth under the covers, and hearing his breathing did not make for the most restful night's sleep. However, she did enjoy some rather exciting dreams. Smiling at Mona, she said, "I have really got to get over myself. Time for a shower." She stood up and ruffled Mona's ears. "Keep Frank in line. You know how boys can be."

After showering and eating, they all loaded into the truck for the trip out to Edgewater Road. Jack pulled out onto the main street of town and headed south. People were walking along the sidewalks, enjoying the brilliant sunshine. In front of a gift store, an older woman was sweeping away some snow that had blown onto her carefully shoveled section of sidewalk. Next to her, a man with glasses and a pretty blonde woman were holding hands and obviously laughing about whatever the older woman was telling them.

Becca couldn't help but smile at how happy everyone looked. A little sun seemed to be a serious Alpine Grove community mood booster. It was a beautiful day and the plows had evidently done more work on the roads, so the pavement was clear and dry. That was good news for her trip back down the mountain later today. Becca was ready to have a more sedate driving experience that didn't involve extreme fear and trepidation.

As they turned onto a road that wound down toward the lake, Becca started to understand why Jack had offered to drive his truck. Because of the angle of the trees and how the road curved along a north-facing peninsula, the road surface received little sun, so there were still large patches of ice.

They parked in front of the house and Becca looked down at her notes. Pat had said the place was a horse property, but there wasn't a barn anywhere. She wasn't exactly a horse expert, but didn't people need a place to put hay and other horsie-type stuff? Not to mention the horses. She turned to Jack. "Are you sure this is 1719?"

"That's what it says on the mailbox."

Becca grabbed her bag. Maybe the notes were wrong. At least she could cross one item off the to-do list. "Okay. Time to get this done." She turned to Jack. "Could you get the dogs? I need to go knock on the door and let them know I'm here."

He gestured toward the quiet dwelling. "It doesn't look like anyone is home."

Becca riffled through her information again. "This is the right place. I was supposed to be here on Wednesday though. Maybe they went somewhere for the holiday weekend."

Jack shrugged and walked around the truck with the dogs. "Maybe."

Becca trudged through the snow, down to the front door. At least today, she was not wearing heels. However, cute flats with dress pants were still not perhaps the ideal wardrobe choice for this activity. Brr. Her feet were going to freeze. She knocked on the door and rang the doorbell. Nothing. Uncle Pat was not going to be happy that she couldn't get inside. Fine. She'd just have to deal with the outside for now. At Jack's place, she'd looked through all the stuff Pat had given her, and it seemed like a lot of information was missing. Where was it? This whole appraisal was such a mess.

With a sigh, Becca pulled her camera out of her purse and started taking photographs of the property. She walked around the entire house, taking notes and photos as she went.

Feeling a little like a criminal, she peered in the windows. It looked like no one had been in this place for quite a while.

Returning to the front, she walked down the path she had created in the snow toward the truck again. Jack was with the dogs and they were all looking up at a huge tree. The image of all three of them standing there amused her, and even though she wasn't supposed to waste company film on personal snapshots, Becca took another picture anyway.

She walked up to the group. "I'm done here and my feet are cold. What are you looking at?"

Jack pointed up at the branches. "Squirrels. Frank is pretty sure that one is making fun of him and that squirrel puree might be a tasty snack."

"Eww. What does Mona think about all this?"

"She seemed interested, but not in an 'I'd like to invite you to dinner' kind of way like Frank."

Becca reached out to stroke the big dog's head. "Oh Frank. This is like the chicken thing, isn't it?"

"The squirrels are busy getting their goodies stored away. I think the snow caught them by surprise too. I'm afraid Frank's going to end up needing to have another learning experience about squirrels."

Becca stood listening to the frenetic squirrel scold them from above. Two more agitated squirrels were scurrying through the branches, chasing each other, leaping from bough to bough. She realized Jack had a point about the forest. Being surrounded by all these trees was relaxing, even when the forest was filled with hyperactive wildlife. The tightness in her chest had been absent for a while. That sensation had been her constant companion for months. When had it gone away?

She couldn't think about that now though. It was time to get home and get back to work. There was so much to do and many lists to make. Item one was to drive home. She took Mona's leash from Jack. "We should get going. I need to get on the road."

They loaded the dogs back into the truck and returned to Jack's place. After collecting her things from his apartment, she put Mona in the backseat of her car and closed the door. Jack stood next to her with his hands tucked into two of his thousands of coat pockets.

Becca looked into his eyes and her stomach clenched. She couldn't bear the idea that she might never see him again. "Okay, I'm warning you. Brace yourself, because I want to hug you."

He stretched out his arms. "Okay. Go for it."

She grabbed him and hugged as hard as she could. Pressing her cheek into his coat, she said, "How can I ever thank you enough?" She let go and shook her index finger at him like an angry schoolmarm. "You have to promise to call me and let me know what I owe for the broken window. And anything else we destroyed at Joel's cabin."

"I'll be going out there to meet him tomorrow. I'll let you know."

"Okay. So I guess this is goodbye then."

"Drive carefully."

Becca crawled into the driver's seat and waved. Jack raised his hand and gave her a half-smile. She pulled away and glanced at her rearview mirror. Jack was walking back toward the door to the ugly apartment building with his hands in his pockets again. She hurriedly wiped a tear from her eye before turning onto the main street to leave Alpine Grove.

Chapter 9

Adjustments

Becca sat at the little writing desk in her apartment, trying to concentrate on the pile of paper in front of her. Her trusty calculator was by her side and she was attempting to figure out the adjustments to a comparable property for this awful appraisal in Alpine Grove. She knew it wasn't a decent comp. The whole project had turned into a morass of miscommunications and mistakes.

The problems weren't all her fault, but the memory of Uncle Pat saying, "That's the wrong house!" kept reverberating in her mind. To his credit, he had tried to remain calm, but he was obviously furious. It was a good thing she was related to him and that he remembered her when she was just an adorable nine-year-old little girl selling cookies for her scout troop. That might have helped him refrain from firing her right there on the spot.

Before Joanne, the senior appraiser, left for her trip home to the East coast, she had dumped a pile of documents about the Alpine Grove project on Pat's desk, and he gave the whole mess to Becca. After going through the sequence of events, it seemed that Joanne had pulled the wrong file and that the house Becca was supposed to have appraised was actually farther down Edgewater Road than the one Becca had visited. That certainly explained some things, including the lack of equine facilities.

A fire engine siren wailed outside and Becca looked up from her calculations. Mona zipped through the doorway into the bedroom. The dog was probably busy crawling under the bed. And Mr. Rap Dude who lived downstairs was playing his dreadful music, so the bass was vibrating through the floor like a heartbeat. It was giving her a splitting headache. Time to complain to the building manager again.

When Becca signed the lease on this place, she hadn't thought about how close it was to the fire station or much about the neighbors. All she'd thought about was what a great deal it was and how lucky she was to find it because the company she worked for at the time managed the building.

Over time, Becca had developed a deep loathing for rap, hip–hop, or whatever it was called. Wasn't there some phrase like 'sign a lease in haste, repent in leisure'? She was repenting a lot, but at least it had been long enough that she was paying month-to-month now. Yes, she should move, but with everything going on, she hadn't had the time or mental energy to deal with the idea of looking for a place, much less moving. The new job, counseling, yoga classes, and everything else had been quite enough. Just the idea of moving was exhausting.

Although taking work home didn't tend to work out well, Becca had opted to give it a try in this case. Uncle Pat was one of the most easy-going people she'd ever met, but he was so angry about all the problems with this appraisal that he'd had to retire to his office and close the door for a while. He *never* did that.

If Pat had any hair left, some of it probably would have turned gray after the events of the day. Becca tried to ignore the tightness in her chest. She had contributed to this disaster. There was no denying it. The countless other appraisals she'd done before had been fine. Even though she was still the new appraiser on the block, she did know what she was doing. Every appraisal assignment involved a lot of details, but Becca was good at details. She always tried to dot every *i* and cross every *t*, and Pat often said how pleased he was with her work. But this stupid appraisal in Alpine Grove seemed to be cursed.

The morning had started off so well, too. The first thing on her to-do list had been to drop off her film at the one-hour photo place on the way to the office. After Becca got her coffee, she went to talk to Pat. As Jack had predicted, Pat found the whole trapped-in-a-snowstorm story amusing. Her uncle shared some anecdotes from Thanksgiving and everything she'd missed with her family. He'd even seemed impressed with her initiative to go out to the Edgewater property even after everything that had happened to her over the holiday weekend.

At lunch, Becca picked up her photos and went back to talk to Pat about the tasks that still needed to be done to finish up the project. The conversation that morning had been so friendly and fun, she hadn't been able to bring herself to tell Pat that she hadn't been able to take pictures of the inside of the house or comparable properties.

Becca was still fretting about that fact when she showed him the photos. But she never had a chance to say anything because Pat had taken one look at the photograph of the front of the house and freaked out. Well, maybe *freaked out* was a little extreme. He was too nice to completely freak out. But he had stroked his smooth skull and started pacing back and forth before he exclaimed, "That's the wrong house, Becca!"

Things had taken a nosedive after that.

After he'd retreated to his office, calmed down, and called the client, he came back to Becca's office with a laptop. Placing it on the desk, he'd said calmly. "Becca, you need to completely start over on this. I got you a one-week extension. They are not happy, but they grudgingly agreed that a blizzard is out of our control. So let's go through everything we have and what you need to do."

They'd waded through the pile of papers. Maybe Joanne had the missing information somewhere. Or maybe not. Pat had said Joanne was dealing with a family emergency, so it was up to Becca to do the appraisal from scratch. He suggested she return to Alpine Grove and take the laptop this time. Because Alpine Grove was the county seat, all the records she needed were there. Becca would need to spend a lot of time at various offices digging up information.

This had to be the worst Monday in her short and not particularly illustrious appraisal career. Becca leaned forward, crossed her arms on the desk, and laid her head down on them. All day, she had been working on breathing deeply and focusing on the *right now*, but it wasn't working. Maybe she really wasn't cut out to be an appraiser, after all. The right now she was experiencing at the moment was definitely lousy. The incessant pounding in her head and chest weren't even in sync with Mr. Rap Dude's horrible music, which was unbelievably annoying. The phone rang and Becca almost fell off her chair. Clutching her chest, she grabbed the receiver and yelled, "What!"

"Becca?"

"Hello. Yes. Sorry. Who is this?" The deep voice sounded familiar.

"Hi, this is Jack. Are you okay?"

"You always ask me that. I'm fine." Becca rubbed her chest. How had she not noticed that his voice was so smooth and mellow? "You just sound different on the phone."

He chuckled. "It's still the same ole me. You wanted me to call you after I met with Joel, remember?"

It had been less than twenty-four hours, but that conversation felt like a lifetime ago. "Yes. Thanks for calling. Is everything okay with the cabin?"

"Yes, Joel is great. He plowed everything out and I cleaned up. Oh, and I measured the window and talked to a glass company about getting a piece cut down that I can use. It's an odd size, so it's going to be ridiculously expensive for such a small thing. I might call around a little more."

Becca picked up her calculator. "Well, a few things were kind of odd about that place."

"True. That reminds me, I found out why it smells like smoke."

Becca pressed a button to clear out the calculator display. "Oh, do tell."

"It was a kitchen fire. Joel didn't really go into detail, but I guess someone threw something at him that was on fire. They had to call the fire department."

"Wow, that sounds like some serious drama at The Shack. Not to mention big excitement for the neighborhood too." A siren screamed outside the window and Becca sighed, hoping Jack didn't hear.

"Your place isn't on fire, is it?"

"I live close to the fire station. If I'd rented this place after I got into property appraisal work, I would have known that. But no. Back then I didn't really think about location and how it affects property values. I can tell you that the boys at the fire department get out a lot. My tax dollars are working hard."

"Are you okay? You sound sort of, I don't know, tired."

Becca put her elbow on the desk and rested her chin on her palm. Tired didn't begin to describe it. "I've had a bad day. It's a long story, but suffice it to say, the whole appraisal is a disaster and my uncle probably wants to kill me. Or at least fire me. The end result is that I have to go back to Alpine Grove."

"Really? But you just got home."

"I know." Becca sat up straight again. "Since I have to go back up there, maybe I could see you?"

There was a long pause and finally he said, "Okay. But I have to work."

"I know. So do I. I'm trying not to think about how much work I have to do. But I should take you out to dinner or something. To say thank you. I mean, you fed me for days. It seems only fair. Maybe we could expand our culinary horizons beyond pizza and tree parts. Are there any decent places to eat?"

He laughed. "You can't get lodgepole fries just anywhere, you know. But there's an Italian place that's not bad."

"That sounds great. It's been a really long day. I came home early to try to get a head start on the appraisal, but I'm not getting anywhere. I should just give up and start packing. Before you say anything, yes, I promise I'll bring warmer clothing this time. Including gloves."

"Can I make one other suggestion?"

"Sure."

"Rent a car with four-wheel drive. Just in case."

Becca smiled. "You know, that's not a bad idea."

Becca steered the shiny blue Ford Explorer down the long driveway toward Kat's house. The guy at the rental place had gotten all animated about the new "Control Trac" automatic four-wheel drive system in the 1995 model year. As far as Becca could tell, this nifty new feature mostly just meant that the thing cost a small fortune to rent. On the other hand, the money would be well spent if the weather turned and it decided to snow again. The Explorer even had all-season radials on it. Jack would be so pleased. Given his comments about her driving, he'd probably be even more excited about the fact that it had air bags. Safety first.

Mona was running back and forth across the backseat, wagging excitedly and pressing her nose at the small window opening Becca had given her. The dog was sniffing so hard that it seemed like she was trying to inhale the forest. Becca turned and looked behind her. "Calm down, Mona. We're almost there."

The snow on the driveway had melted enough that the holes had reappeared. The Explorer clunked heavily down into an especially deep crater and Becca patted the steering wheel. "Welcome to exploring some off-road driveway driving. You're supposed to be designed for this, right?" The rental company wouldn't be amused if she broke the SUV on its maiden voyage.

Becca parked beside Joel's green pickup and got out. The packed snow crunched under her boots and a light breeze was wafting the scent of wood smoke and pine trees through the clearing. Becca looked up at the brilliant blue sky. The only sound was the light whap-whap of a bird's wings as it flew overhead.

The door of the house opened and Kat walked down the front steps with the gigantic dog following behind her. She was bundled up in an over-sized coat, which along with the big dog made her seem especially tiny. Becca waved, "Hi Kat."

Kat walked over to the Explorer and said something unintelligible.

Becca inclined her head. "I'm sorry, what did you say?"

Kat moved closer to Becca and said in a hoarse voice, "New car?" She turned to the dog. "Linus, stop that. Not everyone wants to be leaned on."

"It's okay." Becca stroked the large dog's head. "After my last driving experience here, I decided to rent something a little more suitable."

Mona was leaping around the inside of the Explorer, and Kat pointed at the vehicle. "I think Mona really wants out."

Becca collected Mona from the back and the dog ran over to Linus. The two dogs wagged and looked delighted to see one another again. Becca smiled at the reunion. "I think Mona really enjoys it here. It was like she could tell when we were getting closer."

"I didn't see much of her toward the end of her last stay, but she seemed to settle in with everyone really easily."

Becca reached out to touch Kat's arm. "Joel said you were sick. Are you feeling better? I'm sorry to dump Mona on you so soon."

"It's okay. Mostly I just sound terrible. I talked to a friend of mine on the phone last night and she said I sound like Kathleen Turner."

Becca laughed. "Hey, that's kind of sexy, right? What does Joel think?"

"He said it's fine, as long as I don't go all *Romancing the Stone* on him and hatch a plot to capture Columbian drug lords."

"I was so glad I got to talk to Joel the other day. After wearing his clothes for so long, I felt like I was meeting an old friend."

Amusement flickered in Kat's blue eyes. "I'll bet. He really appreciated the fact that Jack spent so much time cleaning up The Shack. From what Joel said, Jack sounds like a great guy."

"Yes. Even after being trapped with Jack for days, I still like him. At first I thought we might kill each other, but it all worked out."

"Oh really?" Kat looked down at Linus, who sat down next to her, leaning on her thigh.

"It's not like that." Becca gestured dismissively. "Note to self: don't get trapped in a snowstorm with a married guy."

"Jack is married?"

Becca nodded. "Technically. For eight more days."

"Eight days. How, um, specific."

"I'm all about details. I probably shouldn't be saying anything about it, although Jack made it sound like everyone in Alpine Grove already knew."

"This is not an easy place to keep secrets." Kat ruffled the large dog's ears. "So have you met his wife?"

"No." Becca glanced down at Mona. Meeting the legendary Annie was definitely not on her to-do list. "I hope I never do. From his description, she sounds gorgeous."

Kat stroked Linus's head, looking thoughtful. "Sometimes men surprise you. It's not always all about looks."

Becca smirked. "Yeah, right." She twisted Mona's leash in her hand. The dog was quietly sitting at her side. It was as if she enjoyed being back here, happily looking up at the humans and listening to their conversation. "I should really get going. I have so much work to do for this appraisal. They're going to get really tired of seeing me at the offices I have to go to in town. I have to go to the assessor's office, talk to real estate people, stare at records at the county courthouse, and dig up a bunch of other stuff. It's going to take a while."

"Wow, you go, girl." Kat took the leash from Becca. "Let me know if you need anything. We'll be here."

Becca reached out and gave Kat a hug. "Thank you."

As Becca drove the Explorer back toward town, she was feeling a little bad that her dog seemed to like being here a whole lot better than being at home. Maybe Becca just wasn't cut out to be a dog mom. She did work a lot, after all.

Poor Mona. When you're a refugee from an animal shelter, you don't get to pick your new family. They pick you. And in the great spin of the adoption roulette wheel, unlucky little Mona got her.

~

Kat took Mona and Linus into the house. Joel was in the kitchen making a sandwich. As Linus trotted by, Joel glanced at Kat. "Mona looks pleased to be back."

Kat unclipped the leash and Mona ran off to the living room to join the other dogs. "Yeah, she definitely likes it here. I thought she was going to try to break out of the Explorer Becca was driving."

"How are you feeling?"

"I'm okay. Tired, which seems impossible, given how much I've slept lately." She pointed at the sandwich. "That looks good. Now that we have clean silverware again, would you be willing to make me one of those?"

"Sure."

Kat sat down at the table, and a few minutes later Joel joined her, handing her a plate with a sandwich on it. He settled into a chair. "I have to talk to you about something."

Kat paused before taking a bite of her sandwich. "Please don't tell me your sister is coming back. I'm still not up to full strength yet."

"No. I think I need a break from family for a while."

"Thank you." Relieved, she took a bite. Food actually tasted normal again.

"It's about The Shack."

Kat put down her sandwich. "What about it? I thought everything was okay. And you were going to meet Jack again after he got the glass to fix the door."

Joel shoved his plate forward and put his elbows on the table. "Yes. It's all fine. I wondered what you would think about me renting it."

Kat leaned toward him. This was new. "Well, I'm not sure. It's your house. You can do what you want. But if you rent it, you can't…uh…escape there if you want to."

"I know." Joel arched an eyebrow. "And neither can you."

A flush rose on her cheeks. "That was just one time. There were extenuating circumstances. I was stressed."

He gave her a sympathetic smile. "I know. I remember."

"Who would you rent it to? No one wants to go way out there in the winter do they? Your sister doesn't even want to come out here, and The Shack is farther out than this place is."

Joel looked down at the plate. "I was thinking of asking Jack if he wants to rent it."

"Jack? That's a surprise. You'd think he and Becca would never want to see that place ever again."

"He's working on a property right near there."

Kat waved the sandwich in her hand at him. "There's nothing *over* there. What does Jack do?"

"He's a forester. I guess he's doing some work for the people that own the old commune property."

Kat took Joel's hand. "Doesn't Jack already have a place to live? Becca told me he's married. Or he was, I guess. He must have a house or apartment or something."

"He lives in that old brick apartment complex near town." Joel shrugged. "It wasn't like he said he hated it. More like he loves the trees out at The Shack. He told me all kinds of stuff about them. It was really interesting. I guess a lot of logging was done here in the twenties. And he said that it's an unusual habitat. I can't remember everything he said, but I have to say, he really knows his trees."

"Hey, as you know, I like the trees too. I can relate to that."

"I wanted to see what you think before I say anything to him. He might not be interested, so it may not even be an issue. But it would be kind of nice to have someone keeping an eye on the place."

Kat raised her eyebrows. "So people like Jack don't break in?"

Joel laughed. "Yes."

"But what if we got into a huge fight?" She squeezed his hand. "You've always had a place to go if you needed to get away from me. Which I understand. Sometimes I'd like to get away from me too."

"Are you planning on having a huge fight? We haven't had one so far."

"Not huge. More like limited-time disagreements. I suppose there were some adjustments to living together. And maybe some minor snarling." She shrugged. "But you seem to limit your major fighting activity to altercations with your sister."

"True. It's not like I'm incapable of getting into an argument."

"Me neither. I think that's well-documented. Sometimes I speak when I should shut up."

Joel grinned. "Sometimes I shut up when I should speak."

Kat got up out of her chair and moved to sit in Joel's lap, wrapping her arms around his neck. "I know I've said this before, but I don't want you to go anywhere. If you're asking me if I am planning to throw you out, the answer is no. If you want to rent your house, you won't get any argument from me." She gave him a kiss. "And thanks for talking to me about it."

"I've been told that I should communicate more." He tickled her ribs playfully. "There was this mute woman waving a notepad at me."

"That mute woman is feeling much better."

He raised his eyebrows suggestively. "How much better? I thought you were tired."

"Maybe not that tired. Don't you have geeky engineering stuff you're supposed to be working on down in your office?"

"I suppose. But you have this sexy, low sultry voice. I don't really *have* to work right now. Do you have something else in mind?"

Kat nibbled on his earlobe and whispered exactly what she had in mind.

~

After a long day of attempting to sweet-talk information out of numerous Alpine Grove office workers, Becca was looking forward to meeting Jack for dinner. She sat at the Italian restaurant enjoying the aroma of spicy tomato sauce and the warm glow of the candlelight. Jack walked in the door and she waved.

He was wearing a long, dark-colored wool coat that made him look like some type of exotic foreign spy. It was a far cry from the Eskimo garb. After hanging the coat on a hook, he sat down across from her. "You look nice. That dress is exactly the same color as your afghan."

Becca looked down at the teal dress, which in addition to being extremely comfortable and impervious to wrinkles, also had a form-fitting design that showed off her figure. "Thank you." She pointed at the coat. "So where are you supposed to keep your duct tape in that?"

"I'll never tell. How was your day?"

Becca leaned forward. "Great! I got tons of information today. My nagging skills were in top form. It's much more difficult to avoid someone when she is standing right in front of you. Not fighting with voicemail makes a big difference as far as efficiently getting what you need."

"I'm impressed."

"While I was busy harassing county employees, what were you doing today?"

He leaned his elbows on the table. "Same thing I usually do. I was out boring trees."

"Honestly, Jack, you need to get over this being boring thing. I don't think you're boring and I'm sure the trees think you're utterly fascinating."

"What? No." He shook his head. "I mean I was boring trees, as in drilling holes in them. To check the age and quality of the wood. You use a tool called an increment borer. You poke it into the tree and then twist it and pull out a little strip of wood, which gives you a cross-section of the rings of the tree." As he spoke, he indicated the poking and twisting action with his hands.

Becca's eyes widened. "Well, now you really have my attention."

Jack paused in his explanation, and at the expression on her face, he burst out laughing. "Becca!"

He had the most wonderful laugh. Warm, rich, and infectious. Becca wanted to say something funny just to hear him laugh again. She put her fingertip on her cheek and said in a phony high-pitched voice. "Sir, I do not know what you think I am thinking, but I am not the kind of girl who would think such impure thoughts."

Jack exchanged a knowing look with her. "I think we both know..." Glancing toward the front door, he stopped in mid-sentence, a horrified expression on his face.

Becca turned to see what he was looking at. A tall woman with long blonde hair, wearing a ruby red cashmere coat, was striding toward them. Jack struggled to get up. The woman waved him back down into the chair and stood alongside the table. She glanced briefly at Becca and then said to Jack, "Don't bother. How are you Jack?"

Jack said evenly, "I'm fine. I thought you were down at your parents' place."

"I couldn't stand any more of that wholesome family time. Plus, I needed to get back and take care of some things at the house here."

Becca cleared her throat loudly. "Hello. I'm Rebecca Mackenzie."

Jack said, "I'm sorry. Becca, this is my, uh, wife, Annie."

"Well, not exactly," Becca said.

The woman glanced at Becca quickly. "Anne Sheridan. Nice to meet you." She turned back to Jack and reached to touch his cheek, which still sported a fading yellow bruise. "What happened to you?" She ran her fingertip along the side of his face and traced the outline of the bruise with a long red fingernail.

He jerked his head away. "Just an accident."

Becca said perhaps a bit too loudly. "Things might have gotten a little out of hand when we were out at that cabin in the woods."

Annie looked down at her. "Oh really?" She carefully placed a little white box she was holding on the table.

Becca proffered her sweetest smile and raised her eyebrows suggestively. "Oh *yes*."

Annie turned her head to look at Jack again. "I guess you got over that whole idea of being by yourself for a while."

Ignoring the statement, Jack asked, "Why are you here?"

Annie pointed at the box. "I'm just picking up some tiramisu. You know how I love the tiramisu here." She licked her lips. "I doubt you'd forget that."

Jack shook his head, but didn't say anything.

"Well, I should be going." Annie picked up the box. "Jack, I need to talk to you. I'll call you later tonight."

He nodded. "That's fine."

Jack and Becca both watched in silence as Annie left the restaurant. Becca turned to him. "Well, that was awkward."

He sighed. "Sometimes this town is just way too small."

"I'm thinking I want to try some of this tiramisu. Apparently, it's not to be missed."

Jack chuckled and the tense expression on his face relaxed. "It really is good."

Becca gestured expansively toward the room. "So tell me more about how you spend your time having your way with unsuspecting trees."

He grinned. "Dendrology is a lot sexier than people think."

As it turned out, the lasagna was almost as good as the tiramisu. Becca had a great time eating, drinking, and laughing. Jack seemed to forget about the whole uncomfortable conversation with Annie and teased Becca about how her afghan was probably the size of New Jersey by now. After a long day of having to be polite to people, it was great to just sit and talk to someone who already knew all her most terrible secrets.

They got up to leave and Becca watched as Jack put on his coat. "So you must have something in your coat pockets. You always do."

He reached into his pocket and opened his palm to show her a small Swiss army knife. "Don't leave home without it."

Becca laughed and tucked her arm into his. "Never."

They walked outside and stood on the sidewalk in front of the restaurant. The wind had kicked up, blowing Becca's hair every which way. "I should get back to the lovely H12 now."

"It's dark. I'll walk you there."

"It's three blocks away. I think I can make it. This is not exactly like walking around in the mean streets of LA."

Jack locked his gaze with hers. "Humor me."

"Fine." They began walking down the street toward the motel. Becca said, "Have you ever actually stayed at the H12?"

"No."

"It's kind of a dump. But the owners are nice. And when you check in, they give you a condom with your room key."

Jack slowed his pace and turned to look at her. "What?"

"Apparently, it's a progressive type of no-tell motel." Becca huddled against Jack's coat as they walked into the wind. "I told them I was staying by myself, but the lady at the desk just nodded and handed me one anyway. Then she told me to take more from a basket on the counter if I needed them."

"I suppose that is good to know, given my wife's extra-curricular activities."

"You mean your not-exactly wife."

"Right."

"I'm in room 12, by the way. At the end."

They stood in front of the door and Jack put his hands in his coat pockets, hunching his shoulders against the wind.

"Thanks for dinner. That was a lot of fun. Well, except for Annie showing up. Sorry about that. But I still had a great time."

Becca tried to think of something to say. She didn't want him to leave yet. "Where did you park?"

"I walked."

"All the way from your place?"

"It's not that far. And there's no decent parking next to the restaurant."

Becca tugged at the arm of his coat. "It's freezing out here. Why don't you come in for a minute? I want to ask you about something. There's a weird code on the tax stuff I got and I'm not sure what it means. The printouts from their ancient database are really cryptic and not the same as the ones I'm used to in LA."

"Can't you just ask the people at the assessor's office?"

"They might be a little sick of me at this point." Becca tugged at the fabric again. "It's about the land, not the house, so you might know."

Jack shrugged. "Okay. Just for a minute. I should probably get back and make sure Frank is okay."

Becca unlocked the door and they walked inside. She took off her coat, threw it on a bed, and went over to the desk. Picking up a stack of papers, she sat down on the edge of one of the beds and started riffling through them. Jack was standing stiffly with his hands in his pockets, looking decidedly uncomfortable. She looked up at him. "Why don't you sit down? This could take a minute. I made about 300 copies today. Relax, Jack. Take off your coat."

Jack did as instructed and perched on the edge of the desk chair, looking around the room. "You're right. This is not exactly a high-end motel, is it?"

"Not so much." Becca pulled out a paper from the stack. "Aha! Found it."

She walked over to the chair and held the paper in front of him. "See that? What the heck is AG? Alpine Grove? Silver?"

Jack looked up into her eyes. "Agricultural land. Tax exemption." He reached up and gently took both sides of her face in his hands, pulling her head down to his. A delicious thrill went through her as her lips touched his. The kiss was just as electrifying as the first time, not to mention a lot warmer, without all the snow.

As the kiss grew more intense, Becca tried not to fall in an indelicate heap on top of Jack, but it was difficult. As heat coursed through her body, she straddled the chair, wrapping her arms around his neck. She threw the paper on the desk and yanked at his shirt collar. A button flew off and she inclined her head to look into his eyes, which had turned a deep sapphire. "Maybe that lady at the front desk was on to something."

Pushing the fabric of her dress down her shoulder to expose more skin, Jack kissed her neck and mumbled "Maybe so," before moving downward.

Boots

Later, Becca was stretched out alongside Jack, enjoying the warm feel of his skin against hers. She ran her hand down his arm and laced her fingers in his. He pulled her arm around and pressed her hand to his chest, so she was hugging him.

She kissed his shoulder blade. "Are you okay?"

Rolling over onto his back, he pulled her hand up to his lips, kissed her knuckles, and smiled. "I think the answer to that question is fairly obvious, don't you?"

Becca rubbed his calf with her toes. "No, I mean you didn't make it to December seventh. The day that shall live in infamy and all that?"

"I decided you were right."

She flashed a grin. "What? That I should jump you? I'd like to point out that *you* jumped *me*."

He chuckled. "Well, okay, that too. But no, you said that I was punishing myself. I decided you were right and it wasn't doing me any good. I figured out what I need to know. Now December seventh is just an arbitrary date. With a summary divorce, you don't go to court or anything. One day you're married and the next day you're just not anymore. It's sort of strange in a way."

"I suppose it is." Becca propped her head up on her elbow, looking down into his face. "But I'm not sure what you're saying."

"I needed to decide what I want from the rest of my life, so I spent a lot of time alone thinking."

"All that Zen time in the trees?"

"Yes. It was helpful that I got this huge project. One of the owners of the former commune showed me this place near a creek. I spent a lot of time there."

"Aren't you supposed to be boring trees and making grids?"

"Yes." He trailed a fingertip across her shoulder. "But I also am supposed to observe habitat. Forest ecosystems are complex, but I might have done more observation than absolutely necessary."

Becca stroked his chest. "You're such a nature guy."

"True. But going off into the forest turned into an escape. What I do for a living requires it, but I blamed myself for not paying more attention to my marriage. I didn't face things that needed to be faced."

"I think most people tend to avoid things they don't want to deal with."

Jack looked at her thoughtfully as he traced the outline of her jaw with his index finger. "You didn't. This terrible thing happened to you, and you just moved ahead. All the counseling, yoga classes, self-defense classes. Then the new job. I bet you didn't even know how to knit before, did you?"

"No. The fact that I only knit squares and rectangles is a giveaway."

"You were brave. And what you said to Annie about being at the cabin." His lip twitched with suppressed humor.

"The look on her face—well—let's just say I don't think she likes you."

"That's fine. I don't think I'm her biggest fan either. I don't feel very brave."

"Maybe that's not the right word. But you don't run away from difficult situations. That's what I did. There were rumors about Annie for a long time before I said anything. It's a small town, after all. But I didn't want to have that conversation."

"You didn't seem too excited when Cliff got in your face either."

"I know. I hate conflict."

Becca took his hand and interlaced her fingers with his. "All the creatures of the forest should live in harmony, right?"

"Yes."

She searched his troubled blue eyes. "What changed? Obviously, you *did* have that conversation, since you filed for divorce."

"It was just as bad as I thought it would be. Maybe worse. Annie apologized and said it would never happen again. But it's not like I'm going to turn into a different person. I'm still the same boring ole me, and I have no reason to believe she wouldn't start looking for excitement again. I thought about what would happen if we had kids. Right now, we have no children, no house, and haven't really been married that long. Divorce is bad enough without involving kids and a lot of complicated money stuff."

A heaviness settled in Becca's stomach. But she had to ask. "Doesn't she love you? I mean you *did* get married, after all."

"She said she did. That's what I had to think about for so long. I wanted to forgive her and just go back to the way things were when we met." Jack glanced away. "It took a long time to accept, but I think Annie loved who she wanted me to be, not who I really am. And that hurt."

"I'm sorry." Becca laid her head on his chest. The beating of his heart was soothing. "I understand what you mean. When my ex called me a head case after I was attacked, it made me realize he didn't understand who I was either. Not really. It does hurt."

"Yeah." Jack stroked her hair, tucking a strand behind her ear. "But I'm glad I met you. And even glad we were snowed in."

Becca moved her head to look at him. "I know. It was sort of awful and wonderful at the same time. Maybe sometimes it's good to get away from your own life and thoughts for a little while."

He trailed a finger along the contours of her neck. "How Zen. I do notice that you're speaking a lot more slowly."

"I'm relaxed. Apparently the chatterbox in my head runs out of things to say when I'm lying here all warm and snuggly with you. 'Wow' was about as far as I got."

"That sounds good."

"It definitely was. Plus, the fact that you don't think I'm completely nuts is kind of a turn-on."

"Oh really?" He moved his hand across her thigh. "I like that you don't think I'm boring. That dress you were wearing didn't hurt either."

"I figure if you're going to check out my boobs, I should give the girls the opportunity to look their best."

He lifted up the sheet, and looked down. "Very nice. Even better without the dress."

Becca put her palm on his chest. "I hate to kill the mood, but I just thought of something. You said you had to check on Frank."

"I did. But I'm sure he's fine. Probably lying flat on his side on the mattress, shedding, and snoring like a freight train."

"So you don't have to leave right now?"

"No. I should probably go before the sun comes up, since then Frank will start getting agitated about his breakfast. But right now—right this second—there are other things I'd like to do."

As Jack's hands moved under the sheet, Becca leaned to kiss him. "I think I might like these things."

"I think you might."

~

At some dark early morning hour, Jack kissed Becca and slipped out of bed. She rolled over and watched as he dressed and got ready to leave.

He pulled on his long coat and sat down on the edge of the bed. "Can I see you later?"

"My appointment with the owners to see the house isn't until tomorrow. So I have planned a big morning of continuing harassment at a wide range of Alpine Grove offices. Then I have to come back here and enter data into my ever-so-exciting appraisal software. Many calculations will be involved."

He bent to kiss her. "Maybe I could stop by in the afternoon and take you away from all that for a while."

"Away from my laptop?" She grinned. "Gee, twist my arm."

He cupped her cheek with his hand and kissed her again. "See you later, then."

"Say hi to Frank for me."

Later, Becca was hunched over the little laptop pecking at numbers. She double-checked an entry against the number on her calculator display and pounded at the laptop's Backspace key. Software could be so unbelievably annoying.

At the knock at the door, she dropped the calculator on the desk with a little squeak of happiness. Spending way too much time thinking about last night with Jack had completely shot her concentration. She couldn't wait to see him again.

Opening the door quickly, Becca launched at Jack, wrapping her arms around his neck. "Oops, forgot to warn you."

"That's okay. I'm kind of getting used to it." He gave her a quick kiss. "Are you ready to go?"

"It depends. You're dressed like an Eskimo again. Where are we going?"

"You'll see. Wear gloves and bring those Italian hiking boots you told me about."

She picked up her gloves off the dresser and flopped them back and forth. "Ta-da!"

He pointed at the boots on the floor. "Is this them?"

"Yes. Aren't they cute?"

Picking them up, he turned to her. "Are hiking boots ever cute?"

"Just because they have tread, doesn't mean they have to be completely hideous."

They walked out to the truck, where Frank was sitting in the driver's seat. Becca glanced at Jack. "He looks very official."

"Yeah, well, he's not the greatest driver." Jack opened the door and relocated Frank to the extended cab.

"You're so picky about driving skills. So where are we going?"

"Up Misty Meadow Lane."

Becca glanced at him. "Um, I believe I've been there before."

"You've only seen part of it. Plus, it was snowing and you were lost."

She leaned on his shoulder as he put the truck in gear. "If we fall off the road again, I'm not going to forgive you. Neither will my uncle Pat if something happens and I don't get this appraisal done."

"That's why I'm not letting Frank drive."

Jack drove out north of town, and as they wound their way out past fields and long dirt roads toward the forests near Joel's cabin, Becca regaled Jack with stories about the people she'd met that day. It was another gloriously sunny, blue-sky day and everything was snow-crusted and sparkly. Becca wished she'd thought to bring her sunglasses from LA.

They passed the driveway to the cabin and Becca waved toward it. "Hey, it looks so different!"

"I told you Joel plowed when we came out here. I'd love to have a blade like that for this truck."

"Don't they plow your apartment complex?"

"Yes. I suppose it's just a guy thing."

"Hmm. Snow-plow envy. Is this kind of like big chain saws?"

He laughed and reached over to take her hand. "Something like that."

The road dead-ended into a huge snow berm and a cleared area where the plows evidently turned around and went back down the road.

Becca looked at Jack. "You brought me all the way out here to see a pile of snow?"

"We're not there yet. Put on your hiking boots."

"I'm not slogging through snow again. We've done that before and it wasn't a lot of fun."

"I know. This time, you're snow-shoeing. It's a lot easier. I promise."

Becca changed her shoes and got out of the truck. Frank was leaping around, running in circles, and having an all-around fantastic time snuffling his nose down in the snow.

She smiled at the dog's antics. "Well, Frank is certainly enthusiastic about this idea."

"He loves it out here." Jack handed her a pair of snowshoes. "Put these on. Just slip your foot in and tighten the bindings."

Becca did as instructed and clomped around in a circle. "I feel like Bigfoot."

"Follow me. And don't let Frank step on your snowshoes. He gets pretty excited, but having one-hundred pounds of dog on your snowshoe tends to slow you down or pull off the shoe entirely."

"That sounds like the voice of experience talking."

Frank ran up ahead on a trail that led into the trees. Jack whistled and Frank came galloping back gleefully. Becca followed and looked up at the giant trees around them. The afternoon light shifted through the branches and a light breeze caused some of the boughs to creak. She inhaled the pungent scent of pine and let it fill her lungs.

Jack was right. Walking on top of the snow was far easier than walking through it. As she got used to the wide-legged clunky walking rhythm, she forgot she was wearing snowshoes and started to enjoy the experience. The number of snowshoe tracks on the trail and others veering off to points unknown indicated that Jack had been out here recently.

They walked down an incline and the sound of water rushing over rocks burbled below them. Jack leaned against a rock and Frank began a snow excavation project, digging furiously, then lying down in the indentation. The small clearing with the creek running through it had a sense of peace that Becca was at a loss to explain. She turned to Jack. "This is the place, isn't it?"

"Yes. You're the only person I've ever told about it." He gestured toward the creek. "At the risk of getting all woo-woo on you, there's something special about this spot. How it feels. The woman who showed it to me—Bea—owns the gift store in town. She's one of the people who lived at the commune, and she said I'd understand about how they felt about the conservation of the land if I came here."

She clumped over and leaned on the rock next to him. "Thanks for bringing me here."

"You once asked if I'm religious. And I'm not, in the traditional go-to-church kind of way. But in *Walden,* Thoreau said that 'A field of water betrays the spirit that is in the air.

It is continually receiving new life and motion from above. It is intermediate between land and sky.' If there truly is some type of life force, I believe I'm closer to it in a place like this one." He looked down and thumped his foot to remove the extra snow that had collected on the snowshoe. "That's how it feels to me anyway."

Becca moved closer to him, trying not to step on top of his snowshoes with hers. "Can we just stay here for a while?"

"I usually do. There's a place over there where we can sit."

They took off their snowshoes and sat on a section of rock Jack had obviously cleared off earlier. He put his arm around her and she leaned her head on his jacket. Closing her eyes, she listened to the sound of his breathing and the rushing water below. Right here, right now, she was falling in love with Jack. And she wasn't sure what to think about that.

~

The next day, Becca went out to the correct house on Edgewater Road to take pictures. She'd made an appointment and arrived early. Everyone at work always used to tease her about being such a stickler for punctuality, but as a busy person herself, she hated to keep people waiting.

The house was an enormous estate that was set back from the road. Fencing criss-crossed the land, and next to a huge barn several horses were standing in paddocks eating hay that had been thrown into large metal feeders. The horses probably missed grazing in their pastures, which were now a vast expanse of white.

Becca went up to the door and was greeted by an employee who showed her around the house. Becca knew from her research that the place was sixty-five-hundred square feet. As she went through the rooms, she understood why Pat had immediately known the other house she'd visited was not the right place.

The huge rambling ranch house had five bedrooms, five bathrooms, four fireplaces, a wet bar, wine room, and an exercise room with a hot tub and steam shower. After riding all those horses, you probably really needed a hot tub.

As Becca passed through the rooms, she took pictures of the vaulted ceilings and the custom stone work on the fireplace hearths. The shiny sparkling kitchen looked virtually untouched and sported two refrigerators, a commercial-grade stove, and a walk-in pantry. Becca peeked in the pantry. No Twinkies or Chef Boyardee in this place.

She stood at a window in the expansive master suite and looked out across the estate. The house was set on a rise that overlooked the lake. In the opposite direction were acres of beautiful, serene fields with panoramic mountain views beyond. A small creek also ran through the property. With the immense acreage and all the high-end features, the place looked like it belonged in a magazine.

Becca thanked the employee and told him that she'd be outside taking photos for a while. He nodded and closed the door behind her. She wandered the property and continued taking pictures. It was possible she might have wasted a teeny-weeny bit of film on a few extra photos of the landscape and some adorable curious horse faces.

Later at the H12 motel, she was entering data into the laptop again when she heard the knock at the door she'd been anticipating. As she let Jack into the room, she announced, "I know what I want for Christmas."

He pulled her into an embrace. "What's that?"

"This house I'm appraising." She threw her arms around him and returned the hug. "I'm not sure I can add numbers this large. It's just incredible!"

Jack inclined his head to kiss her. "I hope you have some rich relatives, then."

"A girl's gotta have a dream. I need to get my film developed. It looks like there's a photo place near the gift store."

They collected Frank from the truck and walked hand-in-hand down the main street of Alpine Grove, passing cute little touristy shops. There was a big wooden bench in front of the gift store and a woman with light blonde hair was sitting on it with her legs stretched out in front of her, eyes closed. As they got closer, Becca realized that the woman's hair was actually blonde mixed with gray, but it had been highlighted in a way that disguised the gray. Sneaky.

Jack squeezed Becca's hand. "That's Bea. She's one of the owners of the land. I need to talk to her for a second and tell her where I'm at on the project."

"Okay. It looks like she's taking a nap though."

They walked up next to the bench and the woman opened her eyes. She leaped up and gave Jack an enthusiastic hug. "Jack! You caught me sunbathing." She bent down to stroke Frank's head. "Hi Frank. Yes. I know. There's a squirrel right over there. Please ignore him. He's my friend."

Jack tightened his grip on the leash and glared at Frank. Looking back up and turning to Bea he said, "It's good to see you again. The sun is nice, isn't it?"

"Yes. It's like the weather is apologizing for last week." Bea spread her arms wide. "I was trying to collect as much

Vitamin D as possible. In wintertime, I need to get my sun when I can."

Jack gestured toward Becca. "This is my friend Becca. She's a property appraiser."

Becca smiled politely. "Well, technically I'm an appraisal trainee. I work for my uncle. But I've almost completed my hours, so I can get certified. It's very nice to meet you."

Jack said, "Bea, I wanted to let you know that I should have the plans and information to you in the next couple weeks. I thought I'd get more done on it over Thanksgiving weekend than I did, so I'm a little behind schedule."

"Oh that's fine Jack. Did you have a nice holiday?"

Jack glanced at Becca. "Yes, actually. Much better than I expected."

Bea reached out to touch his arm. "I'm so glad, Jack. It's wonderful to see you looking so happy."

Becca said, "Jack took me out to see your land, and it's just beautiful."

Bea nodded. "Yes, it's a special place. That's why we want to make sure it is preserved for future generations to enjoy. Now that my daughter finally has found a boyfriend who isn't a creep, I have hope that there actually will be future generations in my family to see it."

Becca giggled. "I think my mother is starting to despair about me. Did you spend Thanksgiving with your family?"

"Yes. It was loud and everyone ate way, way too much. But it was one of those times I'm glad we live in town, since I guess many people didn't have electricity because of the storm. My husband and my daughter even got along, for the most part. Then Rob fixed something on my husband's computer, which improved his mood considerably. It was a holiday miracle."

Jack laughed. "It sounds like it. We should get going. Becca needs to drop off some film before the photo place closes."

"It was nice to meet you," Becca said.

Bea said, "Lovely to meet you too, dear. I hope I see you again."

Jack and Becca continued down the street and Becca said, "Bea is great. I think I want to be her when I grow up."

"You want to own a gift store?"

"No. But I wish I were that nice. More likable I guess."

"Apparently you're nice enough to people that they give you lots of real estate information. But yes, everyone loves Bea."

"I think some of those people gave me information just so I'd go away. Persistent is not the same as nice. I'd love to just sit around with Bea and listen to her tell stories." Becca squeezed his hand. "So who is Rob?"

"Rob is her daughter Tracy's boyfriend. Tracy works at the veterinary clinic part-time and does something with computers with Rob. I've met Tracy a few times when I've taken Frank in to the vet."

Becca looked down at the dog, who looked worried with his furrowed brow and purposeful stride. "I think Frank is a little concerned that you just used the 'v' word."

"He's just hoping that if we walk faster I'll forget the fact that he's due for his shots."

~

The next day, Becca had a long day of analysis ahead of her. It was time to wax poetic on the numbers and how they related to her opinions on the value of the house in question. Blech. Writing up her conclusions always made her a little anxious. This was definitely not the fun part.

As he had for the last few days, Jack had slipped out of the H12 sometime in the wee hours of the morning. Becca was enjoying her nights with him far too much. Some of her body parts tingled just thinking about it. But now she was starting to feel apprehensive at the idea of leaving in forty-eight hours. It was distressing that her time left with him was dwindling to the point that it was easily measurable in hours. She took a deep breath and stared at the laptop screen, trying to focus on the numbers.

Thinking about being anxious tended to increase her anxiety, which was not good if she ever wanted to get this done. Leaving Jack was the future. Right now, she had to finish this stupid analysis. They probably wouldn't appreciate "The house is gorgeous and I want it" as an accurate estimation of value.

Becca hit a key on the keyboard and the screen flashed once and turned blue with a bunch of white text and long strings of numbers on it. She grabbed the corner of the laptop monitor and shrieked, "A *problem* has been detected? What do you mean *check if my software is properly installed?* It was properly installed two seconds ago, you piece of garbage!" Putting her hand on her chest, she attempted to take a deep breath. It would be fine. Just turn off the laptop and maybe the blue screen would go away.

The little computer did not want to return to service. The black screen that appeared was even worse than the blue screen. At least the blue screen said something other than "C." *C?* What the heck was C supposed to mean? Becca stood up and began pacing the room. She sat on the bed and flipped through the skinny phone book. The only entry under "computers" was for a company in Los Angeles. *Really?* She flopped back on the bed and put her arm over her eyes, trying not to panic. Or cry. It was just a computer. With almost a week's worth of work on it. She sat up. What about that Rob guy?

Becca put on her coat, stuffed the laptop in its bag, grabbed her room key, and ran out the door toward town. She walked into the gift store, where Bea smiled at her from behind the counter. "Hello Becca. It's nice to see you again. May I help you?"

Becca looked around the store. There were lots of sparkly wonderful things that in any other situation she'd love to explore. But now was not the time for shopping. Right now, she had a much bigger problem. "Yes, I hope you can help me. Didn't you say your son-in-law—or whatever—your daughter's boyfriend knows about computers?"

"Yes. Rob. Half the time I don't know what he's talking about, but he is the sweetest man. He and Tracy have an office across the street and down a little ways."

Becca put the laptop bag on the counter. "Do you think he'd help me with my computer? The laptop I'm using died and my appraisal is gone!"

"It couldn't hurt to ask. Go down to the building that has the advertising agency and take the stairs to the second floor. He's probably up there working now."

Becca clutched the shoulder strap of the laptop bag and threw it over her shoulder. "Oh, thank you!"

"My pleasure, dear. I hope it works out."

After committing an egregious act of jaywalking, Becca ran down the street looking at the signs on the plate-glass windows. She found the ad agency and next to it was a stairwell. Zipping up the stairs, she stopped and looked around the hallway. There was an open door with a baby gate across it. She walked down the hall and peeked into the office.

A lanky man in a t-shirt and shorts was sitting at a computer squinting at the screen. He certainly seemed to be a trifle underdressed, considering it was the first day of December. Becca tapped on the open door and a cabinet door slammed. A little wiener dog ran toward her, barking angrily. Becca stepped back away from the baby gate.

The man stood up and walked toward the door. "Sorry about that." He pointed at the dachshund. "Roxy, that's enough! Go lie down."

With a final glare and a surly growl at Becca, the dog turned away and settled into a dog bed, where she could keep an eye on the evil human. The man pushed his glasses up to the bridge of his nose and said, "The ad agency is downstairs. So is the cute dog. I know sometimes people get lost."

Becca said, "I'm not looking for the ad agency or a dog. Are you Rob?"

"Yes."

As she stepped over the gate, she thrust the laptop bag into his hands. "Thank goodness I found you. Bea said you might be here. I have a terrible problem and I hope you can help me. I *really* need your help! There was a blue screen, then there was no screen. With the letter C. What does that even mean? If my appraisal is gone, my uncle is going to really kill me this time."

Rob looked down at the bag in his arms, then at Becca. "Please slow down. I can hardly understand you."

Becca took a breath and looked around the room. "It's got to be 400 degrees in here. Why is it so hot?"

"The building restoration project has hit a little snag. They're working on the heat."

"Do you mind if I take off my coat?"

He sighed. "I'm kind of dealing with a deadline right now."

Becca removed her coat and threw it over a chair. "Please help me. I think my computer died. Could you take a look at it? Just for a minute? Bea said you fixed her husband's computer."

Rob shook his head. "That was just a favor. I don't really do computer repair work."

"Please?" Becca looked into Rob's eyes, which were an unusual and striking hazel color. He also had to have the longest eyelashes she'd ever seen on a man. If Maybelline came up with a mascara that did that, she'd buy it in a heartbeat. She patted the bag. "Just look at it? Please? I'll pay you anything you want if you can fix it. I'm desperate."

He put the laptop bag on a desk. "All right."

Becca grabbed him in a hug. "Thank you so much!"

Stepping back and away from her, Rob pulled the laptop out of the bag, sat down, and plugged it in. He pressed the power button and looked up. "So what happened again?"

"I didn't do anything. Suddenly, there was a blue screen with writing all over it. And numbers. It just sat there and I couldn't figure out what to do. So I turned off the computer."

Rob looked back at the screen, which had the letter C on it.

Becca jabbed her finger at the monitor. "Then it did *that*. A black screen with the letter C. That's not helpful. Does it mean everything is gone?" She threw up her hands in frustration. "I swear this stupid appraisal really *is* cursed."

He tapped a few keys and scowled. "Okay, let me go see if I can find a disk. Maybe I can boot from a floppy and access the data."

"Huh? Boots?" What did footwear have to do with computers?

Rob stood up. "Just a minute. I need to go look for something."

"Okay." Becca walked toward the window, which faced the street. She looked out at the sidewalk below. People were walking around, once again enjoying the sun, and talking to each other. Apparently, everyone else in Alpine Grove had functioning computers.

Jack had told her he was going to be spending the day at his office working on his computer too. He didn't seem terribly excited about the prospect of sitting at a desk instead of wandering around in the woods. *Wait. Jack was supposed to meet her!* She looked up at the clock. "Is that what time it is?"

Rob looked up from the drawer he was rummaging around in. "Yes. The clock works."

Becca grabbed her coat. "I've got to go. I'll be right back. I'm supposed to meet someone. I'm never late. It's rude. Please, please fix the laptop. I promise I'll come right back."

Rob stood up. "I'll see what I can do."

Becca ran down the stairs and out the door to the street. She stopped to catch her breath. Ugh. It was really time to get in better shape. All this running around Alpine Grove was way more physical activity than she was used to. Trying not to pant like a dog, she walked as quickly as she could back to the H12.

Becca crossed the parking lot toward the motel. Jack was pacing back and forth in front of the door to her room. He looked up and raised his palms toward the sky. As she approached him, she said, "I'm sorry!"

He pulled her into his arms and kissed her hungrily. "I was worried about you. Weren't you the one who said that you hate it when people are late?"

"I know. And we have to go back. My computer died. I left it with Rob. I hope he's fixing it."

Jack released her and raised his eyebrows. "Rob?"

"Bea's daughter's boyfriend. The computer-geek guy."

"Oh yeah. Can he fix it?"

"I don't know. He didn't seem particularly optimistic, and I'm not sure what he's doing to it. Maybe something with boots? I don't know. His office is down the street from the gift store." She took Jack's hand. "Come with me. I told him I'd be right back"

"Okay. Frank will be fine in the truck for a few minutes. He's asleep anyway. Let's go." They started across the parking lot and he turned to her. "I hate computers. Having to use one is the worst part of my job."

"Tell me about it."

~

Jack and Becca returned to Rob's office, where they were aurally assaulted by the dachshund again. Becca waved at Rob, who was sitting at her laptop and doing something with floppy disks. "Can we come in?"

"Sure." Rob gave the dog a menacing glare. "Roxy, stop it."

Becca stepped over the baby gate and Jack followed her. They walked over to the desk and Jack introduced himself.

Rob said, "Bea told me about you. You're the forester. She thinks you're great."

"That's good to hear. I'm glad you're the one dealing with this computer problem. I'm useless at that kind of thing." Jack looked around the room. "Is it really hot in here?"

Rob stood up and faced Becca. "I think the hard drive is dying. But I was able to get your recent data files off the machine. The laptop might run for a while again, but honestly, I wouldn't trust it."

"What do you mean?"

Rob handed her a pile of floppy disks. "Here's a backup of everything you did over the last few days. Fortunately, you gave your files names like "Edgewater Appraisal," so I could tell what they were."

"Well, that's what they're about. What else would I call them?"

"Some people get a little too creative with file names. Or not creative enough. Names like *File 1* are never helpful."

Becca rummaged around in her bag for her wallet. "I suppose not."

"You should take the laptop in and get the hard drive replaced."

Becca ran around the desk, grabbed Rob in a fierce hug, and shoved some bills into his hand. "Thank you so much! I don't know what I would have done if I'd lost everything. This appraisal is already so late as it is."

Looking somewhat alarmed, Rob backed away, looked down at the money in his hand, and then began shutting down the laptop. "No problem."

As Jack and Becca walked back outside, Jack turned to her and said, "You really need to stop tackling men you don't know without warning. It stresses them out."

"What can I say? I'm a hugger."

He put his arm around her shoulders. "Maybe you could restrict your hugging to men you *do* know."

She looked at his face. "I know you."

"My point exactly."

They stopped by the photo place, picked up the package of appraisal photographs, and returned to the H12. Becca sat on the bed. "I guess because of this stupid dead laptop, tomorrow I can't finish up the appraisal like I planned. Maybe I should just leave tomorrow instead of Sunday."

Jack leveled his gaze at her. "Do you want to do that?"

"No." She really didn't. The time she had left with Jack was already evaporating far too quickly. "I guess I could leave really early on Sunday and maybe go into the office for a couple of hours after I get back. I'm almost done with it. Do you think Kat might be an early riser? I wonder how early I could pick up Mona."

"You could ask."

She walked over to Jack, sat on his lap, and put her arms around his neck. "That would mean we could spend the whole day together tomorrow. It's Saturday, so you don't have to work."

"I've heard that all work and no play makes me a dull boy. What do you want to do?"

Becca leaned to kiss him. "I think we might be able to think of something."

Sometime in the middle of the night, Jack disappeared to go tend to Frank. The next morning, someone knocked on the door. Becca peered through the peephole, smiled, and let in Jack. As she closed the door behind her, he looked her up and down. "Are you planning to get dressed?"

"Not unless you want me to."

Grinning, he began removing his clothing. "No. Not at all."

Later, they went to go get Frank for a walk near the lake. As they strolled along the shore, Becca couldn't stop thinking about leaving Jack the next day. The idea of not sleeping curled up with him and feeling his warmth next to her made her noisy, lonely apartment seem utterly depressing.

They walked along the shoreline path as Frank cavorted around on the rocky beach. Jack stopped and turned to look at her. He cupped her chin with his palm and caressed her cheek with his thumb. "You're awfully quiet. Are you okay?"

"You always ask me that." She looked into his eyes. "When am I going to see you again?"

"I don't know. I've got to get this forestry management plan done." He scratched his ear. "As you know, I'm a little behind on it."

Wrapping her arms around him, Becca leaned her head on his shoulder. "I'm going to miss you."

He smoothed her hair. "I'll miss you too. But we'll figure something out. Right now, we should just enjoy being here together."

She lifted her head and looked out at the lake. "It is really beautiful. But I'm getting cold."

"Okay. Let's go back to my place. You can contend with my chair while I feed Frank and make us something for dinner."

She laughed. "If I get into that chair again, I might not be *able* to leave."

Inclining his head to kiss her, he whispered, "That thought had crossed my mind."

~

After dinner, Becca sat next to Jack on the mattress. Frank was snoring at their feet, half falling off the mattress onto the floor.

Becca pointed down at the dog. "Honestly, how can he possibly be comfortable like that?"

"Frank sleeps hard. I'm sure he didn't notice when the back half of his hairy body rolled off."

"Kat said I could pick up Mona at seven tomorrow. I guess with that many dogs they get up pretty early. So that means I'll be leaving at six thirty or so." The slightly queasy feeling in the pit of her stomach had returned now that she was talking about leaving. Her departure was getting so close. And there were so many things she wanted to say to Jack, but wasn't sure she should. He was wrong about her being brave about facing hard conversations. She'd rather face twelve uncooperative employees in the assessor's office than risk seeing what Jack's reaction would be when she told him she loved him.

He put his arm around her. "I'm sure Mona will be glad to see you."

"I don't know about that. I think she likes it better out at Kat's place than she does with me. She'd probably be happier in another home."

"I don't think that's true." He squeezed her shoulders gently. "Mona was awfully excited to see you the last time you picked her up."

"You should see her at my place though. It's like Mona is a different dog." Becca shrugged. "I guess really it's more like she's a different dog here in Alpine Grove. A happier dog. I just feel bad for her, like it would have been better if someone else had adopted her."

"You aren't going to give her away, are you?"

Becca shook her head. "I can't do that. I'd miss her too much. That probably makes me a selfish person though."

Jack touched his fingertips to her chin, turning her head toward him. "I don't think you're selfish. Adopting Mona, saving her life, and taking her into your home to care for her seems pretty generous to me."

Becca looked into the deep blue eyes that she'd come to love and mumbled "Thanks" before closing her eyes and kissing him. He took her in his arms and held her close as he tenderly caressed her and brushed his lips along her throat. Although Becca had enjoyed the many energetic and exciting adventures in bed with Jack at the dingy H12, this was different. Slower and more intimate. She relaxed in his arms and let the sensations overtake her. As she touched him, she tried to memorize the contours of his body, so she wouldn't forget.

The next morning, the alarm went off and Becca jolted upright on the mattress. Jack launched up and hit the clock on the dresser, sending it crashing to the floor. He picked it up and crawled back onto the mattress, sprawling out on his stomach. "Well, you wanted to get up early. Ugh."

"All this minimalist living and yet you actually have an alarm clock."

"A loud one," he grumbled into the pillow.

Becca leaned across his back and kissed his neck. "It's definitely not Zen. Even Frank is awake now. I'm going to go take a shower."

Jack's only response was, "Mmfmmfh."

After her shower, Becca left the bathroom and found Jack in the kitchen with Frank, who was staring up at him intently. Breakfast was imminent and the dog was on alert. Jack looked somewhat less rumpled, but seeing him shirtless with all those muscles and wearing nothing except old Levis reminded her of a poster all the women in her dorm had drooled over back in college. Even Jack's bare feet were sexy.

He looked over his shoulder at her. "I have coffee here. Your elixir of awakeness is served."

Becca took a mug and leaned on the dresser, cradling the mug in her hands. "Thank you."

"You're sure you know how to get out to Kat's place, right?"

"Yes, I've been there more than once now. It didn't snow. And I have a map."

He chuckled. "Sorry, but I'm definitely not impressed with your map."

"Neither am I." She turned to look at the obnoxious alarm clock. There really were no more excuses to stay and she was going to be late if she didn't leave soon. "I should get going."

He put down his mug and walked over to her. "Are you sure you don't want me to go with you?"

"No, it's fine. I know you need to catch up with work. So do I."

Enveloping her in his warm embrace, he said, "Drive carefully."

"I will." Becca kissed him and placed her palms on his chest for one last moment. "I'll call you when I get home."

She picked up her suitcase and with her free hand gave Frank a goodbye pat on the head. "You behave Frank. Don't mess with the hyperactive squirrels."

Jack leaned against the door jamb as she walked by. He took her hand, pulling her back toward him. "I'm going to miss you."

Becca smiled weakly. "I'm going to miss you too." She leaned to kiss him hurriedly one more time before she burst into tears. "Bye."

She scuttled down the stairs and out of the building to the Explorer. After heaving her suitcase into the passenger seat, she got in the driver's side and started the engine. Covering her face with her palms, she finally let herself sob. She was such a coward. Why hadn't she told Jack how she felt?

After a few minutes of pretending to warm up the car, but mostly crying, Becca took a deep breath. Pulling herself together, she put the Explorer in gear, pulled out of the parking lot, and headed north.

Becca was glad that it took almost half an hour to get to Kat's house. By the time she was bumping her way down the driveway, she was more or less ready to face the world, both human and canine, again.

Kat was outside with Mona and a number of other dogs who were having lots of fun playing in the snow. Becca got out of the Explorer and opened her arms wide, "Mona!"

The dog went running to Becca and crashed into her, knocking her back into a pile of snow, but Becca didn't care. She hugged her dog and ruffled her ears. "It's so good to see you!"

Kat walked over and extended her hand to help Becca up. "I think Mona is glad to see you again."

"I missed her."

"She was a good girl. Just one of the canine gang again."

"Yes. I notice she's not even on a leash."

"No. Mona doesn't need one here. She's like Linus. Those two won't leave my side. It's like having large furry things glued to you. I can't go anywhere alone. Mona has become one of the Velcro dogs."

Becca laughed. "I love that. It makes me feel so much better. Thanks for letting me pick Mona up so early."

"It's no problem. As you can see, everyone is very much awake." Kat looked at Becca quizzically. "Are you all right?"

"Yes." Becca looked down at herself. Sure, she was distracted this morning, but she seemed to be dressed okay. "What do you mean? I'm fine."

Kat motioned her hand along her face, indicating Becca's eyes. "I think you might want to redo your mascara."

Becca rubbed her lower eyelids with her fingertips. "Oh. Oops." She looked at the blackness on her fingers. "Wow. Well, that's not pretty, is it? I'm okay. I'm just having trouble leaving."

"I had that problem when I first got here too. In the end, I just stopped leaving, which solved the problem."

"Really?" Becca looked at Kat intently. "I mean, I hated Alpine Grove. Every time I had an appraisal assignment here, I'd get lost. And then when my uncle made me come up here again over Thanksgiving, I was totally furious."

"And now?"

Becca waved her arms toward the trees. "It's so quiet and beautiful. At The Shack, at first the quiet made me want to tear my hair out. But something changed while I was there. I don't know. It sounds so silly, but now I just feel like I can actually breathe here. It doesn't hurt that Mona is so happy too."

Kat put her hand on Linus's huge head. "And that Jack lives here?"

Becca looked down and stroked Mona's head. "Well, yes. But I don't think that will work out."

"How many more days until he's not married now?"

"Four. But I don't think he feels the same way I do."

Kat stroked Linus's fur slowly. "Did you ask him?"

"No."

"Maybe you should."

Chapter 11

Other Plans

As Becca drove back toward Alpine Grove, she thought about what Kat had said. No one could be as tender and loving as Jack had been last night without feeling *something*. It couldn't just be lust. He couldn't be that good an actor, could he? Becca certainly wasn't, given her tendency to spill her guts to Jack on a regular basis. Maybe he really was moving on. From what he'd said, it sounded like his marriage was truly over.

To leave Alpine Grove and return to the city, she had to drive through town right by the turn to Jack's apartment complex. Maybe she should stop and talk to him. It didn't seem right to leave things unsaid. She didn't even know when they were going to see each other again.

Becca sat up straighter in the Explorer's plush bucket seat and readjusted her hands on the steering wheel. Jack was probably still there at the apartment hanging out with Frank, so she could just stop by, say what she needed to say, and give him another goodbye kiss. She wanted one more kiss. Okay. It was a plan. Everything was better with a plan. Turning to look at Mona in the backseat, she said, "Mona, we need to make one more little stop before we head home." Mona wagged her tail, indicating her support for the idea.

Becca turned down the side street toward Jack's building and stopped the car. Jack was standing in the parking lot

223

facing Annie, with his hands in the pockets of his long dark coat. Becca couldn't see his face very well, but his head was bowed. She backed up a few feet and parked the car, trying to decide what to do. Should she walk up and make a scene? Jack said she was brave, but there was a fine line between bravery and utter stupidity. Even she wasn't gutsy enough to have *that* confrontation.

Becca got out of the Explorer and walked a little way down the sidewalk, so she could stand casually next to a tree out of sight. Okay, yes, she was behaving like a stalker, but given the body language between Jack and Annie, there was no way she was leaving without finding out what happened next. Then, after Annie went away, she could still talk to Jack.

As usual, Annie looked gorgeous. That woman would never be caught dead in a grubby old flannel shirt. Her long blonde hair fluttered in the breeze and although Becca couldn't hear what she was saying, Annie was gesturing wildly at Jack, emphatically making a point. He shook his head and whatever he was saying appeared not to go over well with Annie. Becca gave a little internal cheer for Jack sticking to whatever he was saying.

Annie shook her head and flipped her hair back with her hand. She reached into her coat pocket, pulled something out, and handed it to Jack. He took it with both hands and gazed into Annie's face with a look of incredulity. Annie grinned at him and he moved forward, wrapping her in a hug.

Becca put her hand over her mouth and waited. The time frame for a "friendly" hug had officially been exceeded now.

That was the type of hug that could evolve into a lot more than a hug. Annie stepped back away from Jack smiling, nodding, and still holding his arm possessively. Becca had seen enough. More than enough. It was time to go now.

Moving back behind the tree, she ran back to the Explorer, and got in. Throwing the vehicle into reverse, she backed into a driveway and turned around. Mona fell off the backseat and glared at her from the floor. "Sorry Mona, but we've gotta get out of here *right now*."

As Becca drove down the mountain back toward the city, it seemed like she went through every possible emotion. Well, except happiness. But shock, confusion, disappointment, sadness, shame, anger, and jealousy were well covered. The chatterbox in her brain was working overtime. How could she be such an idiot? *Do not* fall in love with a man who has not gotten over his wife. It was obvious from his face that no matter what he might have said or done with Becca, he was still in love with Annie. His *wife*. Of all the bad choices Becca had made in her life, this had to win some sort of prize for stupidity.

By the time she pulled into the parking lot of her apartment building, Becca was emotionally exhausted. It was going to be a relief to immerse herself in work and forget about everything. She grabbed her suitcase and laptop and unloaded Mona from the back. As she opened the door to her apartment, a fire truck went by, its siren wailing off into the distance. A car honked, there was a screech of tires, and then a lot of shouting from the sidewalk below.

She set her laptop next to the desk and looked up to see Mona skittering off to the bedroom. "Welcome home, little dog."

After unpacking and eating something, Becca's world seemed a little bit brighter. She loaded Mona and the laptop back into the Explorer so she could return the car and go to the office. At least her little cave of an office at Radcliffe and Associates was quieter than her apartment.

At the office, she copied the files from her floppy disk backups onto her own desktop computer and set to work, while Mona snoozed under the desk. It was hard to focus and her write-up was probably not as good as it should have been, but later that evening, at last, all the photos were scanned, the data was entered, and the appraisal was finally finished. Becca held the printout in her hands, and then set it down in her out-box. She leaned forward and flopped her arms across the desk. That had to be the longest, most complicated appraisal trip ever.

After a few moments of sitting there, silently thanking the computer gods for cooperating, she stood up wearily and peeked under the desk. "Okay Mona. I'm finally done. Let's go home."

~

Monday, Becca went back to work and gave Pat the bad news about the demise of the laptop's hard drive. He was philosophical about the computer issues, but thrilled to see the finished appraisal. After he read it over, he offered a few instructions for improvements she could make next time. But he signed off on everything and left to take the appraisal to the client with a happy little spring in his step. Becca was just glad that she never had to see the stupid thing again.

Now that the gigantic and fashionably late appraisal was finally off her desk, Becca turned to the other smaller assignments that had been filling up her in-box in her absence. They were all local and since she didn't feel like driving, she busied herself accessing a few online databases. When more information was online, her job would be so much easier. Of course, in tiny towns like Alpine Grove, it could take decades for them to embrace the wonders of the World Wide Web. But she wasn't going to think about that place anymore. Pat would just have to get someone else to do those appraisals in the future. As she went through the piles of papers, she tried to ignore the tightness in her chest by working on her deep-breathing exercises. It was beyond time to get herself back to a yoga class.

That evening, instead of going to a class, Becca decided to fully embrace the Monday blues by getting into her jammies and spending some quality time with a restorative quart of ice cream. She sat in front of the TV, which she had turned up extra loud to drown out the din from Mr. Rap Dude's latest CD acquisition. Fortunately, there was a re-run of the *Friends* Thanksgiving episode she'd missed. Ross and Rachel were busy arguing on the screen when the phone rang. Clutching the ice cream container to her chest, she rammed the spoon into the frozen goodness and picked up the receiver.

Jack said, "Hi Becca. I guess you made it home okay?"

Becca put the ice cream container on her desk. "Yes."

"I thought you were going to call."

"I got busy. Appraisal stuff. You know."

"I know." He paused. "Are you okay? You sound sort of…different."

Becca jammed the spoon into the ice cream. "Stop asking me that. I'm fine. What do you want?"

"I just wanted to talk to you."

"Okay. Talk."

Jack paused again. "Well, I miss you."

"Yeah, right."

"What do you mean? I do. Are you sure you're okay? Did something happen?"

Becca jabbed the spoon into the ice cream more forcefully. She was starting to slash a serious fissure into the Chocolate Ecstasy. "You lied to me."

"Lied? I don't think so. About what?"

Becca slurped some chocolate off the spoon and rammed it into the container again. "I thought you were moving on."

"I am. Actually I wanted to talk to you about that. I talked to Joel today."

"What does he have to do with that?" The ice cream was beginning to melt around the gash she'd created. Becca scooped up a slippery hunk of ice cream and slurped it into her mouth. "I mean moving on from your marriage."

"Oh. Well, yes I said that. And I am. Three more days."

"I don't think so."

"Yes. I told you. On Thursday it's all final. Remember? Pearl Harbor Day."

"I know that. Do you think I wasn't paying attention?"

"No. You always pay attention." Becca could hear the smile in his voice. "That's one of my favorite things about you."

"That's nice. Tell it to you wife."

"What? Annie?"

"Yes. The woman you love. Remember her? The one you said you didn't love, but that you obviously still do. The one you lied about."

"I never said I didn't love her."

"What? Well gee, Jack, that's just fantastic to hear *now*. I have no idea what you were doing with me. Just a little revenge sex to get back at Annie or something? Whatever it is—or was—I wish you hadn't. And I *really* wish I hadn't." Becca slammed the spoon into the ice cream one last time. Her stomach churned, and it was a toss-up whether she was going to be sick or burst into tears in a horrendously mortifying way. "I've gotta go."

She hung up the phone, threw the ice cream in the sink, and went to bed. The sound of the TV and Mr. Rap Dude's horrible tunes reverberated in her head. Putting a pillow over her ears, she curled up under the covers and cried quietly for a while. The phone rang a few times and the answering machine clicked on. Mona jumped up on the bed, curling up into a ball next to Becca. The little dog *never* got up on the bed, but it seemed like she knew something was wrong. Becca reached out from under the covers to touch the dog's soft coat and stroked it until she fell asleep.

The next morning Becca woke up with an ice-cream hangover. Consuming copious amounts of dairy products for dinner was not a good idea. In addition to having a crampy, queasy stomach, her eyelashes were gluey from all the crying. Ugh. She needed to get to work. Coffee. Shower. Now.

Before she walked out the door with Mona to go to work, she pressed the button on the answering machine. At the sound of Jack's voice, she hit the erase button and unplugged the machine. There was no way she was talking to him again.

Over the next few days, Becca made an effort to resume her normal life. It was time to figure out what she was going to do next. She was getting close to having enough hours to get her certification as a residential appraiser. It was sort of unbelievable. Her goal had been to complete the 2000 hours within a year and it looked like it was actually going to happen.

Becca was sitting at her computer in her office, trying to ignore the date in the corner of the screen letting her know that today was December seventh. The day that would live in infamy. Jack was now divorced. Unless he'd changed his mind. Becca had gone to the library and done a little research on summary divorce. Or dissolution, as the state called it. Apparently, if one party or the other filed a form, the divorce process could be stopped. Maybe that's what they were talking about in the parking lot. Probably. What was the un-dissolving of a marriage? Reconstitution? It sounded like a chemistry experiment.

Shaking her head, Becca chastised herself for dwelling on that topic *again*. That was not a train of thought she should be following. Right now, she needed to find a new apartment. Mr. Rap Dude had been expanding his CD collection into even louder and more obnoxious music every day. Mona was starting to look anxious when it was time to leave her spot under the desk and go home. It was so sad. Poor Mona.

Because Mona was so unhappy in the apartment, Becca had looked into some yoga classes that were in the afternoon instead of after work, so she could let Mona stay at the office under the desk and nap. Becca tried really hard to listen to the instructor, but at the end of the class when they did corpse pose and she was supposed to clear her mind, she couldn't. It never worked. Her thoughts tended to drift to being in the loft in Joel's cabin with the sound of Frank snoring and Jack sprawled out on the sofa downstairs. Clearing her mind was going to take some effort. She'd just have to keep trying.

Pat tapped lightly on the door of Becca's office, disturbing her from her thoughts. She looked up at her uncle. "Hey, what's up?"

He was holding some file folders in his hand. "I want to talk to you about a new assignment."

"Come on in to my palatial office."

"I know. Now that it's looking like you're going to get your certification, maybe we can think about finding you a better space. Or maybe move some of these file cabinets out of here. Some of the files stored in those things are really old. I can look into off-site storage."

Becca knew he'd never do that. Storage cost money and Pat was not exactly known for his willingness to part with cash. His thrifty nature undoubtedly benefited the business though, keeping the overhead low. "Sure, Pat. I can make a few calls about that if you want."

He leaned on one of the cabinets. "That would be great. How's the apartment hunt going? Did you look at that place I told you about?"

"Yes. The apartment was okay, if a little boring. But I think the neighborhood is going downhill. I talked to one of the people who lives there. Or, actually, I think she is moving out, since she was loading stuff into her car. Anyway, she told me someone drove by and shot at the first-floor windows."

His eyes widened. "Oh Becca, I'm sorry. I never would have suggested it if I'd known that."

"You know what they say—location, location, location."

Pat placed the files he was holding on the stack in her in-box. "On another note, I got another job on a place in Alpine Grove. You did such a great job on the Edgewater house, they seem to have told their friends."

"Well, that's good news for you, particularly if their friends are as loaded as they are."

Pat smiled widely. "It seems so. It's a summer place. They need an appraisal for tax reasons, which means it could be a little complicated."

"The dilemmas of the filthy rich, huh?"

"Something like that. Anyway, since you seem to know every nook and cranny of the county and the real estate offices up there in Alpine Grove, I'd like you to take it. By the time you're done, you'll probably get those last few hours in and I can sign off on everything. You'll be an official residential appraiser!"

Becca shook her head. "I'm not going to Alpine Grove again. I'm never going back there again."

Pat crossed his arms across his chest. "Is this about Jack?"

She looked up quickly. "What? No. I told you, I met him because of the snowstorm. He fed me trees, remember?"

"I know. So why does he keep calling? I think Jenny is starting to get the hots for him. Or his voice anyway. She claims he sounds like a hottie on the phone."

"Our sweet new receptionist shouldn't be flirting with callers, should she?"

"This guy is very persistent, and you won't take his calls. Jenny said he claims you won't talk to him at home either. But maybe you could tell him to stop harassing us. This is a place of business, you know."

Becca straightened some papers on her desk. "I'm sorry, Pat. I'll talk to Jenny."

"You are so stubborn. This is just like when you were a kidlet, and I couldn't make you go to bed when you stayed over at our house. Would you just talk to the guy, Becca?"

Becca shook her head. "Can't Joanne do Alpine Grove appraisals, now that she's back?" Becca pointed at her in-box. "I've got all this other stuff to do. I'm so behind! In fact, I'm coming in this weekend to get caught up."

"You don't have to do that." Pat uncrossed his arms. "We've talked about this, Becca. I don't expect you to work weekends. In fact, I don't *want* you to work extra hours. It's important to have some balance between work and the rest of your life. You need to consider your health."

Becca raised her eyebrows. "You didn't seem to have a problem with me working Thanksgiving weekend."

"That was an extenuating circumstance. And believe me, I got a long lecture about it from your mother." He waved at her desk. "You know none of that is going to take you very long. It's just piddly stuff and you're here *all* the time as it is."

"I really don't want to go back to Alpine Grove. My car isn't up for it. What if it snows again?"

"I'm sure you'll figure something out. Rent another one of those four-wheel-drive things. Just think about it, will you? Joanne is so distracted with what's going on with her mom's illness, I don't want to overload her."

Becca sighed. "I'll think about it. I appreciate you putting your faith in me."

He reached across the desk and gave her shoulder a little squeeze. "It's been easy, Becca. You're very good at appraisal work. I know you can do it."

As Pat left her office, Becca looked down at Mona, who had raised her head and appeared to be listening to the conversation. "Well Mona, that makes one of us. Because no matter what Pat says, I am *not* going back there." Mona wagged her tail and cocked her ears, giving her an encouraging look.

~

That Saturday, Becca was sitting at her desk, typing numbers in her appraisal software program. It was incredibly boring, but she needed to get caught up. If she ever found a new apartment, she'd need to take some time off to pack, so it was better to get a little ahead of things now. So far, the to-do list for the apartment-hunting program was utterly depressing. The only apartments she could afford were either in a slum or had some tragic flaw like roaches the size of small cats scampering through the kitchen. That place had been particularly disturbing. It was all she could do not to run screaming out of the complex. Instead, she'd managed to retain some small level of professional decorum and politely explained to the property manager that she didn't think the apartment was a good fit.

Maybe she should just stay where she was. Her apartment was located in a safe neighborhood. And it certainly had great fire protection. She could buy a big package of ear plugs. Of course, then she wouldn't be able to hear the TV. Maybe she could get headphones for the TV. But Mona was miserable there. Becca put her forehead down on the desk and took a deep breath, trying to get the chatterbox in her head to just shut up for once.

Mona emerged from under the desk and faced the door, wagging her tail. Becca raised her head and Mona looked back at her expectantly. "We just went outside, Mona. Come on. You can't possibly need to go *again*."

A noise came from the hallway and Mona moved toward the door. Becca's heart began beating loudly in her chest. No one was supposed to be here. Pat had said he was spending the day watching football, and no one else *ever* came in on the weekends. There was another clunk outside the door and Becca leaped up from the desk and looked at Mona. "Did you hear that?" Mona wagged in response. "You did! What kind of lousy watchdog are you?"

Becca ran toward the door and pushed the button on the lock. She crouched down next to Mona. "You're right. Good girl! Just be quiet and they'll go away. No one knows we're here." She put her hand to her throat and sat down on the floor with a thump. Oops. They probably heard that. She put her arms around Mona's body and squeezed her eyes shut. Wait a minute. What was she doing? She was like one of those idiots in scary movies. The ones that get chopped up into little pieces because they were dumb enough to go hide in a closet. Those were the characters on the screen you ended up yelling at. "No, don't do that, you fool! He's right there with the chain saw!" Was she really that much of a brainless moron?

Leaning her forehead on the dog's side, Becca tried to stop what was happening, but it wasn't working. She couldn't breathe and the pounding in her ears was deafening. Her heart was beating so hard, it was like it was going to explode out of her chest. She tried opening her eyes. Maybe her vision would just go back to normal this time. Maybe not. Tears leaked out of the corners of her eyes as she shut them again. *Oh please, no. Not again.* More noises arose from the hall, but they were starting to sound far away. Someone was shaking at the door knob. They were going to get in. It was really going to happen. She was going to die in an appraisal office. Uncle Pat would probably find the pieces of her lifeless body on Monday. That would be horrible. *I'm so sorry, Pat!* At least she'd fallen in love before she died. But she'd never told Jack how she felt. He'd never know.

There was a distant sound of swearing, a popping noise, and then something hitting the floor. Mona was pushed away and there was pressure on Becca's upper arms. Someone who sounded like Jack was saying, "Becca! Look at me! Open your eyes. Look at me *now*!"

She opened her eyes and saw Jack kneeling in front of her. His face was inches from hers and his blue eyes were intense. Everything was blurry, but it looked like he was wearing a leather jacket and a faded Harley Davidson t-shirt. Maybe she really was dead. The biker look on Jack was totally hot. At least she'd die with a sexy memory of him. A fuzzier-than-usual version of Frank pushed his huge slobbery head into her face. Okay, maybe she was still alive, after all.

Jack pushed Frank away and said, "Frank, get out of the way." He turned back to Becca. "Are you okay?"

Becca took a deep breath. Then another. Her vision cleared and she shook herself out of his grasp. She wasn't dying and it wasn't a sexy biker dream. But she was angry at Jack. "What are you doing here?"

Jack sat back on his heels and rubbed his eyes. "Trying to find you."

"How did you get in here?"

"Your uncle let me in."

Becca looked around. "Where is he?"

Jack sat down heavily on the floor next to Frank, who was taking up most of the remaining floor space. "In his office, I guess. He said I had ten minutes, then I had to get out."

"I can't believe he let you in here."

Jack put his elbow on his knee and rested his forehead on his hand. "I think he's a little sick of me."

"Why are you harassing my uncle? And me? What is your problem?"

He lifted his head to glare at her. "My problem is you. Why won't you return my phone calls? Why won't you talk to me? I've been worried that something happened to you."

"There's nothing to say. Go be with your wife. That's what you want, isn't it?"

"No. And that's ex-wife, by the way."

"So what, now you can just live in sin or something? That's probably more exciting, right? Gotta keep it exciting."

Jack reached out to touch her arm. "Becca, what are you talking about?"

Becca pushed his hand away. "Your wife! You love her. I saw you. And then you said it yourself."

He shook his head. "Saw what?"

"Before I left, I was going to stop by your place and say… well…stuff. But I saw you in the parking lot with Annie. You gave her this huge hug." Becca put her hand over her face for a moment, then looked at him. "That was not just a friendly hug, Jack. We huggers know these things. I thought you were going to jump her right there in the parking lot, so I left."

Jack looked down and stroked Frank's head thoughtfully. "I had no idea you were there."

"Well, that was obvious. You certainly looked happy though."

"Annie gave me a photograph."

"What? Of her naked?"

He scowled. "Jeez Becca, no. It was a picture of Annie's brother, his wife, and their new baby. They've wanted kids for so long, and I had no idea Sarah was even pregnant. Annie said they want me to be the little girl's godfather."

"What? Okay. That's nice, I guess." Becca took a deep breath. "But why were you in the parking lot?"

"She came up to the apartment, but I wouldn't let her in. Frank was barking, so I told her we needed to go outside to talk."

"You wouldn't let her in?"

"No. She'd been leaving messages about getting back together. There's a form you can fill out to stop the divorce. I never called her back. Then she just showed up."

Becca nodded. "I read about the form. I figured you'd do it."

"Why would I do that?"

Becca raised her palms toward the ceiling. "Hello? Because you love her."

"Of course I do. I'm sure I always will in some way. Don't you have more than one person in your life that you love? That doesn't mean I want to live with her again. Much less be married to her. I'm not *in love* with her, which is a good thing because, against my better judgment, I've fallen in love with you."

Becca put her hand on her chest. "*What?* What did you say?"

Jack turned to look behind him down the hallway. He lifted his hand and waved slowly. "Hi, Pat."

Pat walked up to the doorway and Mona and Frank stood up to greet him. Pat stroked Frank's head and asked, "Why are you two sitting on the floor?"

"I only have one chair. A guest chair won't fit in here," Becca said.

Pat said, "Are you done yet? I'm missing my game. Jack, your ten minutes are up. Get out. Becca, go home. Your mother will kill me if she finds out you were here on the weekend again." He shook his finger at Becca. "Don't you dare come back here on the weekend, or I'm going to change the locks on this place and *not* give you a key."

They stood up and Becca said, "I'm sorry. We're leaving. Go back to your football. I promise I'll lock up."

As Pat stomped off down the hallway, Jack bent to pick up something off the floor. Becca touched his arm. "What's that?"

He opened his hand to reveal a small pocket knife in his palm. "Swiss army knife. Really, Becca, who locks herself into an *office*?"

Becca leaped into his arms, causing him to stagger back a step. She looked into his eyes. "Oh Jack, please don't ever stop carrying those things around. I'm in love with you, too. *So* in love with you—and all your seven-hundred pockets!"

~

Jack loaded Frank into the truck and followed Becca to her apartment. As they wound their way through city traffic, Becca couldn't quite believe Jack was here in Los Angeles.

Having him here was contextually bizarre. It didn't feel right to take the forester out of the forest.

She opened the door to her apartment, and Frank and Mona ran in. Frank amused himself sniffing one of the many boxes that littered the floor. Jack looked around the space and smiled at Becca. "It's very you."

"A little too much me, I think. I'm trying to clear out some stuff."

He pointed at one of the boxes. "Are you moving?"

"Not yet. I haven't found a new apartment. But I thought I'd get a head start on packing. And giving some stuff away. For example, I really don't need to keep the clothes I wore in high school. Just because my best friend gave me a sweatshirt doesn't mean I have to keep it forever."

Downstairs, Mr. Rap Dude fired up his tunes and the beat started reverberating through the floor. Mona ran to the bedroom, Frank looked distressed, and Jack looked down at his feet. He looked back at Becca. "That's horrible. And really loud. Are the speakers down there facing the ceiling or something?"

"Now you know why I'm looking for a new place. I've tried talking to the apartment manager and Mr. Rap Dude himself, who, I can report, is really quite a piece of work. At this point, all I have managed to do is create an inter-apartment feud."

Jack walked over to Becca and took her into his arms. "Could I persuade you to spend the night somewhere else?"

"Twist my arm. Where can we go? We can't just leave Frank and Mona here."

"I wasn't sure if I'd be able to find you or if you'd talk to me, so I have reservations for me and Frank at a dog-friendly bed and breakfast inn near Santa Monica. Bea knows the owners."

"Does she know everybody?"

"Seems like it."

As the music vibrated below, Becca put her arms around Jack's neck and kissed him. "I can't believe you're here. Let me pack some stuff and we can go."

As Becca ran around her apartment collecting things, Jack stood in front of Becca's desk and kept an eye on Frank, who was still in the process of ensuring that all of the boxes passed the sniff test. Jack looked through the books on the desk, picked one up, and started riffling through the pages.

Becca stopped and motioned toward the books. "I went to the library. I thought maybe embracing simplicity and learning about feng shui would help me feel better about my apartment. I don't think I want to take simplicity to the level you do because I'm really quite fond of furniture. But I thought maybe clearing out some of the clutter would help."

"I think convincing the guy downstairs to move out would be the first step toward better feng shui flow. How do you stand this? I'm getting a headache." He held the book up to her. "*Walden*?"

"I was supposed to read it in high school, but I went for the *Cliffs Notes*. After you talked about it, I wanted to check it out. Some of it is interesting, but he gets really boring about beans."

Jack laughed. "I know. That's pretty tedious. I like to just flip through it, read a couple of sentences that catch my eye, and think about them." He looked down at the page. "This is one of my favorite passages: 'I learned this, at least, by my experiment; that if one advances confidently in the direction of his dreams, and endeavors to live the life which he has imagined, he will meet with a success unexpected in common hours.'"

Becca reached out to touch his arm. "So are you advancing confidently?"

"I'm working on it. For a long time, I stopped dreaming." He glanced at the book in his hand. "But I'm starting to have some ideas again. There could be some advancing. It might not be confident advancing yet, but it's a start."

"Baby steps?"

"Something like that."

After Becca gathered her stuff, they loaded themselves and the dogs into Jack's truck. As they headed north on the Pacific Coast Highway, Becca leaned her head on Jack's shoulder and watched as the sun descended into the ocean, shooting rays of orange and gold across the sky. What was she doing? Jack would never be able to stand living here and there was no way she could live in Alpine Grove. When would they even see each other again? She sighed. The chatterbox needed to shut up for a while. Right now, it was just good to be here, feeling his warmth and watching the sunset. Although she knew she loved him, the future with Jack, if there actually was one, was a question for later.

They turned down a tree-lined street into a residential area of Pacific Palisades and found the bed and breakfast, which was a restored colonial house with shingles and white trim. The owners were welcoming and Becca and Jack checked into the "pet suite," which had a huge four-poster bed and a fireplace. Dog bowls were set up in the corner and a little basket was filled with treats and canine hors d'oeuvres.

A bottle of wine and two glasses sat on a tiny tiled bistro table.

Becca walked to the large window and looked out at the ocean. "Jack, this is amazing. Way nicer than the H12. And after thirty seconds, I already like this better than my apartment. Do you think they'll let me move here?"

Jack took off his leather jacket and threw it on the bed. "I doubt it. The room is just for one night."

She moved away from the window and locked her gaze with his. "Then we should make it a very good night."

He grinned. "Let's see what we can do about getting you to speak more slowly again."

Becca put her arms around his neck. She drawled, "I love you," as languidly and deliberately as she could.

He bent his head and whispered in her ear, "I love you too."

~

When Becca opened her eyes the next morning, the sun was streaming through the windows. Jack was sitting in a chair reading and Frank and Mona were sitting in front of him, staring intently. Becca sat up and curled her hands around the plush down comforter, not wanting to leave the cozy nest. "Hey there. Why didn't you wake me up?"

"I took the dogs for a walk. Frank attracts a lot of attention around here."

"Most people have little poodles or Chihuahuas, not Bernese mountain dogs. He probably stands out."

Jack came over to the bed and laid on his side next to her. He cupped her cheek with his hand. "I was hoping you'd do something for me."

"I think I already did quite a few things."

He grinned. "Well yes, and thanks for that. But I'd really like it if you could go to a doctor. You scared me yesterday and I'd like to know you're okay."

"I've seen doctors. They tell me that I have a syndrome. It was triggered by a traumatic event and I need to make lifestyle changes. Or take drugs that mess with my brain chemistry and have side effects. I didn't like the sound of 'lowered libido,' for example. I'm a fan of my libido and I don't think you'd be too excited about me losing it, either. Yoga and counseling had fewer unpleasant potential consequences, so I opted for that."

"Did any of the doctors mention antacids?"

She nodded. "Yes, but that doesn't make any sense. My stomach is fine. Well, most of the time. I learned recently that having ice cream for dinner is not necessarily a good idea."

Jack pushed a lock of hair back from her face. "I went to the library and looked up your syndrome. Actually the librarian did. That woman is really into research and she dug up a bunch of medical information from databases on the Internet. Anyway, chest pain like you have can be acid reflux. If it gets bad, you think you're having a heart attack and that increases your anxiety."

"Thinking I'm going to die does have that effect on me."

He kissed her tenderly. "Please think about it, okay? I don't want anything to happen to you."

"Thank you for doing some more breaking and entering on my behalf. If the whole forestry thing doesn't work out, you can always become a criminal."

He laughed. "No thanks. I'd miss the trees too much. You know how I like *Thuja plicata*, and there aren't any in prison."

"I suppose cedars *do* tend to be in short supply in the penal system." Becca snuggled up to him. "Do we really have to leave? I'm becoming very attached to this comforter. I think it has a thread count of three million or so. I want one for Christmas."

"Well, at least it's less expensive than the house on Edgewater Road. I'm glad you're managing your expectations."

"Pat wants me to do another appraisal in Alpine Grove. I told him no, but that was when I never wanted to see you again."

Jack touched his fingertip to the base of her throat and ran it downward. "It seems you've changed your mind."

"Yes. Would it be okay if I stayed with you for a week or so? Maybe I could bring a desk. Or a bed. Sleeping on the floor that close to piles of Frank fur has some downsides."

"Actually, I'm moving. I tried to tell you, but you hung up on me. Then I told your answering machine. Didn't you get my message?"

Becca sat up straight in bed. "You're going to Colorado?"

"Apparently, you did *not* get my message."

She slumped back down on the pillows. "You're really leaving? I can't believe it. After everything that has happened you're going to move a thousand miles away?"

"I'm not going to Colorado. When I went back to put in the new window glass at The Shack, Joel asked me if I wanted to rent the place. I said 'yes.'"

Becca threw her arms around his neck and hugged him hard. "That's wonderful. I'm surprised he did that. He had it all closed up for winter."

"He said that I was the only person he'd ever met that seemed to like the place as much as he did."

Becca leaned back against the pillows and patted the comforter absently. "It does smell like smoke, I suppose. That's a bit of a turn-off at first."

"There's probably something that can be done about that. I figure I'll set the mad researcher librarian on that question and see what she comes up with. And yes, you can stay there with me. It's kind of a long drive to town though."

"I don't care. I'll get snow tires. Or those studded tires. Maybe tire chains? It doesn't matter. I can't wait to see the place again."

"Good. Because we should probably check out soon. I have to get home."

She gripped the edge of the comforter. "Okay. I'll call Pat and tell him I'll do the appraisal. He'll be thrilled. Once it's done I'll have enough hours to get my residential certification. It looks like I'm going to achieve my goal to become an appraiser in 1995. Pat wants to throw a huge Christmas party to celebrate."

Jack kissed her. "Was there ever any doubt? Once you set your mind to something, you seem to do what it takes to make it happen."

"Pat says it's because I'm stubborn."

"Like a mule. But it's part of what makes you who you are."

She reached out to caress his soft beard. "Kind of like how you smell like a Christmas tree most of the time is part of who *you* are."

He laughed. "Not exactly, but okay."

Chapter 12

Get Happy

After checking out, they went back to Becca's apartment so she could call her uncle and pack up some things. She opened the door and as usual, the beat of booming music was thumping from below. Mona shot toward the bedroom and Becca sighed. "I wish I could say it's great to be back here, but Mr. Rap Dude is really making it easy to take a vacation."

Jack closed the door behind him and looked down at the floor. "No kidding. Pack fast."

Becca gave Jack a sidelong glance. "You know, I'm just so happy I could jump for joy." She started jumping up and down, waving her fists and making a special effort to land on the floor as hard as possible. "Come on Frank, what do you think? Aren't you happy?"

Frank wagged his tail warily, furrowing his brow. Becca waved her hands at the dog and ran around the sofa, "Okay, let's run to the bedroom and get Mona! Run Frank, run!"

Jack leaned on the desk with his arms crossed. "This is a little passive-aggressive isn't it?"

Becca and Frank ran by and Becca gasped, "No way. We're just having fun, right Frank? And the fact that this dog has to weigh at least a hundred pounds has nothing to do with it."

Frank leaped in the air and landed with a great thump on the floor. Turning, he ran back to the bedroom and barked a few times. He returned with Mona following him, making rrr-ing noises and wagging her tail. The two dogs engaged in some play bowing and barking, running around the sofa and chasing each other.

Becca grabbed at Jack's elbow, "Come on. Let's do speed packing. I'll race you to the closet"

He grinned and ran after her back to the bedroom. "Okay, but if you say the words jumping jack, I'm leaving you here."

Becca stopped, turned, and tackled him onto the bed so she was lying on top of him. "I would never do that. And if you leave me here, I'll just buy some duct tape, drive up to Alpine Grove, and break into your house."

Jack flipped her over and leaned down to kiss her. "I'm sure you would."

"If you keep doing that, I'm going to lose focus here. I have to pack."

Cupping the side of her neck with his hand, he stroked her cheek with his thumb. He brushed his lips lightly across hers one last time and pushed himself up off the bed. "Fine. And they say I'm the dull one."

After stopping by the office to pick up the folders with the appraisal information, they made the trek out of the city back up to the mountains. As they drove through downtown Alpine Grove, Becca considered the businesses and storefronts passing by her window. It was surprising how many of them she actually knew now. During the several times she'd been there, she'd probably met more people in Alpine Grove than she'd ever met in her apartment building the whole time she'd lived there.

Jack drove north of town toward The Shack. After days of melting, there was significantly less snow on the ground and it had a more compressed, dimpled look, like a mattress pad. The sparkly drifts of pristine snow had been replaced by stodgy-looking icy berms along the side of the roadways. The trees were no longer flocked and the deep green color of the pines contrasted with the whiteness of the rest of the landscape.

Finally, they turned down the long driveway and slowly made their way to the clearing, where the late afternoon sun was starting to disappear behind the cedars. The Shack sat in its cozy little corner of forest looking almost exactly the same as it had the last time Becca had seen it. She clasped Jack's arm. "It's so good to see this place again!"

As they unloaded the truck, Becca noticed that at least one thing was different. The ugly blue tarp now covered a sizable stack of firewood. She walked to the door and looked up at the little overhang that covered the landing. She had been so very grateful for it and now she knew who had put it there. The pane of glass in the door had been repaired and it looked like someone had cleaned the other panes as well. Jack unlocked the door and opened it. "Welcome back."

Becca walked in as Frank and Mona charged by her into the room. The large dog claimed his favorite spot on the old rug while Mona busied herself inspecting the exciting new space. She wagged and looked up at Becca expectantly. Becca bent to ruffle the dog's ears. "I hope you like your little vacation retreat, Mona, because we're going to be here for a few days." The dog wagged and ran off toward the kitchen to resume her explorations.

Jack flipped on a light and Becca pointed at the lamp. "Okay, electricity is an exciting change."

"Wait 'til you go to cook something. Functional appliances."

Becca looked around the room. The only new piece of furniture was the body-sucking chair. "What did you do with the mattress?"

"I leaned it against the dumpster behind the apartment building. An hour later, it was gone. Maybe there's another guy out there getting divorced who needed it."

Becca leaned against the back of the sofa. "I'm guessing moving in didn't take long."

Jack smiled. "No. Joel offered to help and it took about ten minutes. Getting my dresser up into the loft was kind of a pain though. By the way, Joel left something he wanted me to give to you."

"Really?"

"Yeah, it's on the bed. Go up and see."

Becca climbed up the ladder, walked to the bed, and squealed. Joel's old flannel shirt was folded up neatly on the end of the bed. She leaned over the railing. "He's giving it to me?"

"Yes. He took the rest of his clothes out of the dresser, but he said you should have that."

She held the shirt to her chest. "Thanks, Mr. Tall Guy."

〜

Becca sat on the sofa knitting, the pink yarn flowing through her fingers. Her enormous teal afghan was wrapped around her like a cocoon. It had seemed right to bring it with her. Maybe she'd leave it here for Jack. She looked up when she heard tapping on one of the glass panes of the door. Joel's tall outline was visible outside. She waved and yelled "Come in!"

He walked through the doorway, closed the door behind him, and stood with his hands in the pockets of his jeans. "Hi Becca. Is Jack around? I brought that last load of wood for him."

"He's outside with the dogs somewhere. I'm sure he'll be back in a minute. Frank woke up and stuffed his nose in my face looking anxious. You know that look?"

"All too well."

"Sorry I didn't get up. My toes are so happy in this afghan, I didn't want to ruin the mood. But it's your house, anyway. I'm sure Jack would want you to feel welcome to stop by any time."

"I don't want to disturb your privacy." Joel looked around the room. "It looks nicer in here. After I moved out my stuff a few months ago, it was a little bare."

"Why don't you sit down?"

Joel glanced at the recliner and walked over to the ladder to the loft. He half sat, half leaned on the steps, and rubbed the side of one of his legs. "What are you knitting? It's very, uh, pink."

Becca held up the wool, which had the color and fluffy consistency of cotton candy. "It's a baby blanket."

"*Really?* Wow. Congratulations."

Becca raised her eyebrows. "Um, no. It's not for me. It's for Jack's goddaughter."

"Oh, okay." He pointed at the table that was now covered with piles of paper. "I had my desk there, too."

"Yes. It's great that there are so many phone jacks in here. I can connect to the Internet from almost any corner of this place."

"I may have overdone it on the wiring. Have you thought about getting a file cabinet?"

"I know." Becca shook her head. "It looks like something exploded over there. Now there's not even any space left for the laptop. Not to mention no place to eat. Jack's going to be relieved when I go back home and all my piles of papers are gone."

Joel shrugged, but didn't say anything. He rubbed at something on the side of the ladder.

Becca directed her knitting needles toward the windows. "I just hope it doesn't snow again. I've got to get back home before this weekend."

"I think it's going to snow later today, but it will probably be fine by Friday."

"But they said flurries."

"They're wrong." Joel shifted his placement on the ladder, stretching out one of his long legs in front of him. "By the way, thanks for inviting us to the Christmas party your uncle is having, but I don't think we can go. Kat is worried about the dogs and cats."

Becca sat up straighter. "That's what she told me. But you *have* to come! It's not that far." She extracted herself from her afghan cocoon and walked to the table. "You can find someone to take care of the critters."

"I don't know. Maybe."

Becca handed him an envelope. "This will convince Kat. Oh and I keep forgetting. It would be great if you could take the Twinkies back. I know Jack isn't going to eat them."

Joel sighed. "There's some here too?"

Becca got a grocery bag and went to the pantry cabinet. "Yes. You must really like them."

"No, I don't. A few people stayed here after I moved out."

"Oh yeah, Cliff said that. One of them must have a serious sweet tooth." Becca heaved a few snack cakes into the bag. "When did you buy this place?"

"Six or seven years ago after my sister moved here. The listing said The Shack itself had no value, but it had electricity and a well."

"Speaking as an appraiser, electricity definitely has value. So does a well."

"I know. Back then, The Shack was just a log shell that had been sitting here empty for about ten years."

"What happened?"

"The people who built it ran out of money before they finished it. Interest rates were really high and no one was interested in buying a half-done cabin. It had been sitting on the market so long, the price dropped low enough that I could pay cash. I wanted a weekend project."

"Well, from what I can tell, property around here was a lot less expensive then too. That was before everyone wanted a summer house here." Becca paused in her pantry clean-out. "This was your weekend project? Do you mean you finished this place *yourself?*"

"Yes." Joel pointed to a spot on the floor. "For years, the table saw sat right there. It was like camping out. I didn't get to the electricity and plumbing until I moved up here full-time and could hire pros to help."

"I can imagine." Becca looked up. "So you built the loft and everything?"

"Yeah, when I look around, I still notice the things that are a little off." He tapped the side of the ladder. "See, here's a pencil mark that isn't supposed to show, but you can see it because the step isn't quite spaced right with the others."

"I had no idea. Kat said you were an engineer."

"That too." He grinned. "But she likes the fact that I can fix things."

Becca gestured toward the room. "So she knows you built this whole place?"

"Yes. She was annoyed that after all the times she'd been out here, she'd never even seen the loft. So she came with me when I was shutting it down for the winter and asked me about every, single, little thing I built."

The door opened with a whoosh and Frank and Mona charged into the house, followed by Jack. Frank shook off some snow and settled onto his favorite rug. Mona went over to Becca to say hi.

Jack walked over to Joel and shook his hand. "I see you brought wood."

"This is the last of it."

"Even better, he's taking the Twinkies away," Becca said, holding up the grocery bag. "Joel was just telling me how he built this place."

Joel said. "I just finished the inside."

Jack gestured toward the kitchen area. "You made all the cabinets?"

"Yes. Nothing in this place is a normal size. Or particularly square, so I had to build pretty much everything. My neighbor Cliff was having a guy with a Wood-Mizer come out to get some wood turned into boards. So I had lumber cut from some logs here too. I had a huge stack of stickered lumber drying out back for ages."

"I was wondering if the logs for the house were cut from the property," Jack said.

"Probably. That's what I was told." Joel stood up and looked at Jack. "So are you ready to stack that wood?"

"Sure. Let's go."

The two men tromped outside, leaving Becca inside with Frank and Mona, who were both looking a little too interested in the grocery bag full of snack cakes. Grabbing the bag, she put on her coat and boots, went outside, and put the bag in the cab of Joel's truck. She was not going to let him get away without taking those stupid Twinkies with him.

Chapter 13

Decisions

Friday morning, Becca began gathering her stuff together for her return to LA. It had been a wonderful vacation, but the queasy feeling in her stomach had returned now that she had to leave. It was going to be even more difficult not to cry this time. Trying to steel herself against the inevitable weepy factor, she picked up her bag of knitting and placed it on the table, which had been cleared of her piles of papers. The appraisal was done, and she knew Pat would be pleased with it. Jack had pointed out a couple of aspects related to the land, which had helped her do a better job of conveying what the place was like.

The door opened and Mona and Frank rushed into the room, rrr-ing, and shaking snow off themselves. Apparently they'd had quite a wrestling match out there. Jack closed the door behind him and took off his coat. "So have you got everything? We should probably hit the road."

Becca sat down on the sofa and looked down at her hands in her lap. "Yes. I think so." *Do not cry. Do not.*

He sat down next to her. "Are you okay?"

"Yes. No. I don't know."

"What's wrong?"

"I've been trying to stay in the moment and all that. I really have." She shook her head. "But I can't stop thinking about it. How is this ever going to work?"

"This what?"

"You. Me. Us. I know I love you, but when am I ever going to see you again? Weekends? That's not going to work. It's too far. And as we know, the weather doesn't always cooperate."

He took her hand. "Maybe you'll get another appraisal job up here."

"Maybe. My uncle claims there's more work here, but I don't know."

"Plus, once you have your license, you can be an appraiser anywhere in the state where you have experience, right? You've done enough appraisals in Alpine Grove. Why not here?"

Becca looked into his eyes. "Don't you think I've thought of that? You know I can't live here."

"Why not?"

She waved her arms. "For one thing, how much work could there be in this tiny town? Where would I find clients? *How* would I find clients? I have no clue. And apart from work, what else would I do? I'm not all outdoorsy like you are. There's almost no shopping and only two restaurants, or something like that. There's nothing to do. I'd go nuts!"

"What do you want to do?"

"I want to...I don't know. Work. Have fun. Normal stuff."

Jack wiped a tear off her cheek with his fingertip and leaned over to kiss her. "According to your uncle, you're doing a lot more working than having fun."

"Well, I *could* have fun. Go out. Do stuff."

"True. Do you?"

"Not really."

He gazed into her eyes. "Becca, only you can decide what's important to you."

"Oh sure. That's easy for you to say. You have the trees and all that."

"Maybe you weren't paying attention, after all."

Becca leaned away from Jack and reached down to stroke Mona's head. "That's not true. Of course I was paying attention!"

"I don't think you get it."

"Get what?"

"I decided to stay here because this is where I want my life to be. But by making that choice, I gave up the ability to see my friends and family in Colorado as often, so it wasn't an easy decision to make."

"Then why did you stay? Was it me?"

"Not exactly. But after we were trapped here in The Shack, I realized that I had to be happy on my own. It's not the responsibility of my friends and family to make me happy. Or Annie. Or you. It's mine. At some point while I was sitting at the table extracting pine nuts, I realized I was actually content. Okay, I was also hungry, but I was basically content. There's something about Alpine Grove that feels like home, and I knew I didn't need to go back to Colorado. I could be happy here if I just let myself. That sense of peace was what was most important to me." He leaned forward and put his elbows on his knees, looking at the floor. "I'm probably not explaining this very well."

"I guess I didn't realize how close you were to moving away."

He looked up at her. "I told you that's why I didn't buy furniture."

"So what are you suggesting? I should just drop everything and move to Alpine Grove?"

"I can't answer that for you. You have to decide what you want. Figuring out what you want to do with the rest of your life is something you need to do yourself."

"But you said you love me."

"I do. But contrary to what John Lennon might say, love is *not* all you need." Jack leaned back on the sofa and slouched down. "I learned that the hard way."

Becca put her hand on his arm and leaned over to kiss him. "I do love you though. This vacation has been wonderful, even though I was working on the appraisal. I don't suppose you'd like to move to LA, would you?"

"Nope. But it has been great sharing a loft with you." He put his hand on hers. "You were right. I like it up there. It's nice not having Frank stomping all over my mattress too."

"Sorry we have to spend tonight at my place. But the Christmas party tomorrow should be fun. Pat knows how to throw a great holiday bash."

"It sounds like he's excited about celebrating your new full-fledged appraiser status too. I think he's really proud of you."

"I'll probably have a lot more work to do and be able to make more money."

"I'm sure you'll be great at it."

"Maybe." Becca leaned her head on his shoulder. "We haven't answered my main question though. When you return here after the party, will I ever see you again?"

"I don't know. But I'm not going anywhere, so you can visit whenever you like. I'll be here."

She lifted her head to look into his blue eyes. "I know." And she also knew that they'd get busy with their lives and it was only a matter of time until he met someone else or just forgot about her entirely. Lowering her head to his shoulder, she closed her eyes and allowed another tear to slide down her cheek.

~

Joel stood in front of the large window staring out at the ocean view. Kat came up behind him and wrapped her arms around his waist. She leaned her cheek on his back. "I can't believe we're here. It's our first vacation together."

He turned, enveloped her in his arms, and bent down to kiss her. "No kidding. You know I'm way too cheap to splurge on a place like this. I can't believe Becca gave us a free night's stay."

Kat squeezed his waist. "She thinks you saved her life."

"I think that was Jack."

"You and The Shack helped."

"I don't know about that, but I'm glad to be here with you."

"I wish I could take that comforter home with me. It's like crawling onto a poufy pillow. I'd have enjoyed that when I was sick."

He stroked her cheek. "Please don't get sick again for a while, okay?"

"I'm not planning on it. I told Maria we'd meet her at four. She said that no one is at the fern bar then, so she can talk for a while before we go to the party." Kat stepped back, took his hand, and swung it back and forth. "I want to walk on the beach first. It's been so long since I've heard the ocean. Let's go down to the pier and wander around for a while."

"Okay. Do you know where this fern place is?"

"It's not too far from where I used to live. But it can be a pain to get there, depending on traffic. You'll get to scare some more LA drivers with the blade on the truck. It will be fun in a 'my truck is older than your truck so I don't have much to lose' kind of way."

Joel laughed. "No doubt."

Later, they were walking hand-in-hand along the beach. Even though it was chilly for LA, Kat took off her shoes and carried them in her other hand. It was necessary to feel the sand in her toes, even if it was cold. She looked up at Joel. "It feels weird walking with you without having five or six dogs around."

"I know."

"I hope Cindy is coping with everything okay. Thanks for asking her to take care of the house. I really hope Johnny doesn't burn it down."

"Cindy walked the dogs before. I'm sure it will be fine."

"It's about time she did something to help *you* for a change."

Joel shrugged. "I don't know about that."

Kat stopped and turned to look up into his face. "I do. I love our house and being with you, but we might want to go on a trip again sometime. It's good to establish a precedent with her as our official house-sitter."

He smiled. "That's true. Where do you want to go?"

"I'm not sure. I haven't done much traveling, but I'd love to go sit on a beach somewhere and drink mai tais. Hawaii would work. Or Fiji. Maybe a tiny island in the Caribbean? I wouldn't mind going to Europe either. I don't know. It's just that certain important life events merit traveling. Celebrations. Vacations. Those are great excuses for trips to exotic, faraway places."

"Sounds like fun."

Kat leaned her head on his chest. "As long as I'm with you, I think it would be."

Later, they walked through an archway of ferns into the Fern Oasis. Maria waved from behind the long bar. Pushing aside an especially large frond, she ran around the bar and stretched out her arms for a hug. "Hey, girlfriend!"

They embraced and Maria looked down at the bag Kat was carrying. "Did you bring groceries? You do know that more drinking than eating happens at this establishment, right? They aren't too fond of it when customers take the potluck approach."

Kat placed the bag on the bar. "These are for you. Think of them as a housewarming gift."

Maria went back around the bar and peeked into the bag. "That's outstanding! How many are in there?"

"Seventy-five," Joel said. "We counted."

"Actually, you bought them," Kat said. "You're like the Twinkie fairy, leaving cases of snack cakes wherever you go. But after Joel's nephew stayed with us, we determined they needed to return to their rightful owner. Six-year olds and Twinkies do not mix."

Maria took the bag and put it behind the bar. "Thanks. I went through my stash over Thanksgiving weekend. Sometimes you can't stop at just one, you know."

Kat said, "So it seems. How's the job search going?"

"Not so good. I may be hanging out here with the ferns longer than I thought. I'm a little discouraged, if you want to know the truth. And they really don't have many hours for me here." She opened her arms toward the room. "And as you can see, we are not exactly jam-packed with clientele. In fact, this whole place could go under. Then I've really got a serious situation. On that note, would you like a drink?"

Kat pointed at Joel. "He's the designated driver, but you can give me something. What about the swizzle thingie you told me about?"

"Queen's Park Swizzle. But it's got a lotta rum in it. You sure?"

Kat spread her arms expansively. "I'm on vacation. For two whole glorious days I have no responsibilities whatsoever! I need to live it up. Plus, as you know, social situations tend to stress me out. It might be better if I'm a little loosened up before we go to this party. I've never met Becca's uncle or anyone else who is going to be there. It could be uncomfortable and awkward, and I hate that, since sometimes I say stupid things and people think I'm weird."

"Okay. But don't say I didn't warn you." Maria turned away and began combining ingredients into a tall glass.

Joel looked at Kat. "Take it slow, please. You're a small person."

Maria handed the drink to Kat. "Here's looking at ya."

Kat took a sip and made a face. "Whoa. Ahem. So, I had an idea on your employment situation."

Maria leaned her elbows on the bar. "I'm all ears. In eight days my rent is due. But who's counting?"

"Remember the guy who owns the ad agency? Michael?"

"You mean the Marlboro man? The totally hot guy?" Maria fanned her face with her hands. "Oh yeah. He was so very nice to look at."

Kat glanced at Joel, who raised an eyebrow slightly in response. She took a sip of her drink. "Yes, Michael. He has a secretarial problem."

"Huh? What do you mean?"

"He can't find anyone to answer his phone and keep his advertising agency office organized. Or I guess he found a couple of people, but they quit. I went to the library the other day and Jan was complaining about it. She's his girlfriend, remember? She hates doing that kind of work, and refuses to have anything to do with it. And she has her job at the library anyway, which she loves. So now Michael is begging Tracy to just come in and answer the phone sometimes when she's not working at the vet clinic. But she doesn't have much time, because she's also got that computer job with Rob."

Maria gestured toward the doorway. "Wow, it's sure a complex little world up there in Alpine Grove, isn't it?"

"Why don't you apply?" Kat handed Maria a piece of paper. "This is the number at the agency. You'd be good at it. I mean, if you were able to keep a nut job like Mark under control, this would just be child's play for you. Give Michael a call. You've already met him at our house, so you might have an in with him."

Maria looked down at the paper. "While it is definitely true that I did excel in working for a man who was certifiably insane, and I could certainly do this job, there's a major issue here. I don't want to move out there to the middle of nowhere. That might work for you and Mr. Rustic Engineer here. But I am more of an urban-type dweller. My social life would take a serious nose-dive if I were to relocate there."

Kat sipped her drink. "You liked visiting. And the cost of living is a lot lower. You could rent a place for a quarter of what you're paying here. Maybe less. And Michael is even talking about profit-sharing. He's desperate for someone good. And I know you are great at planning and keeping an office running. I saw you do it."

"I appreciate the vote of confidence, girlfriend, particularly given my current career trajectory." Maria rested her chin on her palm. "But I can't even get up there. From what you said, it's an ice-skating rink. It is definitely not the right environment for Greta. She is a sensitive automobile. Miatas are like that, you know."

"You can buy my car. Or borrow it for the winter. I've been driving Joel's truck anyway. That old thing and I have come to an agreement. Or more like a detente. I cuss at it a lot and then it moves."

Joel poked Kat in the ribs. "Be nice. That thing is what's getting you back home."

Kat grabbed his hand and pushed it away from her. "My Toyota is kind of stuck in the driveway right now, but we could pull it out. And even though it's not great for my place, my car would be fine if you live in town, since it has front-wheel drive."

Maria twirled a tiny paper umbrella in her fingertips. "Nothing personal, but your car does not work with the image I'm trying to convey to the world. More specifically, the fifty-percent of the world who are male and might think I'm fine. I cannot look fine in a beat-up Toyota."

"You could still drive the Miata in the summer. Anyway, just think about it." Kat sucked on the straw to slurp up the last of her drink. "That was good. Can I have another one?"

"No!" Joel said, putting his arm around Kat's shoulders. "We should probably get going."

Kat got up and sashayed around her barstool. "I feel gooood. So good, so good."

Maria grinned. "You knew that you would, now. Have fun at the party, girlfriend. I'll talk to you soon."

Kat took Joel's hand, did a pirouette underneath his arm, and waved back at Maria. "Enjoy those Twinkies!"

Chapter 14

Changes

After the big Christmas party in LA, Jack went back to Alpine Grove and Becca returned to her life. She had lots of fun celebrating Christmas with her family and even better, Mr. Rap Dude must have gone away somewhere for the holidays. Her apartment was much quieter, although the firemen were still vigilantly protecting the city. The lack of loud music was definitely an improvement though.

Mona was sleeping on the floor and Becca was sort of watching TV, but mostly remembering her vacation in Alpine Grove, when the phone rang. Jumping to answer it, a little thrill went through her at the sound of Jack's voice. She said, "I was just thinking about you."

"You're just dreaming about having some of my incredible *Pinus contorta* fries, aren't you?"

Becca laughed. "Well, maybe that too. Some parts are edible, you know. How are you?"

"Wondering when you're coming back to visit. It was fun meeting your family at the party, but I was thinking it would be nice to spend New Year's together here."

"Yeah, my mom thinks you walk on water. Even Uncle Pat has forgiven you for being such a pest."

"He spent a lot of time talking to me about some football game. I didn't have the heart to tell him I hadn't watched it."

271

Becca giggled. "Your secret is safe with me."

"So what about New Year's?"

"I have a lot of stuff I should do here. I'm hoping I can find a place to live, so I can give notice before the first. A lot of people are on vacation though."

Jack sighed. "Did you go to the doctor yet?"

"Not yet. Everything has been closed for Christmas, but I have an appointment tomorrow."

"Okay. Let me know how it goes."

They chatted for a while longer about the party and a few Alpine Grove happenings, and then said good night. Afterward Becca lay in bed staring at the ceiling. A siren wailed in the distance and Mona scuttled under the bed. What was she doing here? Now that she had her license, she could be an appraiser anywhere she had experience. Jack had suggested that idea and she'd rejected it. But maybe it would work. What if she worked from The Shack? But that was completely impractical. It was miles out of town and there was no place for any of her furniture, much less her work stuff. But as she had predicted, the long-distance thing wasn't working. Phone calls weren't enough. She missed Jack.

She rolled over in bed and dialed the number to The Shack. After several rings, Jack answered in a sleepy voice. Becca said, "It's me again. I'm sorry to wake you up."

"No problem. I can just close my eyes and pretend you're lying here next to me."

"I changed my mind. After my doctor's appointment, I'd like to drive up and see you. Nothing's happening at work this week anyway, and I'd like to greet 1996 with you. Would it be okay if Mona and I stayed there?"

"Of course. Always. Like I said, my loft is available to you any time."

The next morning, Becca talked to her uncle Pat about taking more time off and went to the doctor. Although she liked her doctor, the woman was annoyingly stern about health topics. At the appointment, she'd had no sense of humor at all, and what she said was more than a little disturbing. But what was Becca supposed to do? She had to earn a living somehow. Was she supposed take a vow of poverty and live in a convent or something? That wasn't going to happen. Apart from it not working as a career choice, becoming a nun had other serious downsides as well.

After being lectured by the doctor, Becca loaded up Mona and drove to Alpine Grove. It was a good thing it was such a long drive. She had a lot to think about.

As Becca drove through downtown Alpine Grove, she noticed a For Lease sign in the window at the ad agency. Didn't Rob say that they had office space available? The beginnings of a plan started to form in her mind. She turned down a side street and parked the car. "Be good, Mona. I'll be right back."

Becca walked into the ad agency and a seriously gorgeous man looked up from the desk. She tried not to stare, but wow. The guy looked like he should be on magazine covers. "Um…hi." An extremely furry white dog leaped out from somewhere in the back and ran up to her, skidding to a stop. The dog sat proudly looking up at her and smiling. The creature looked like a roly-poly stuffed animal. Becca bent to pet the soft white fur. "Oh, you are the cutest, most fluffy thing I've ever seen!"

The man pointed at the dog. "That's Swoosie and I'm Michael Lawson. Can I help you?"

Becca straightened. "Maybe. I saw the For Lease sign in the window. I'm, well, maybe looking for office space. Just a small office really. All I need is enough space to hold a couple of file cabinets and a desk. Oh, and it looks like you allow dogs. That would be perfect for me."

"Do you want to take a look? We finally got the heat fixed, so it's not a sauna anymore. It's nice not feeling like I'm part of the cast of *Lawrence of Arabia*." He sighed. "But that was a whole lot of money I wasn't expecting to spend. Restoring an old building sounds a lot more romantic than it really is."

Michael led her up the stairs to the offices. She peeked into Rob's office and waved at him when he looked up from his computer monitor. "I see Rob is still here."

"Yeah, he's got a deadline. Poor guy is a little stressed, I think."

Becca nodded. "Been there."

Michael fixed his gaze on her. "So what do you do?"

"I just got my residential property appraiser's license. I work for my uncle in the city."

He unlocked a door and turned on the light. "This one might work. Why do you need an office here? Are you going to open your own appraisal business?"

"No. I thought about that, but I'm going to keep working for my uncle. I've had quite a few assignments up here and it seems like he's getting more Alpine Grove clients. I could work on those projects. But I need to cut back on work. I know that if I started my own business, it would be a lot of effort to get it up and running and then marketing to find clients. Knowing me, I'd become obsessed with it. I need to slow down and spend some time focusing on my health for a while."

"That sounds like a good idea. Having just gone through the process, I can tell you that starting your own business is a pretty major undertaking. If I didn't go running with Swoosie, I'd probably be a basket case again. The business and restoration stuff is starting to level out, although if I don't find some decent administrative help soon, I think my girlfriend is going to kill me. But it's a lot better than what I was doing before because I can set my own hours." He smirked. "Not to mention that I can fire clients who make me miserable."

Becca glanced out the window. "It sounds like you've got it figured out. I did some work from home—well, not my home—but a place north of town. The problem is that it's not very large. Papers were everywhere. As I do more appraisals, the paper problem is only going to get worse. And if I have an office, I can just close the door and forget about the mess. I need to do a better job of leaving work at work."

"I do like that about this building." He gestured toward the brick walls. "At the end of the day, I lock it up and leave."

They went back downstairs and Michael handed her information about the rent and a rental agreement. "Let me know what you decide."

"I will. I need to talk to someone first."

Becca got into the car and drove north out of Alpine Grove. Fortunately, last week's snow had been plowed away and the roads out to The Shack were clear. She slid her way down the driveway and the car glided to a stop next to Jack's truck. It might be time to get those snow tires. She let out

Mona, who sniffed at the huge new plow blade attached to the front of Jack's brown pickup.

The door opened and Frank bounded out of the cabin. Mona play-bowed and barked, running around the truck and encouraging the big dog to chase her.

Jack came out wearing his Eskimo coat. Becca ran toward him and launched into his arms. "I missed you!"

He kissed her and said, "I was ready for you this time. I missed you too. It's so good to see you."

"I'm glad to hear that because I need to talk to you."

Jack collected her luggage, called the dogs, and they all went inside. Becca sat down on the sofa and took Jack's hands, pulling him down so he was sitting next to her. "I was thinking about Thoreau and I wanted to ask you something."

He raised his eyebrows. "Is this a trick question or a test? It's not like I memorized the book, you know."

"No. You said you stopped dreaming for a while."

He nodded. "Yes. But things are better now. I told you that."

"I know. But I think I did the same thing. I thought about what you said. I haven't ever stopped to consider what I really want. With my life, I mean. What my dreams are. I just kept working because I was good at it and that's what I always have done."

"I noticed."

"After I went to the doctor, I thought about what happened when I had my panic attacks. When I felt like I was going to die, the thing I regretted most was that I'd never been in love, that no one would ever love me, and I'd never have children. I was so upset because there were all these experiences I hadn't had in my life yet."

"Well, someone loves you now." Jack squeezed her hand and looked into her eyes. "Wait. Did the doctor say something? Are you okay?"

"Yes. She gave me a prescription for some antacids, which might help. We'll see. Mostly I got a big lecture about how I needed to slow down and make some serious life changes."

"More yoga?"

"That might help, but it's more than that. The bottom line was that stress kills. She said what I've been doing isn't enough and she doesn't want me to end up as some premature death statistic. So she wants me to drastically cut back on work and focus on dealing with my health and anxiety issues."

His hand tightened on hers. "You're going to be okay, right?"

She nodded. "Then I remembered that passage you read from Thoreau. The going confidently in the direction of your dreams one. On the drive here, I thought about it. In the life I imagine, I'm not anxious and you're there. That's what I want. It's like I feel right now, sitting here with you. When we were trapped here, yes, I was definitely hungry, but mostly when I'm here with you, I'm not bored or wanting to go out somewhere or buy something. I'm just content. Happy."

Jack tilted his head. "Are you saying what I think you're saying?"

"At the risk of inviting myself, would it be okay if I stay with you here?" Becca smiled at his puzzled expression. "Not just on vacation, but for good?"

"What about your apartment and all your stuff?"

"During my de-cluttering program, I set aside some personal things that I don't want to give up. But I also talked to my mom about doing a major yard sale next month.

Except family gets first dibs on everything. She was excited about that concept and I think the idea will spread through my family tree like wildfire. None of that matters, anyway. Some things are more important than things. My health, for one, and being with you, for another."

Jack grinned. "So you're saying you want to shack up with a boring forester in The Shack?

"Yes, I am. As long as the boring forester is you."

He gathered her in his arms and kissed her. "Yup. Same ole me."

Thanks for Reading

Thank you for dedicating some of your reading time to *Snow Furries*. I hope you enjoyed the adventures with Becca, Jack, and Kat and I wanted you to know that I'll be writing more books that will feature Kat, Joel and various other residents of Alpine Grove who bring dogs to the new boarding kennel. The fifth novel, *Bark to the Future*, is available along with ten other books in the series.

If you would like to be notified by email when I release a new book, you can sign up for my New Releases email list at SusanDaffron.com.

I know that not everyone likes to write book reviews, but if you are willing write a sentence or two about what you thought of *Snow Furries*, I encourage you to post a review at your favorite book vendor site or share a message with your social networking friends.

If you would like to share your thoughts about the book with me privately, you can reach me through the contact page on the SusanDaffron.com web site.

I look forward to hearing from you!

~ Susan C. Daffron

Acknowledgements

Writing a novel is never easy and I'd like to thank my husband James Byrd for his support and encouragement throughout the writing and publishing process.

I'd also like to thank my alpha and beta readers for their eagle-eyed reading and great feedback:

- James Byrd
- Cynthia Daffron
- Dian Chapman
- Kathy Goughenour
- Kate Turner

About the Author

Susan Daffron is the author of the Jennings & O'Shea series and the Alpine Grove romantic comedies, a series of novels that feature residents of the small town of Alpine Grove and their various quirky dogs and cats. She is also an award-winning author of many nonfiction books, including several about pets and animal rescue. She lives in a small town in northern Idaho and shares her life with her husband and three really cute dogs.